As Long as the Rivers Flow

As Long as the Rivers Flow

JAMES BARTLEMAN

ALFRED A. KNOPF CANADA

PUBLISHED BY ALFRED A. KNOPF CANADA

Copyright © 2011 James Bartleman

All rights reserved under International and Pan-American Copyright Conventions.
No part of this book may be reproduced in any form or by any electronic or mechanical
means, including information storage and retrieval systems, without permission in writing
from the publisher, except by a reviewer, who may quote brief passages in a review.
Published in 2011 by Alfred A. Knopf Canada, a division of Random House of Canada
Limited. Distributed by Random House of Canada Limited, Toronto.

Knopf Canada and colophon are trademarks.

www.randomhouse.ca

Library and Archives Canada Cataloguing in Publication

Bartleman, James, 1939–
    As long as the rivers flow / James Bartleman.

Issued also in an electronic format.

ISBN 978-0-307-39874-1

    I. Title.

PS8603.A783A75 2011   C813'.6   C2010-904198-4

Text design: Leah Springate
Map: Paul Dotey

First Edition

Printed and bound in the United States of America

10 9 8 7 6 5 4 3 2 1

LOCKED IN A NIGHTMARE, Martha was a child again at the Indian residential school on James Bay where she had lived for ten years, from the age of six to sixteen. The priest who had summoned her to his office for "special spiritual instruction" was sexually assaulting her.

In her terrorized state, her little-girl self tried to call for help, but the words would not come. She also knew, within her dream, that she was far from home and no one in the church-run school would come to her rescue even if they heard her cries.

"Please, please don't," she finally managed to say, and woke up.

Lying back exhausted, Martha wondered if her anguish would ever end. Although more than three decades had passed and she was now middle-aged, with children of her own, she still remained a prisoner of the priest who had whispered that he loved her as he violated her body. She had tried to forget the trauma of those years by losing herself in the oblivion of alcohol and the ecstasy of religion, but nothing had worked.

———

While Martha lay awake fighting the terrors of the past, her daughter, Raven, in the next room, was emerging slowly from a restless sleep. Sensing that she was not alone, she opened her eyes to find three spectral figures gathered around her bed, silently gazing at her with expressions of yearning and loneliness so unbearably intense that she was forced to look away. She knew that they were friends from her class at school who had recently taken their own lives. Just six weeks before, she had joined them in a collective vow to die when they turned thirteen. Her birthday and those of the others had come and gone, and she was now the only one still alive.

The apparitions faded away, leaving Raven grieving for the loss of her friends, feeling guilty for having not yet carried out her part of the pact, and uncertain whether she wanted to live or die.

At that same hour, it was early morning in Quebec City. Father Lionel Antoine, the priest who had abused Martha when she was a little girl, was alone in a chapel preparing to celebrate his first mass of the day. Now in his eighties, he was still in good health, at peace with himself and happy to be back in the province of his birth. Living quietly in a home for retired priests and respected by the members of his order, he derived great comfort from participating in liturgical acts of worship, talking about the old days and sharing meals with friends who, like him, had returned from their mission posts across Canada and abroad, wishing to spend their last years at home.

Father Antoine often thought back to the decades he had spent at an Indian residential school in northern Ontario. He had done things to the little girls in his care that had not been proper, but that was in the past. He was certain God had forgiven him and that the incidents had been long forgotten by everyone concerned. What was important to remember, he told himself, was that the little girls he had called to his office in those years had loved him

Contents

~

To the memory of the Native youth who have taken their lives as a result of the Indian residential school experiences of their parents and of the parents of their parents before them.

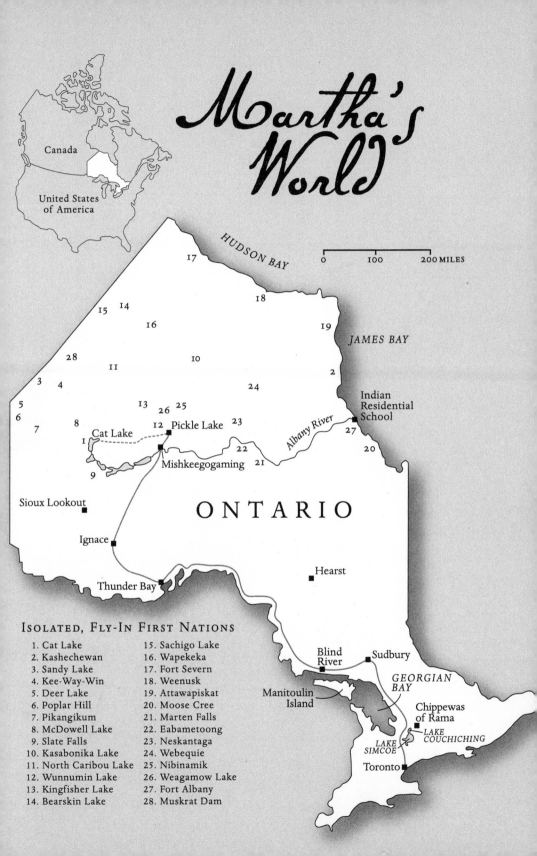

Martha's World

Canada

United States of America

HUDSON BAY

JAMES BAY

17

18

15 14

16

19

28

11

10

2

3

4

24

Indian
Residential
School

5

13 26 25

23

6

8 12 Pickle Lake

27

7

I Cat Lake

22

20

9

Mishkeegogaming

21

Albany River

Sioux Lookout

ONTARIO

Ignace

Hearst

Thunder Bay

0   100   200 MILES

Blind
River

Sudbury

*GEORGIAN
BAY*

Manitoulin
Island

Chippewas
of Rama

*LAKE
COUCHICHING*

*LAKE
SIMCOE*

Toronto

ISOLATED, FLY-IN FIRST NATIONS

1. Cat Lake
2. Kashechewan
3. Sandy Lake
4. Kee-Way-Win
5. Deer Lake
6. Poplar Hill
7. Pikangikum
8. McDowell Lake
9. Slate Falls
10. Kasabonika Lake
11. North Caribou Lake
12. Wunnumin Lake
13. Kingfisher Lake
14. Bearskin Lake

15. Sachigo Lake
16. Wapekeka
17. Fort Severn
18. Weenusk
19. Attawapiskat
20. Moose Cree
21. Marten Falls
22. Eabametoong
23. Neskantaga
24. Webequie
25. Nibinamik
26. Weagamow Lake
27. Fort Albany
28. Muskrat Dam

and had wanted him to show his affection for them in the way he had. He had become quite attached to all of them, especially the one who had been his favourite, but whose name he now found hard to remember.

PART ONE

The Early Years

~

1956–1991

I

First Memories

"*IKWESENS, GEEYAWAAN! IKWESENS GEEYAWAAN!* It's a little girl!
It's a little girl!"

As the midwife held up the newborn baby for the happy mother,
Mary Whiteduck, to see, the infant began to howl. That was the
signal for Isaac, Mary's husband, who had been nervously waiting
outside the family cabin throughout the night, to push open the
door and enter.

"A strong and healthy child," the midwife told him. The
beloved Anishinabe elder had been delivering babies at Cat Lake
Indian Reserve in northern Ontario for as long as anyone could
remember. "Someone to take care of you and Mary when you reach
my age."

The news travelled fast in the tiny settlement that spring morning
in 1956 on the shore of Cat Lake, some one hundred and fifty miles
upstream from the Albany river. Within minutes, relatives, friends
and neighbours came to offer their congratulations, the men standing around outside the cabin to smoke their pipes and gossip and the
women going in to drop off small gifts and admire the baby.

That evening, in honour of the addition to their community, everyone gathered around a campfire to laugh, tell stories, drink tea and eat country food—fish, game and berries harvested from the land. Several days later, a respected elder and long-standing friend of the family came to their home and, in a ceremony involving much meditation and prayer, named the baby Martha.

Four months later, the sky was filled with the cries of geese departing for the south, and Mary and Isaac prepared to join the annual fall exodus of families leaving for their traplines. Isaac fine-tuned the ancient, temperamental Johnson outboard motor, made some last-minute repairs to the family's eighteen-foot square-stern freighter canoe, and loaded it with guns, axes, saws, traps, clothing and provisions. The couple closed the cabin where they spent their summers and said goodbye to the handful of people remaining behind, mainly the sick and elderly who would not be able to survive a hard winter on the land. They tucked their infant daughter into the beaded deerskin cradle bag of her *tikinagan*, the cradleboard that would serve her as baby carriage and crib for the first two years of her life, and took her on her first trip across Cat Lake and downstream to the small lake and trapping cabin that had been in Isaac's family for generations.

Martha's earliest years passed in a blur. Her first distinct memory was of playing on the shore in front of the family's cabin in the bush when she was five. The wind changed direction, the sky grew black and great cracking sounds blasted out of the clouds followed by stunning flashes of light. She burst into tears and her laughing mother ran to pick her up and carry her inside just as the storm burst over their heads and giant raindrops swept across the water to soak them.

"Don't be afraid, my daughter," her mother said, as she removed her wet clothes and dried her off. "That was just the Thunderbird flapping his wings and shooting lightning bolts from his eyes. He does that when he is fighting his enemy, the giant water snake. Never forget that he's a friend of the Anishinabe people, for he provides the rain for Mother Earth and all her creatures to drink."

To cheer up her up, she added, "Now I'm going to tell you a story about Nanabush."

Martha immediately stopped crying, for her mother had told her tales before about the exploits of this part-human, part-spirit son of the West Wind and grandson of Gitche Manitou, and she loved them. Some of them were serious, about how he helped the Anishinabe people by creating animals and plants for them to eat, and others made her laugh. Martha preferred the comical ones and her mother launched into a long, involved tale about the time he once invited the animals to a feast, and didn't tell them until they arrived that they were the feast!

The little girl wasn't sure the story was all that funny, especially if you were an animal, but she laughed just the same.

In a visit some months later that would remain forever etched in her memory, friends of her parents came to their cabin at the time of the Great Moon, when the fiercest and coldest winter winds blow upon the land. After snowshoeing through the bush and across the frozen lakes from their home on a nearby trapline, they pushed open the door and entered, smiling broadly.

"*Bojo! Bojo!* Hello! Hello! We've come to visit. We were going crazy over at our place, with our kids away at residential school and never seeing anyone from one moon to another, and we decided to come see you!"

"*Ahaaw! Ahaaw!* Welcome! Welcome! What a pleasant surprise!" said Mary. "Take off your things and make yourselves comfortable. I'll have some hot tea ready for you in a minute."

The guests took off their parkas, unlaced and removed their moosehide boots, and settled down to relax on the bed. Isaac dug out his can of Old Chum pipe tobacco, and soon the two couples were sipping hot tea, smoking their pipes and gossiping.

As soon as she could, Mary excused herself and set about making supper.

"You're in luck. I've got a rabbit stew already warming up on the back of the stove. We'll have that with some bannock and fried fish." With her kerchief holding her hair in place, she cheerfully mixed Robin Hood flour, Maple Leaf Tenderflake lard, Royal baking powder, Sifto salt and ice-cold lake water in a tin bowl to make fried bannock in a heavy, fire-blackened, cast iron frying pan. The first course prepared, she handed it around, encouraging everyone to eat it while it was still hot and greasy, and started work preparing a large, fresh pickerel she had caught that morning while ice-fishing.

"Let me help you," the visiting wife said. "You shouldn't have to do all that work yourself."

"No, no, please sit down, you're my guest," Mary told her. "I can't tell you how happy I am you're here. The winter is so long and we never see anyone."

Mary scaled, gutted and cleaned the fish, cut it into fillets and used the same pan to fry them in bubbling lard. When it was golden brown and crispy, she called everyone to the rough, handmade table and served a meal that Martha would never forget: rabbit stew, fried fish and more bannock on tin plates with mugs of sweetened tea and Carnation evaporated milk in a room lit by the soft yellow light of a coal oil lamp and smelling of freshly scraped and curing hides, wood smoke and pipe tobacco.

It was time to get down to some serious visiting and Martha climbed up on the always welcoming and comfortable lap of her father and listened attentively and quietly as the grown-ups talked.

Beginning with the subject that interested them the most, the men engaged in some low-key bragging about how many beaver, marten, mink and muskrat they had trapped that winter. They moved on to talk about blizzards that had blown up when they were far from home, about shelters they had thrown together to ride out storms, about waking up in the mornings to dig themselves out into brilliant sunshine, and about fierce wolverines, pound for pound the most powerful animals in the bush, raiding their traplines, stealing bait, springing traps and never being caught.

"But no matter how tough things are for us now," Isaac said, "things were worse for the ancestors before the arrival of the Hudson's Bay Company. They had no market for their furs and no guns and axes and all the things we take for granted today. The summers when everyone got together would have been the best time of the year since there was fish to eat for the entire community at Cat Lake. But I don't know how the families made it through the winters out in the bush all by themselves. Up here in the north, the people didn't have any wild rice or maple sugar to store away like our cousins, the Anishinabe to the south. It would have been hard for the hunters to bring down enough moose and deer with their spears and bows and arrows in the deep snow to feed their families and they would have had to rely on rabbits, beaver, squirrels and any small game they could get their hands on. No wonder not many people lived more than thirty winters in those days."

The women said nothing for a while and then asked the men whether they thought they would get enough money from the trader for their furs to pay their debts and outfit themselves for the next year. The men did not know and changed the subject to hunting.

"I got two deer last fall," said Isaac. "They were pretty skinny and we don't have much meat left in our cache. I guess we'll have to live on rabbits and fish. We could have a tough time feeding ourselves before we make it back home."

"I'm okay this year," said the visiting trapper. "Shot a big bull moose some time ago and have plenty of meat stored away. Last year it was a different story. Couldn't get any big animals and it was a bad year for rabbits. When the thaw came, we had no meat left. I couldn't even go fishing, the ice was so soft and dangerous. Thankfully, I stumbled across a bear that was still hibernating and it was easy to kill him. Sure saved the family from going hungry or even worse. I offered a sacrifice of tobacco and a prayer to its spirit master to be sure he wasn't offended."

Isaac reflected for some time on what had been said, and puffing studiously on his pipe, told an old story about someone from the reserve who had not paid proper attention to the rituals he was supposed to follow when he killed an animal for food. The spirit of the animal had become angry, he said, and had placed a curse on the hunter making it impossible for him to bring down other game and his family had starved.

"The old folks were right," the visitor said, "when they said there were two worlds, the one we live in, and the Skyworld—the one we can't see, where Nanabush lives with the spirits of the dead.

"I know some Anishinabe people today don't agree with the old wisdom. But they're mainly people who spend too much time mixing with whites and believe everything the missionaries tell them."

"Those of us who live on the land know better," said Isaac. "There are things out here that the people on the outside will never understand. I never feel alone because Gitche Manitou is present everywhere—in Mother Earth, Father Sky, Grandfather Sun, Grandmother Moon, the stars, the trees, the plants, the rain, the snow, the streams, the lakes, the trees and the rocks."

"There's something else. I've always thought the elders were right when they said the Anishinabe people were related to the animals." .

"I wonder what it'd be like to visit the Skyworld," said the visitor.

"You'll know soon enough when you die."

"I mean, now, when I'm still alive."

After several more puffs on his pipe, Isaac said, "Only the shamans had the power to travel to the Skyworld and come back alive. And the missionaries drove them away long ago. That's too bad, because they helped people. If you were sick in your body or in your head, they could travel to the other world and find ways to cure you."

"I've heard that," said the visitor. "Did you know that the shamans were the people who painted those Thunderbirds, fish and animals on that rock wall on the other side of Cat Lake back home? Nobody wants to talk about it, but some of those pictures have great power. There's one place, I bet you know it, where there's a reddish-brown image of the ancestors paddling a canoe. It's really spooky."

"I know it," said Isaac. "I believe you. I've been over there at night when I could've sworn I heard drumming coming from inside that rock wall. Gives you a strange feeling. I deal with it by putting tobacco in a crack in the wall under the canoe and by praying to Gitche Manitou whenever I pass by. Also helps with the fishing."

Several long months later, the lake in front of the cabin was black with rotten ice and the sky was filled with formations of honking Canada geese flying north. One night as she lay between her parents in bed, Martha heard the sound of the south wind in the black spruce trees, and her father murmuring to her mother, "It won't be long now. It won't be long now."

When she got up in the morning, the ice was gone from the lake, and grey, cold waves were beating on the shore. It was time to return to the reserve. With Martha helping the best she could, her parents pushed the canoe into the water, loaded it with furs, utensils and other things they would need back at Cat Lake, and attached the old outboard motor to the stern. Martha took her place in the bow, her favourite spot, her mother settled down in the centre and her father took a seat beside the motor, his loaded gun beside him in case he came across game. As they always did when departing for the reserve in the spring, they left their cabin unlocked and stocked with supplies to help any lost hunter in need of shelter who happened by.

Two days later, after forcing their way upstream to Cat Lake, they saw the reserve off in the distance. As they neared the shore, friends and relatives who had already made it home from their winter homes in the bush came out of their cabins to greet them.

"Welcome home."

"How was the trapping?"

"There are still a few families who haven't made it back yet."

"Martha, how big you've become!"

"Come and see us when you get settled."

After unloading the canoe and moving into their summer cabin, Martha's parents, their daughter in tow, visited the Hudson's Bay Company store to sell their furs. Martha looked on as the trader, a white man, graded the winter's take. He entered a figure in a big black book and winked at the little girl.

"Looks like your daddy did really well this year," he said in broken Anishinaabemowin. "Maybe he'll buy you a treat!"

Martha nodded her head solemnly, acknowledging the attention the trader was giving her. She knew him well for he had lived in the small community for as long as she could remember and had married a local woman. Although he could be gruff at times, he was well liked by everyone because he had made an effort to learn Anishinaabemowin and was good to his wife and children.

"Another season like that," he said, turning to her father, "and you'll be out of debt. Now have a good look around. I got lots of new stock. All the usual traps, guns, ammunition, fishing gear, axes, clothing and food. I've also got something else that should interest you. Some new Johnson outboard motors have come in. You could use one. That old piece of junk you've been using could break down completely and leave you stranded some day. Or worse. It could conk out when you're in the rapids. You could get yourself killed! Whatdyasay?"

"Maybe another year," said Isaac. "When I've paid off all my bills."

"Look at these sultana raisins and dried fruit," the man continued, ignoring Isaac's comment. "My wife tells me they go really good mixed in bannock. Better get some now before I run out. Take anything you want. Your credit's good here."

Isaac poked around for a while in the tiny building that smelled of furs, coal oil and chewing tobacco, and picked out a small bag of hard candy.

"These are for you," he said to his daughter. "We'll come back later to stock up on food and other supplies for the winter."

Spring turned into Martha's last summer of innocence before she was sent off to residential school, and she experienced to the full the uninhibited joy of shouting and laughing with children she had not seen since the preceding fall. Every day, she ran, played tag and spent endless hours in the water swimming and splashing. At times, she joined her friends on canoe rides. Occasionally, an adult would take her with him when he went fishing. She was never home until after dark but her parents never worried.

Then it was time for the annual visit of the Indian agent. More than half a century before, a flotilla of canoes, each one flying a Union Jack from its bow, had arrived at the summer encampment of the Cat Lake people. The boats were filled with Mounties, in full ceremonial dress, and self-important white officials wearing pith helmets and draped in mosquito netting as if they were on an expedition into the heart of Africa.

"Your great father, His Majesty King Edward VII," they told the people, "is concerned about the well-being of his Native children who reside here in the northern wilderness. As a sign of his immense compassion, he has asked us to come here to sign a treaty with you that will protect you for all time. In return for ceding your rights to this land, every man, woman and child will be immediately handed a cash payment and a reserve will be set aside for your exclusive use.

"All you have to do," they said to the people who did not know how to read and write and who had no concept of rights and land ownership as interpreted by the commissioners, "is to put your mark on this document and each year a representative of the Crown will visit you and give you more money."

The people did so, unknowingly authorizing outsiders to take the mineral and forest wealth of their lands and game wardens to enter their traditional territory to interfere with their trapping and hunting way of life. And every year that followed, the people of Cat Lake held a celebration to mark the anniversary of the treaty and the visit to their community of the Indian agent to pay the treaty money.

Preparations for the festivities of 1962 began when the men draped sheets of canvas over a frame of birch saplings to make a tent big enough to accommodate everyone and moved stoves and tables into place. The children collected kindling and firewood and picked blueberries and raspberries to make into pies. The women set to work, preparing in advance communal meals of boiled moose meat cut into strips, venison stew, fried fish, berries, bannock and tea as well as local delicacies such as boiled *tripe de roche*, a gooey favourite made from dry black moss mixed with berries and well-cooked fish pounded into powder with everything liberally drenched in fish oil.

On the morning of the big day, the children gathered on the shore and scanned the sky for the arrival of the float plane carrying their guests. Eventually, someone with sharp eyesight saw a speck far off in the sky.

"It's them. The *zhaagnaash* are coming! The white men are coming!"

As the float plane approached the lake, the Indian agent, a short, trim, red-haired bureaucrat in his mid-forties with a handlebar moustache and nervous, pale blue eyes, was sitting beside the pilot trying to pick out, from the mass of green foliage along the shore, the cluster of log cabins that comprised the settlement.

A self-made man, the Indian agent had left school and home in the depths of the Great Depression when his father lost his factory job and could no longer feed his family. After years of riding the rails looking for work and living by his wits, he joined the army when war broke out in 1939, discovered he had a talent for managing men, progressed through the non-commissioned officer ranks, and was eventually ordered to report for duty as a drill sergeant at Camp Ipperwash, a newly constructed recruit training base on the shore of Lake Huron in southwestern Ontario. He had relished converting squads of awkward farm boys and factory workers into polished, well-drilled soldiers who responded like puppets to his shouted commands on the parade grounds.

It was not his fault he had never made it overseas to participate in the actual fighting. He had volunteered to go, but his superior officer had taken note of him, had liked him and had blocked all

efforts to ship him out, afraid he would not find anyone as compe-
tent to replace him. When the war ended, that same officer, who
had joined the government department responsible for Indian
Affairs when he was demobilized, remembered him and told him
that his employer was hiring former military personnel to work as
Indian agents running Indian reserves across the country.

"You probably don't know anything about Indians, but that's
not a requirement," he told him. "You don't even need a high school
education to get one of these jobs. Veterans are given preference
and we're looking for tough, well-disciplined managers to deal
with childlike people who are still living a hand-to-mouth existence and need help to prepare them to join the modern world.

"Just get yourself the proper forms, fill them out and put me
down as a reference. I'll make sure you get taken on."

The former sergeant jumped at the chance to move up in the
world and become a federal public servant with its job security and
guarantee of a good pension. And it wasn't true that he didn't know
anything about Indians. He had met plenty of them living in hobo
jungles and working in lumber camps and tobacco fields when he
wandered the country in the 1930s.

In those days, he considered it unfair that Indians, even war veterans, were legally prohibited from buying beer, liquor and wine in
government outlets and from drinking in beer parlours and bars like
white Canadians. So when he had a little cash, he would sometimes
do a little discreet bootlegging, buying a few bottles of cheap wine
from a government liquor store to sell to his Indian acquaintances,
at a good profit of course, to compensate himself for the time, effort
and risk involved. Sometimes, to show that he was not prejudiced,
he would even accept an invitation to have a little drink with them.

Once he had even spoken up for the Indians, even if none of
them knew about it. Like everyone else on the base, he was vaguely

aware that Camp Ipperwash had been built on land seized from Indians at the beginning of the war. He had no problem with that. After all, everyone had to make sacrifices for the war effort, and Indians were having their lands taken from them all the time anyway. But when he caught some recruits using tombstones and crosses for target practice in the abandoned Native cemetery, he was furious.

"There may just be a bunch of dead Indians buried here," he told them, "but how would you like if some strangers came along and shot up your family graves?"

After joining Indian Affairs, the new bureaucrat was pleased to discover that the hierarchical work culture of his workplace was similar to that of his beloved army. Only instead of drilling green soldiers on the parade grounds, he was ordering Indians around on their reserves. Like the recruits, the Indians could do nothing about it. They had few rights, not being allowed to vote in federal elections or even to keep their children at home to be educated. As an Indian agent, he had the authority to decide whether his charges could leave their reserves, own property, attend university, sell their livestock or even organize themselves politically. Although he sensed there was something indecent in that, he actually enjoyed lording it over so many people.

Now, as the plane landed, he looked forward to celebrating another Treaty Day. In the seats behind him were a Mountie decked out in a scarlet tunic sprinkled with badges, striped breeches and polished knee-high boots and spurs, and a clerk, who sat with one hand on a cash box.

After disembarking from the aircraft, the Indian agent shook hands with the chief and introduced his travelling companions. The chief formally presented the band councillors, and everyone moved to a table set up in front of the Hudson's Bay store by the trader.

"How's the wife and kids?" asked the Indian agent, trying to make small talk.

"They're okay."

"Someone told me the winter up here wasn't too bad. How did your people make out? Get lots of fur?"

"Everyone's done okay, I guess."

The clerk bustled around opening his ledgers and checking the cash box as the Indian agent asked the chief if the water had been high in the spring, if the fishing was good, if the elders were receiving their old age pension cheques on time and if many babies had been born since his last visit. The chief, who had met the Indian agent many times on other Treaty Days and did not like him, continued to answer in monosyllables.

When all was ready, the two white officials sat down and the Mountie took up a position behind the table, standing at attention, when not swatting mosquitoes and black flies, and doing his best to lend an air of formality to the occasion. The people, dressed in their best store-bought clothes—calico dresses with colourful floral patterns for the women and plain white shirts and trousers and braces for the men—waited patiently as the clerk checked their names off a list and handed over their treaty money: four crisp, brand-new one-dollar bills to each member of the band.

Afterwards, the chief asked everyone to gather around, and as he did every year, officially welcomed the visitors to the community, speaking in Anishinaabemowin for the benefit of his people, with the trader translating his words into English for the delegation.

"I thank the people who have come such a long way to be with us today to celebrate the treaty signed by our grandfathers so many years ago. We are always happy to receive our treaty money. But the money is not the important thing. Having the opportunity to celebrate the treaty itself is what counts. We don't want it ever to be forgotten that our grandfathers were promised by the white man that the treaty would last for as long as the rivers flow, the sun shines and grass grows.

"The treaty, however, is being ignored. We are a patient people but the mining, lumber and pulp companies are taking minerals and wood off our traditional lands and we get nothing, not even jobs. You are our friend and we ask you to tell the big chief in Ottawa to help us."

As the chief spoke, the Indian agent stood stiffly erect, his hands clasped behind his back, staring off into the distance as if he were back on the parade grounds listening to a report from one of his corporals. When the speech was finished and the translation rendered, he turned to the chief and gravely delivered his judgement.

"You know I tell it as it is and I don't mince words. Of course I'll pass your message up the chain of command, just like I've done with your other ones over the years, but I gotta tell you now, as your friend, that no one's gonna listen. For one thing, you should read the fine print in this treaty before you start complaining. Maybe you'd see that you don't have as many rights as you think you have.

"Another thing you gotta realize is that the world has moved on since your treaty was signed. Two world wars, the Great Depression, and the arrival of the motor car, airplanes, lots of things. Just this year, the government put a satellite up to explore the skies and paved the highway across Canada from the Atlantic to the Pacific.

"And no one, not even way back here in the bush, can stand in the way of progress. Maybe you'll find it hard to understand, but nobody in Ottawa believes in these old treaties any more, and the day is coming when there'll be no more reserves, and you Indians will be just like the Italians, the Dutch and the Chinese—no better and no worse off than anyone else."

As the people applauded without conviction, the chief handed each visitor gifts of deerskin moccasins with rabbit fur lining, beaded moosehide winter gloves with beaver pelt trim and birchbark needle boxes embroidered with porcupine quills and sweetgrass.

"My people would be honoured if you would stay and help us celebrate Treaty Day this evening," said the chief. "I'd love to visit," was his answer, "but I'm a busy man with many other reserves to visit and we just got time for a quick bite."

The visitors, led by the chief, walked over to the big tent, ignored the *tripe de roche* and wolfed down generous helpings of fried pickerel, bannock and venison stew. After a few sips of hot tea, they hurried to their waiting aircraft, promising to spend more time with the community the next year.

The first evening, the people got together in the tent to eat, to drink endless mugs of tea and to talk and laugh, just as they did every year after the departure of the white people from Ottawa. When the feast was over and the dishes cleared away, everyone pitched in to remove the tables and make ready to dance and sing. Two men pulled out fiddles and began to play and step-dance to the rhythm of country music. Delighted men, women and children took to the floor, singing the words to the tunes, dancing jigs and forming themselves up into groups of eight to square-dance.

After the sun had set and it was dark, the people made their way to the beach to sit around a great campfire and listen to the old stories. Anxious not to miss a word, Martha worked her way through the crowd and found a spot at the feet of the elders who had pride of place on logs drawn up around the fire. She sat spellbound as the storytellers related the great myths of the Anishinabe people: how Muskrat created the world, how Frog brought the seasons into being, how Dog became the friend of man, how Thunderbird shook the heavens, how Nanabush came to be the messenger of Gitche Manitou and played tricks on humans and animals, and much, much more.

The second night was reserved for a traditional celebration and the mood was solemn. The people stood silently in the tent after the feast as the chief pounded rhythmically on a water drum. Fashioned out of an empty metal nail keg, half filled with water and tightly covered with a water-soaked moosehide, it throbbed out hauntingly for miles across the lake, summoning the ancestors to come join the celebrations. Other drummers joined in, striking smaller drums with their hands and shaking rattles made from discarded Carnation milk cans filled with small stones. Someone called out that the spirits had arrived, and the people began to chant the old songs and to shuffle solemnly in single file around the inside of the tent.

Afterwards, around the campfire, an old man, entrusted with the evening's storytelling, asked the children to sit on the ground in front of him, promising to tell them a few things they would never forget.

"Last night," he said, after taking a seat, "you heard stories about Gitche Manitou, the Great Spirit, and his supporters and the good things they do for the Anishinabe people. Tonight, I'm going to tell you some things normally too awful for kids to hear. About monsters and bad things. Anyone who doesn't want to listen should leave now."

Of course, no one left, and the old man leaned forward and earnestly whispered to the children that an evil spirit, almost as powerful as Gitche Manitou, was at that moment hiding in the shadows disguised as a toad and secretly listening to what was being said.

"That spirit's name is Madji Manitou," he said, "and it has many wicked followers. The water serpent that chases away the fish and upsets the canoes of fishermen in storms and drowns them is one of them. It is the master of the bearwalkers, the witches who arrive in a ball of fire and take possession of the minds and bodies of people. Everyone is afraid of bearwalkers because they cast spells on people they don't like and make their hair and teeth fall out. They even cause sickness and death. They're easy to recognize because they dress in black, are really old and are always in a bad mood.

"Madji Manitou is also the ruler over the Wendigo, the monster I am now going to tell you about tonight. And you better pay attention and not make me mad because maybe I'm a bearwalker. After all," he said, as the children laughed nervously, "I'm an old man, I dress in black, I'm bad-tempered, especially to little kids, and I know all about Madji Manitou.

"The Wendigo," he continued, "is a half-human, half-devil monster at least ten times the size of a man, with breath that reeks of rotten human flesh.

"You kids have all smelled animals who have been dead a long time in the bush or in the lake. Well, the Wendigo smells even worse. It stinks and it isn't even dead! Its favourite food is fresh, living, human meat. During the spring thaw, human-hunting is really good. The snow is deep and wet and it's hard for people to get around. The moose and deer can wait for the snow to melt, holed up in the swamps eating cedar branches. But the food supplies put away in the fall by the trappers are low by then and sometimes their families have nothing left to eat."

The old man suddenly leaped to his feet and lunged at the children as if he were the Wendigo, gnashing his teeth, snarling and beating his chest. And as the children screamed in terror and ran off crying and stumbling over the rough terrain beyond the light of the campfire, he cried out, "Watch out for the toad! Watch out for the toad!"

Barely able to contain their laughter, the parents went to bring them back, telling them the old man was just pretending.

"Oh no I'm not," he said, frowning and picking up a hemlock bough that he hurled into the fire, releasing a shower of sparks that flew upwards like fireflies in the night sky and a cloud of smoke that left the people downwind choking and coughing.

"Just imagine the scene, kids," he continued, addressing himself directly to the children whose frightened eyes reflected the flames. "Just imagine the scene," he repeated, leaning forward again, his voice barely audible.

"The poor trapper is struggling through the snow. Each step is pure agony since the wet snow sticks to his snowshoes, and they become harder and harder to lift. His rifle and pack get heavier and heavier, and he becomes weaker and weaker, and soon he can barely move.

"All of a sudden, he smells something so horrible it can't be described! He hears whistling and bellowing that shatter the winter silence and freeze his blood. The earth begins to shake under his feet.

"What's this? It's the Wendigo itself rushing at him, crashing through the bush, thumping the snow with its giant feet and hurling trees high up in the air.

"The trapper raises his rifle and fires off a clip of .303 steel-jacket bullets. They hit the Wendigo.

"Splat, splat, splat! They go right through its body, leaving great wounds and covering the snow with chunks of torn flesh and blood! But they heal right away and the monster keeps on coming.

"The trapper can now see its huge, ugly fangs and the dirty slobber that hangs from its mouth. The stench is unbearable.

"He doesn't have time to reload. He throws his gun away, grabs his axe and hurls it with all his might at the Wendigo, burying its razor-sharp blade deep in its hairy chest. The fiend stops, but only for a moment, then pulls the axe from its body and tosses it far off into the distance.

"Grabbing hold of the luckless trapper, it rips off his arms and legs. Just like you kids tear off the arms and legs of deerflies! And as the victim lies watching, helpless and in unbearable pain, the Wendigo gobbles them down on the spot, without even putting salt and pepper on them!

"Usually the trapper dies and there is no more to be said. But if, despite his horrible wounds, he manages to escape and makes it back to his cabin, the story gets even worse.

"For never forget, kids, if someone is bitten by a Wendigo, that person turns into a Wendigo with a great hunger for fresh human flesh. If the family does not get away in time, the new Wendigo will eat them for dinner and not even cook them first!"

After a pause to let the children relish the horror of the old man's tale, the other adults joined in to exchange stories handed down over the years about times of great hunger and starvation in the bush, and about people known to their parents and grandparents who were supposed to have been Wendigos. However, before going too far, the parents told their children that it was time to go to bed, warning them that if they did not obey, the Wendigo would get them!

Martha and the others had heard enough in any case, and satis-factorily thrilled, returned to their homes to have nightmares about human-eating monsters until dawn.

Indian Residential School

ONE EVENING TOWARD THE END OF AUGUST, Mary took her daughter on her knees, and in the softly cadenced tones of Anishinaabemowin, asked her to pay close attention to what she was about to tell her: *Ndi kwesencisim gda dwenmin chi bsindman wha wiindmo naan wewenah.*

"You're now a big girl of six," she said. "It's time for you to go away. Tomorrow, a float plane is coming to take you to a place far from here run by white people who will teach you to read and write. The older kids have already left and you will be the only one going.

"I can't tell you too much about what it'll be like since I never went to school. My family lived so far back in the bush when I was your age, the Mounties couldn't find us. But you'll have friends and relatives there, and so you shouldn't be lonely. You've been a good girl and I want you to do your best to get along with the others. Your father and I will see you next summer when we get back from the trapline."

The trembling mother hugged Martha and burst into tears.

Martha was only a little girl with big, bright, black-wet eyes, blue-black hair, dark brown chubby cheeks and pudgy hands. In height, she did not even reach the waist of her mother.

What was school anyway? Apparently she had to go there but she had only a vague understanding from overhearing the conversations of the older kids about what that meant. None of them liked it. Did that mean it was a place where kids were sent to be punished? If so, why her? She had been a good girl. Her mother had just told her so herself.

Trusting, affectionate and with a ready smile, Martha looked up at her mother with inquisitive eyes and remained silent. Surely the person who loved her more than anyone else in the whole wide world did not mean it when she said she would be going away and not be home again for such a long time?

But the next morning, Mary prepared her daughter to depart, dressing her in a new calico dress, putting up her hair in braids, helping her pull up the long stockings she wore each day to protect her legs from mosquito and black fly bites, and slipping onto her feet a pair of moccasins she had made for the occasion and decorated with red and blue beads in the shape of flowers. After Isaac gave Martha a long and silent hug, Mary led her to the beach.

Soon a float plane appeared in the sky, circled the lake, came in for a landing and taxied to the shore in front of the reserve. The pilot switched off the motor, stepped out onto a pontoon and tossed a rope to the trader, who had pushed his way to the front of the crowd of curious onlookers.

The trader snubbed the aircraft to a tree, and went over to where Mary and Martha were standing. "It's always tough when the kids leave home for residential school," he told Mary. "Especially when it's for the first time. The sooner we get this over with, the better it'll be for everyone."

The little girl did not want to go, and hid behind her mother. But to her surprise, her mother allowed the trader to take her hand and lead her to the pilot.

Like the Indian agent, the pilot had served in the armed forces during the war. But he had joined the air force and not the army and had been sent overseas immediately after flight training to fly Spitfires in the RCAF. When the fighting ended, he had come north in search of a job, arriving just as the region was being opened up by bush pilots flying single-engine de Havilland Beaver airplanes on the lakes and rivers that blanketed the Precambrian Shield, using pontoons in summer and skis in winter. In time, he bought a second-hand Beaver for himself and started his own small business, happily flying prospectors working for mining companies into remote lakes in search of gold, silver and nickel deposits, doctors and nurses visiting the sick in Native settlements, Mounties investigating crimes committed in the bush, and fishermen from the big cities in the south looking for trophy catches.

He was less enthusiastic about the work he obtained from the Canadian government ferrying Native kids to and from residential schools, even if it paid well. He had married a Métis woman soon after he arrived in the north and they had six children who attended a local school in a white community, and he couldn't imagine what it would be like if he wasn't surrounded at all times by his large and loving family. There was something fundamentally wrong with separating kids from their parents, but he had a living to make, a contract to do the work, and if he didn't do it, someone else would snap up the business. Thankfully, his dark aviator sunglasses would hide his uneasy eyes from those of the little girl.

The pilot carried Martha into the aircraft cabin and buckled her into a back seat.

"It's okay, little girl," he told the uncomprehending child, "Nobody's gonna bite you. We're just going on a nice airplane ride. Once we're in the air, we'll fly higher than the birds and it's so clear you'll be able to see everything."

He locked the door and took his place behind the controls as the trader untied the mooring rope and shoved the aircraft away from the shore. After putting on his headphones, he waved goodbye to the people, gave Martha a smile of encouragement and turned the key in the ignition to fire up the motor.

The roar of the engine and the sight of the propeller slashing the air panicked the little girl and she began screaming for her mother. But her mother stood unknowing on the shore, squinting into the sun, with her calico dress billowing out behind her from the back draft of the rotating blades and with her hands on her head to keep her kerchief from flying away.

The pilot was all business, needing to attend to the flight of the aircraft, and he paid no attention to Martha as he taxied across the river, swung the aircraft around to face the wind and gunned the motor. The pontoons slapped the oncoming waves, and the aircraft, shuddering, climbed laboriously into the sky. With one hand, he adjusted the controls, and with the other, he pulled back the stick to bank the aircraft away from the rock face with the pictograph of the ancestors on the other side of the lake. After making a run over the reserve, he set his course for the Indian residential school at the mouth of the Albany River, six hundred miles to the northeast on the shores of James Bay.

Earlier in the week, Martha had seen this same aircraft come and go, taking glum kids off to school. Each time, she wondered what it would be like to ride in the sky, but as soon as it was out of sight, she gave the matter no further thought. But now she was up among the clouds and did not like it. One minute she was standing with her mother on the shore, all dressed up and secure in her familiar surroundings, and the next, she was being carried away against her will to a place where none of the other kids wanted to go.

The aircraft droned on and she grew drowsy and fell into a troubled sleep, dreaming that the man with the hidden eyes carrying her away was a Wendigo. She then dreamed that she was just having a nightmare. Yes, that was it. This was just a nightmare like the ones she had been having since the old man told the scary stories around the campfire earlier in the summer.

She was really in bed back at the family cabin and would soon wake up and run to her mother and tell her about her frightening dream, and her mother would hug her and say not to worry. Her mother would promise to make her a dream catcher and put it on the wall over her bed to catch such awful dreams before they frightened her.

The aircraft began to pitch and buck as it ran into thermal air currents rising off lakes and rivers on the hot August morning. Martha was jolted awake but believed that she was still trapped in her nightmare. Convinced the Wendigo had decided to take her back to its cave and eat her there, she cried out, begging it to return her to her mother. But the pilot paid her no heed and the aircraft ploughed ahead remorselessly through the deceptively clear morning air, plunging, jerking and heaving, but in no danger of falling from the sky.

After what seemed like an eternity to the frightened girl, the aircraft began its descent. The pontoons touched down, the aircraft bounced upwards, returned to the water and settled down into the wake. The pilot taxied to a dock where a figure dressed in black awaited. After securing the aircraft, he turned to his now-sobbing passenger.

"There, there, little girl. There's nothing to be afraid of. We've arrived."

Martha did not understood the meaning of his words, but knew from the tone of his voice that he, at least, was not a Wendigo.

The pilot unbuckled the little girl, lifted her from the aircraft and stood her on the dock.

"Here's a welcoming committee of one," he said, as an unsmiling creature with unfriendly eyes, her head framed in something black and white and dressed in a black dress that came down to the ground, approached.

Martha screamed and tried to hide behind the pilot as the apparition, which seemed to be floating rather than walking, advanced toward her. It had a large cross dangling from a rope belt around its waist, and a string of wooden beads and a smaller cross hanging down from its neck. This, Martha thought, if not a Wendigo must be a bearwalker. For bearwalkers were mean-looking and dressed in black, were they not?

The pilot tousled her hair, told her not to worry and shooed her toward the nun.

"Another wild one straight from the bush, I see," the nun said. "We'll soon tame her."

She seized Martha by the shoulders and shook her.

"Now you behave yourself or I'll give you something to really cry about."

Hysterical and convinced she was now in the hands of a bearwalker, Martha howled all the louder. The nun shrugged her shoulders, took her by the hand and dragged her up the road to the residential school, a three-story clapboard structure, inconceivably gigantic and foreboding. After pulling the little girl up the steps, she jerked her through the front door and hauled her down to the basement. Martha fought all the way. The nun tried to reason with her, shook her and yelled at her but Martha continued to shriek, her attempts to escape ever more frantic as the nun tried to remove her clothing and make her take a shower.

Another nun, Sister Angelica, tall, with broad shoulders and wide hips and opaque black eyes, who was herself Native, stepped in to help. Like Martha, she had spent her winters as a child on the family trapline and her summers at her home community. Like Martha, she had come bewildered and fearful to this same residential school when she was six, but unlike Martha, she had not put up a fuss on arrival.

In fact, it would not have occurred to her to disobey the nuns. Before being taken away to the school, her parents had taught her obedience by starving and beating her for the most minor offences. Sometimes, when they came home drunk, they hit her with their fists and threw her across the room of their shack for no reason other than for just daring to exist. When she arrived at the school and the nuns saw her naked little body, they were shocked by her badly healed broken bones, burn marks and masses of bruises.

"*Quelle bande de sauvages!*" they said. "Only the most primitive people would do such things to their own children."

When her parents, returning home from the bootlegger's one early winter night, took a shortcut across a lake where the ice was thin and fell through and drowned, the nuns told her that God had punished them for mistreating their daughter. And in time, since the little girl was quiet, obedient, and gave every appearance of being devout, the nuns groomed her to follow in their footsteps.

"In the history of the Church," they told her when she was old enough to understand, "many Indian women have accepted the call to become nuns." They related to her the story of Kateri Tekakwitha, an Algonquin woman in the early years of New France who, despite persecution from her own family and community, had lived a life of such exemplary piety and service to others that she had become an object of veneration for members of the faith. It was the little girl's duty, they said, to become a nun and to devote her life to the education of Native children.

She accepted their guidance. When she was eighteen, she was received as a novitiate at a convent in Quebec City and emerged five years later as Sister Angelica. When in due course she was sent back to teach the younger students at her former school, she made it one of her goals in life to find other potential nuns from among the Native students.

Sister Angelica slapped Martha across the face to get her attention, looked into her eyes and whispered urgently to her in Anishinaabemowin.

"God has sent you here for a purpose," she said. "Now just do as you're told and you'll be happy."

It would be the last time Sister Angelica would speak to her in their language. Martha, however, even if she recognized the words, in her confusion did not understand what the nun meant. Sister Angelica, who was trying to prove to the other nuns that she was now a fully assimilated and civilized person by beating the children in her care, slapped the little girl again.

The two nuns took her in hand, yanking off her clothes, throwing her calico dress, stockings and moccasins into a garbage bin, pushing her into the shower and releasing a wall of water on her as she lay on the floor. They dragged her out, towelled her off and sat her down on a chair. While her colleague held her down, Sister Angelica took a pair of shears and cropped off her braids and molded her remaining hair into a Robin Hood cut. After pouring coal oil, stinging and foul smelling, on Martha's scalp "to kill the lice," the nuns led the sobbing child to the girls' dormitory where they outfitted her in government-issue undergarments—white blouse, grey skirt, black stockings and black shoes— to make her look like every other girl in the school.

After they left, other girls, friends and relatives from home, gathered around, anxiously trying to comfort her and telling her the nuns were neither bearwalkers nor Wendigos, but in her state of agitation and rebellion, she did not want to believe them.

When she refused to eat her dinner and sobbed throughout prayers that evening, Sister Angelica strapped her. As she did so, the nun told the little girl that every student had to follow the rule of silence.

Martha cried herself to sleep that night. The next day she wept during prayers, over breakfast and in class, each time receiving a strapping from Sister Angelica. By the end of the first day, physically and psychologically drained and with the palms of her hands swollen and red, she accepted the view of the older girls that the nuns were not bearwalkers. They were only horrible women wearing black dresses that dragged on the floor.

Martha also saw that she was not the only one being punished. For that same day, she saw nuns strap children with leather belts, slap them with open hands, hit them with pointers, and force them to eat their vomit after being sick on their plates.

The nuns would have been surprised if anyone had told them they were being cruel. For they all came from large Quebec farming families where ties were close and kisses and love were lavished on them by their parents, uncles, aunts and grandparents. But in the briefings they received before leaving to work in the residential school, their superiors told them that the Church had learned hundreds of years ago that the best way to save the souls of Indians was to take the children away from the bad influence of their parents and educate them with a firm hand.

"Your task will be hard," they said. "Indian children are like little animals and need strong discipline. You will sometimes have to be harsh but it will be for their own good."

Thus, as the nuns beat their little victims, they assured them with an air of morose selflessness they were being chastised for their own good and for the love of God, and they sincerely believed that they were doing the right thing.

Martha learned to obey the nuns without question and the punishment stopped, but she still missed her mother and was desperately lonely. One night, she closed her eyes and pretended that she was back home in bed, drinking in the wild smell of the balsam needle mattress and snuggled up under soft bearskin covers between her parents. And when morning came and she pushed open the door, she saw images from the time before she had been sent away that she thought had been lost to her forever: The first dusting of snow on the black spruce trees, the outstretched wings of crows, ravens, pelicans and eagles framed against the late fall sky, the lake so calm it had turned to glass, and ice newly formed along the shore.

And her father, as was his practice after visiting his fishing nets in the early morning, was on the beach cleaning northern pike, whitefish and pickerel and throwing the scraps to the gulls circling overhead. She ran to him and he picked her up and he hugged her and he told her he would never let anyone take her away again. She smiled and fell asleep, happy to be home again, if only in her imagination.

On other nights, Martha recreated in her mind the storytelling sessions she had attended the previous summer around the campfire back on the reserve. She saw herself edging closer to the fire as the flames glistened cheerfully on the face of an elder sitting on a log happily telling the legends of her people. She watched the gentle old man sip from his mug of black tea and rise to his feet to demonstrate how Muskrat dove down into the waters to bring back a handful of mud out of which the world, known as Turtle Island to the Anishinabe people, was formed. She marvelled as he described how the first man and woman emerged out of the body of a dead animal to people Turtle Island. She looked on with rapt attention as he pointed up at the Milky Way and said it was actually the handle of a bucket holding up Turtle Island and a bridge across which the souls of the dead crossed on the way to the Skyworld. She laughed as he described how Nanabush turned stones into butterflies to bring delight into the lives of unhappy kids just like her. She fell asleep with a smile listening to him tell her that the Anishinabe people had lived in harmony with nature since the beginning of time, and she should never forget that Gitche Manitou was the Great Spirit.

She then discovered the joys of making up her own stories and creating her own imaginary friends. Lying in her cot in the school dormitory with only the sounds of the other lonely children sleeping around her, she imagined she was back in bed in the family cabin. It was the middle of the night, and in the distance she could hear the reassuring howl of a wolf singing her a friendly serenade. Closer to home, an owl hooted, telling her it would be keeping watch over the family's cabin throughout the night.

But what was this noise? Could it be that a little animal was lost, homesick for its mother and whimpering outside the cabin door? She eased herself out from under the covers and crawled out of bed, being of course careful not to disturb the sleep of her parents. She tiptoed to the door, pushed it open and stepped outside. There, sitting in the welcoming moonlight, was a baby bear.

The little bear said his name was Makwa, and his parents had sent him off to bear residential school far from home. He had been lonely and had been badly treated, but he had managed to escape.

When he reached home, however, he discovered that his parents had died. He was thus sad and needed a new family.

"Why, you can be part of my family and be my friend," said Martha. She brought the little bear into the cabin and introduced him to her parents who welcomed him as if he was one of their own. From then on, Martha always had a friend and was never lonely. The two friends then came across a little raven, named Kagagi, who had fallen from his nest and he likewise became part of their family. The three became inseparable playmates and had many adventures.

On one of their adventures, they met the beaver who lived in a nearby marsh. Mr. Amick was his name and he was busy cutting down birch and poplar trees to repair his dam and to stockpile food for his family to eat over the winter. At his invitation, the three friends visited his lodge in the middle of the pond, taking deep breaths, swimming under the water to the entrance, and by some magic not getting wet. Once inside the cosy living room, they met the many members of the Amick family and spent an afternoon drinking black tea with sugar, eating hot, fried bannock filled with raisins and discussing all manner of interesting things.

It was not long before Martha carried over into her daylight hours the world she had created for her nighttime relief and comfort. She would wake up early while the other girls were still asleep and let her mind run free, searching for a suitable adventure to begin her day. Once, she thought of flesh-eating monsters and journeyed back in her imagination to the family cabin to discover that it was late winter and there was no food to eat. To make it worse, there was a gigantic Wendigo lurking outside, hiding in a tree just waiting to devour anyone who left the safety of the cabin.

A nun rang a bell to summon the girls to rise and go the bathroom. Martha put her story on hold as she washed and dressed but eagerly returned to it afterwards during morning prayers. As she recited the rosary along with the other children, she saw from behind her closed eyelids her father pacing up and down in the cabin trying to come to a decision on what to do. She begged him not to go outside for he would surely suffer a horrible death. But he paid her no attention and began his preparations to leave, telling her that even if the risk was great, he had to hunt to feed his family. Besides, he wasn't afraid of any old Wendigo. After all, if it dared attack him, he would shoot it with his rifle.

By the time Martha was eating her breakfast, her father had gone out the door and was struggling on his snowshoes through the snow, holding his rifle at the ready, anxiously watching out for the Wendigo and looking around for game. Ahead of him on the trail was a caribou. He lifted his rifle, aimed, pulled the trigger, and the animal fell. After offering a prayer to Gitche Manitou, he pulled out his hunting knife and started to cut it up into steaks. But suddenly he saw the Wendigo sitting on a branch of a tamarack tree, licking its lips, preparing to jump on him and tear him limb from limb.

Just as the tension became almost too hard to bear, the bell rang again ordering the children to their classrooms. Once again, Martha was obliged to set her story aside and pay attention as the nuns led the students through their lessons. But afterwards, as she carried out her obligatory chores, washing dishes and sweeping floors, she returned to her make-believe world.

Fortunately Kagagi had been watching the dramatic happenings from a nearby pine tree and the little raven flew as fast as he could to the cabin and tapped excitedly on the window with his beak.

"Come quick! Come quick!" he told Martha. "Your father is in great danger."

Martha climbed onto the back of Kagagi, who had grown as big as the cabin, and the two friends rushed to the rescue, snatching her father from the claws of the Wendigo just in time.

Martha and Kagagi turned to face the angry Wendigo. Kagagi swelled to the size of a mountain and cried out in a voice of thunder, "Take that, you bad Wendigo," and stomped him to death.

Martha, Kagagi and her father returned to their cabin with a supply of caribou meat as well as a bag of flour that they just happened to find lying on the trail, and the danger of starving to death or being eaten by the Wendigo was over.

And after one imaginary adventure ran its course, Martha would embark on another, and another and another, blotting out as much as she could the dreary daytime life of the school until it was time to go to bed and she could escape to her nighttime world of fantasy.

Sister Angelica, not suspecting that the little girl inhabited a parallel universe, mistook Martha's serene demeanour and look of preoccupation for a natural sense of piety and allowed herself to hope. Perhaps Martha would become a novice at the convent in Quebec City where she had taken her vows. Perhaps she would return one day as a sister and become a teacher. It would be wonderful to have another Indian at the school who had risen above her lot in life who could be her friend and serve the Church.

3

Father Lionel Antoine

SHORTLY AFTER CHRISTMAS, Father Lionel Antoine, responsible for the spiritual direction of the children and the nuns, took an interest in Martha. Lost in her own world, the little girl had not paid him much attention. To her, he was the fat, balding grown-up dressed in black who was constantly dropping into her classroom to stare and smile at the girls and make them feel uneasy. He was the priest who led prayers in the mornings and evenings in the chapel and who conducted the long church services on Sundays. He was also, she noticed, the one person the nuns treated with unfailing deference, and someone the older students made fun of behind his back.

What Martha and the others did not know was that Father Antoine was a lonely and deeply troubled man. That had not been the case when he was a child and adolescent. His parents, now long dead, had lavished love and praise on him when he was growing up, and he was well liked and known in his village as someone with a wry sense of humour, who was a passionate fan of the Montreal Canadians and their star players, Howie Morenz and Sylvio Mantha.

At the dances held every Friday night in the church basement, he had been a favourite of the older ladies, whom he never failed to ask to join him on the floor. He was always among the first to volunteer his services at the suppers and bingos organized by the Church to raise funds for missionary work abroad. An eager reader and passionate lover of books, he had haunted the village library, developing an interest in the history of the Church, in medieval music, in village life in New France and in nineteenth-century French novels. He had even put together an impressive personal library that he never tired of showing off to friends and relatives.

Most important, all his life he had been devout and had obtained consolation from his faith and joy from singing in the choir. He loved the beauty, mystery and ceremony of the Latin liturgy, the harmony and balance of the holy words chanted by the priest, and the scent of incense and the flickering of votive candles. On the day of his confirmation at the age of thirteen, he was overcome by the presence of the Holy Ghost and underwent a life-altering religious experience. He knew from that moment his vocation was to be a priest serving God in a small, rural parish, just like the one he called home.

When he told the village curé, his parents, his friends and relatives, they rejoiced with him. The curé marked him out for special favour, making him an altar boy, obtaining a scholarship for him to go to a classical college boarding school for boys in a nearby town, and using his influence in the Church to have him accepted at a seminary in Quebec City.

His happiness and sense of fulfilment would have been complete were it not for an obsession that disturbed him greatly—as long as he could remember, he had been attracted by prepubescent girls. As an adolescent at his classical college, he did not find his feelings unnatural. He joined in the laughter as his friends repeated the smutty stories they heard their older brothers tell when they went home on weekends.

But when he was in his early twenties at the seminary, he found he could not stop himself from fantasizing about little girls, and only about little girls. He sensed that his feelings were unnatural and sought the advice of an older priest, his confessor.

"My son," the priest asked him, "have you ever done anything improper with a little girl?"

"Of course not, Father."

"I would not worry too much. You are probably just going through a phase in your life that you will outgrow. You should pray for strength to resist your weakness, and remember, never, ever, act out your fantasies."

However, despite much fervent praying, the seminarian's obsession became stronger, and incidents occurred, all of which were hushed up. In one instance, the parents of an eight-year-old girl walked into the vestry of their church to find him fondling their daughter who was sitting partially undressed on his knee.

The girl's mother swept the girl up in her arms and the father punched and kicked the seminarian as he fled the room.

"*Espèce de maudit salaud!* Don't think that because you're a member of the Church you can do such things to a little girl! I'm going straight to the police. *Tabarouette!*"

The police, however, were reluctant to lay charges against a future member of the clergy and asked the bishop to smooth matters over.

The bishop received the angry parents at his official residence.

"I have asked you here this morning," the bishop said, "because I want to express the remorse of the Church for the actions of the young man. I understand your anger and I must tell you I would feel the same way if I was in your shoes. However, I am a bishop and must think of the well-being of the Church. If you press charges, its reputation would be damaged. As good Catholics, you wouldn't want that, would you?"

When the parents grudgingly nodded their concurrence, the bishop quickly told them to condemn the sin and pray for the sinner.

"Leave the matter in my hands," he told them. "I promise you that that young man will never do such a thing again. You can be certain that the Good Lord himself would want it dealt with in this way."

The parents nervously glanced at Pope Pius XI smiling beneficently at them from a framed photograph hanging on the wall and quietly left the premises.

Since the seminarian was so widely read, so ardent in his faith, so passionate about the Church, its music and its history and such a good candidate in every other way, the bishop allowed him to be ordained when the time came. But to ensure he would cause no future scandal, he sent him to an Indian residential school in northern Ontario, where presumably he could do no harm, to cater to the spiritual and moral needs of the children and teaching staff, all of whom were nuns.

Father Antoine was so pleased at escaping arrest and being allowed to accept his calling, he embraced with great energy his new duties—at least for a while. In his daily routine, he celebrated Holy Eucharist, led prayers, delivered sermons, heard confessions and taught catechism to the children, preparing them to take their first communion and, later, for their confirmation. In his free time, he read the books from his library that he had brought with him from home.

Every Saturday, alone in his room, he listened to *Hockey Night in Canada*, broadcast on the CBC Northern Service from the Forum in Montreal where the home team, with their new generation of superstars such as Maurice "Rocket" Richard, Toe Blake and Elmer Lach, played their home games.

But as the years passed, and as the 1940s became the 1950s, his enthusiasm waned. Some nights he would turn from the book he was reading to think of the life he could have had as a priest in a small Quebec village if he had not been found out. He would imagine himself knocking on the door of a farmhouse on a cool, dark, fall evening. Supper would be over but the family of twelve would not yet have gone to bed. The children would be playing cards on the kitchen table, the mother and her eldest daughter would be drying the dishes, and the father would be listening to the latest agricultural news on the radio.

A child would answer the door and would cry out in pleasure on seeing him. "Mama, papa, *c'est monsieur le cure! Venez vite! Venez vite!*"

Mama and papa would hurry to the door. "*Entrez, s'il vous plaît. Entrez. Quel plaisir de vous voir. Quel honneur vous nous faites de votre visite.*"

As they ushered him into their modest home, repeating over and over how honoured they were by his visit, mama would ask him to sit in the parlour but he would say "No, no, no, I would love to join the family in the kitchen. Don't forget, I am a son of the land and know the best place to be in a farmhouse."

He would enter the kitchen and pull up a chair to the table, the cards would be quickly cleared away, the radio switched off, and mama would soon be serving him a cup of freshly brewed coffee and a piece of homemade *tarte au sucre*. He would joke, laugh, gossip and dispense wise counsel throughout the evening as the fire in the big cookstove roared, as grandpapa puffed on his pipe on a nearby rocking chair and chuckled, and as the family dog stretched out in comfort at his feet.

The scene would shift and Father Antoine would be celebrating midnight mass on Christmas Eve before a standing-room-only crowd of the faithful who had defied the arctic temperatures and snowdrifts to come to church. The mood of the villagers would be joyful and passionately spiritual, for Christ the Saviour was born at midnight and they had gathered together, missals in hand and wearing rosaries, just as their ancestors had over the centuries in France and in Quebec, to receive Holy Communion, to pray, and to sing the traditional carols.

Closing his eyes, Father Antoine would hear once again the words of the *Huron Carol*, composed by the great Jesuit missionary and martyr Saint Jean de Brébeuf, who had been burned at the stake by the Iroquois with a necklace of red-hot hatchets around his neck in the early years of New France. It was his favourite hymn and he never failed to be inspired by its call to Christians "to take heart, for the Devil's work was done."

> *Chrétiens, prenez courage,*
> *Jésus Sauveur est né.*
> *Jésus est né, Jésus est né,*
> *In excelsis gloria!*

Outside the door to the church there would be a Christmas tree decorated with holly, wreaths and coloured lights. Inside, there would be a Nativity scene of a miniature village in ancient Palestine, with Mary, Joseph and the baby Jesus surrounded by the Three Wise Men and shepherds with their sheep and lambs. A sweet smell of incense and flowers would fill the church, rows of candles would be blazing on each side of the sanctuary and the bells would be ringing.

And he, Father Lionel Antoine, beloved shepherd of his parish, would be there, tending his flock on one of the most important and joyous celebrations of the French-Canadian religious calendar year.

Then the desolate sound of the wind, blowing day and night out of nowhere over the foul-smelling, salt-water mud flats separating the school from James Bay, would bring the priest back to earth. Loneliness would engulf him, and he would put down his book, rise from his chair, and begin wandering aimlessly through the deserted halls. As he passed the dormitories, he would hear the muffled sobs of some frightened, homesick student and would feel a sense of solidarity mixed with envy. Both of them, student and priest, he could not help thinking, were prisoners in exile from their homes serving out harsh sentences. But the child would be free to return home after ten or twelve years while he was condemned to remain in his prison until he retired.

As the years went by, Father Antoine grew bitter, and he shut himself up in his bedroom and adjoining office, emerging only to say mass and teach catechism. He let himself go to seed, bathing infrequently, allowing an unkempt beard to take root on his face and wearing the same clothes for weeks at a time. He gave up reading and even stopped listening to *Hockey Night in Canada* on the radio, even though the Montreal Canadians year after year were now winning the Stanley Cup.

These changes did not go unnoticed by the nuns. In an effort to cheer him up, they dipped into the budget allocated for the children's food and sent away for expensive, high-quality meats, butter and vegetables. Soon they were preparing, and anxiously delivering to his office, meals of roast beef covered in rich gravy, meat pies and tomato sauce, homemade bread lathered in butter, mashed, roast, and French-fried potatoes, baked beans and bacon, hot, heavily buttered toast, apple pie with whipped cream, roast chicken and braised Canada goose.

Naturally, with such a rich diet, the good Father became fat. When he became fat, he became remorseful, aware that in the eyes of the Church, gluttony was a venial sin only, but still, something to be ashamed of. He felt even worse when he went one day into the dining hall where the students were eating their evening meal. What a stink. What flies and cockroaches. What minuscule portions. What unappetizing dishes of lumpy mashed potatoes, greased bread, cornstarch pudding and powdered milk. The food was not fit to eat by any civilized being.

For a few moments, he felt a twinge of conscience—what the nuns gave him was so much better. He soon got over it, however, when he remembered that at their homes back on reserve, the children subsisted on a diet of game, lard, bannock and tea—fare, in his opinion, that was vastly inferior to what they received at the school.

The day came, almost inevitably, when he could no longer control himself and he molested a little girl. At first he was afraid because she fled his office in hysterics and told the nuns that he had hurt her. But no one believed her and he realized that he was free to do anything he wanted without fear of sanction. The Indian girls were under his control, and the nuns, even if they were to take the word of a child over his, would never think of calling the police or reporting him to his superiors. He was after all, a priest, and they had been trained to obey priests without question. In any case, the residential school was far from Quebec and if word was to trickle out to his superiors, the worst that would happen, he was now convinced , would be that he would be transferred to another residential school where he could carry on as before.

He thus informed the nuns that in his village, *le curé* had played a big role, when he was a boy, in helping him deepen and enrich his religious sensibilities. He wanted to do the same for a select group of Indian girls because, he said, more needed to be done to encourage religious vocations for women.

"I will pick them out myself," he said. "All you have to do is to bring them to me in my office and I will provide them with private spiritual guidance."

Pleased to see him show interest in his work, the nuns followed his instructions conscientiously and, over the years, sent a steady stream of hand-picked little girls to his office where, after passionately and sincerely professing his fatherly love to each in turn, he sexually assaulted them. Only, he told himself, his actions did not really constitute assault since he was always gentle. He was not, he convinced himself, an ogre, even if his little visitors sometimes cried. He was certainly not a pedophile, since in his way of thinking, pedophiles preyed on little boys and not on little girls.

To the delight of the nuns, Father Antoine emerged from his depression and began to smile again. He had, they concluded, finally adjusted to life at the school and found a reason for living.

One day early in the new year, Sister Angelica told Martha that Father Antoine wanted to see her. The nun knew why, for she had been among the little girls he had summoned to his office when she was a student at the school. At the time, she had accepted what he did to her passively, and being gullible by nature, had believed him when he told her that he loved her. Even though the priest had dropped her when she became a teenager, she remained fiercely loyal and passionately attached to him. She had never told anyone, not even the other nuns, about what took place behind his closed door.

In her opinion, Father Antoine had caused her no lasting harm and so she did not intend to warn Martha about what lay in store for her. Besides, the priest's attentions, she had come to believe, had constituted a sort of test or rite of passage that you had to go through before you could go on to greater things in life. She wondered, however, if Martha would be up to the challenge.

Martha, oblivious to what awaited her, dutifully made her way to Father Antoine's office along a corridor lined with reproductions of paintings of Jesus suffering on the cross, and knocked on the door.

"*Entrez!* Come in!"

Martha turned the handle and pushed open the door. Inside was a desk so enormous she could not see over it, and to one side a small table on top of which were a half-empty glass filled with what looked like red water, several slices of thickly buttered bread and a half-finished plate of meat and potatoes. On the wall behind the desk was a large black-and-white photograph of a group of people, a smiling young priest in the middle, standing in front of a big house. Shelves crammed with books covered the other walls. And sitting in front of the table eating his dinner was Father Antoine himself.

The priest put down his knife and fork, wiped his mouth with the back of his hand and examined the little girl carefully from head to foot. Smiling gently, he motioned for her to close the door and come to him.

"*Ma petite fille*, you are so timid. But you are not here because you did anything wrong. You will not be punished. I have been watching you ever since you arrived and know you had a hard time at the beginning. You have coped well and seem to have a religious nature. I spoke to Sister Angelica who told me she has observed the same thing in you. I want to spend some time with you, and to help you in your spiritual growth.

"Here, come sit with me."

Martha drew nearer, and the priest, after pushing the table to one side to give himself room, pulled her onto his lap and held her close.

"Did you know, *petite Marthe*," he whispered into her ear, "that you are named after a pious and famous woman in the Bible?"

Although Martha had made great strides in learning English, she did not understand what the priest was saying, and if she had, she would not have cared.

She only knew that she had been hauled against her will onto the lap of someone whose body smelled of sour milk, whose breath was stale, whose teeth were dirty, who had bread crumbs on his unshaved chin and who had hairs protruding from his nose and ears.

"*Marthe, Marthe*," the priest said earnestly. "I have no friends here and neither have you. You are so sweet and innocent and we can make each other so happy."

Martha squirmed, trying to escape, and was frightened and uncomfortable when he thrust his hands under her clothing, and with a fixed mirthless smile, did things to her that she knew were not right.

"Now, *ma petite Marthe*," the priest said afterwards, as if she were his accomplice rather than his victim, "you are never to say what goes on here between us. I asked you to sit on my lap because I wanted to show you how much I love you."

He lowered the silent girl to the floor, opened a drawer in the desk, extracted a candy and gave it to her saying, "I keep a supply of these right here and I'll give you one every time you come to see me."

Returning to his chair, he sat down and resumed eating his dinner.

Martha made her way to the door, pushed it open, let it close behind her and stood still for a moment. She then hurled the candy to the floor, burst into tears and fled crying to her dormitory where she threw herself on her bed and buried her head in a pillow.

"Well, Martha, what do you think of Father Antoine?" asked Sister Angelica when she came to see her shortly afterwards. "He's a nice man, isn't he? Did he speak to you about the love of God? Did he give you a candy? Did he ask you to come back? You're such a lucky little girl!"

Martha turned her face away and refused to reply.

That night, while not fully understanding what had happened, she felt dirty. And try as she might, Martha was no longer able to use her imagination to escape the reality of life at the school.

The next week, when Sister Angelica came to her after class to tell her Father Antoine wanted to see her again, Martha began to cry.

"I don't want to go. He did things to me I didn't like. He scares me."

Sister Angelica tried to reason with her. "There is no reason for you to be afraid. Father Antoine is a holy man who spends his nights in prayer. He has only the best interests of the little girls in mind when he asks for them!"

When Martha remained unconvinced, she took her by the hand and led her, still whimpering, to the priest's office and pushed her in the door. In the weeks and months that followed, Martha, who had concluded there was no one who could protect her at the school, walked alone and dry-eyed to meet the priest each time he called for her.

In late June, when Martha returned home to spend the summer with her parents, she was anxious to tell her mother that the people at the school were mean to the kids and that it was an awful place. Her mother, however, despite the reassuring words she had offered to her daughter the preceding August, was well aware that children were badly treated at the school. But her way of dealing with painful matters was to pretend they did not exist. She certainly did not want to endure the mental anguish of listening to her daughter talk about her sufferings. There was nothing she could do to help her daughter anyway. There was no way out for her.

Thus, she avoided any mention of the school, and when Martha tried to tell her that Father Antoine was undressing and touching her where he should not, she refused to listen.

"Don't say that! Don't say such things! I don't want to know. Priests don't do things like that! You're just looking for an excuse, making up stories not to go back at the end of the summer." Taking her daughter by the arm, she squeezed it hard saying, "What's come over you? You used to be such a good girl. Now you don't care about your family!" Martha was frightened. The loving mother she had known before she was taken away to school had been replaced by an angry woman inflicting pain on her.

"Don't you know the government is sending us money every month as long as you stay in that school," said her mother, continuing to berate her. "We are poor people and the money will keep coming every year until you turn sixteen. Don't you understand we have a debt at the Hudson's Bay Company store, and that money pays for our flour, baking powder and lard. You'd better get used to the idea, because you're going to be at the school for many years to come!"

Afraid to talk back, Martha nodded her head to signify she would do as she was told. She had expected her mother would refuse to let her return to the school when she heard how horrible a place it was. Now she was in trouble for complaining and would have to spend years at the mercy of Father Antoine.

Just when it seemed matters could not get any worse, her aunt took her aside.

"Little Joe, my boy, has just turned six and must go to the school this fall. I know, and you know, that kids are not always treated well there. They can be lonely and they can be bullied by the big boys and hit by the nuns. I don't want him to go but I have no choice. The trader has warned me that the Mounties will come and take him away if I try to hide him. I know it's a lot to ask, but could you keep an eye on him and protect him for me? Don't let him get lonely. He's so small for his age and is so attached to me, he couldn't cope without you."

Martha had just turned seven, and she knew that there was little she could do to help her cousin. She couldn't even take care of herself. But looking into the anguished eyes of her aunt, and being by nature compassionate, she promised she would ensure no harm came to Little Joe.

Her aunt hugged her. "I'm so happy," she said. "You've always been a kind and gentle girl. With you looking out for him, I know he'll be fine."

A truly terrible year began for Martha and Little Joe. With her mother and aunt looking on, Martha and the boy climbed aboard the float plane that came to take them away at the end of August. This time she knew it was not a Wendigo, and was able to reassure Little Joe that nothing bad would happen during the flight. That would be the last time she would be able to help him.

At the dock, they were met by the same nun who had greeted Martha a year before. Without a word, she took Little Joe's hand and led him up the hill to the residential school, motioning Martha to follow. At the door was Sister Angelica, waiting to assist her colleague in preparing the boy for his new life. When Martha offered to help, Sister Angelica paid her no attention.

Soon Martha heard the screams of Little Joe as the nuns undressed him, pushed him into the shower, cut off his braids and poured coal oil on his head. She held her head in her hands as she heard shouting, slaps being administered, renewed howling and silence. Later a grim-faced Sister Angelica led him into the dining room. He smelled of coal oil, his hair was shorn, he was dressed in regulation clothing and his face was covered in welts and swollen from crying.

Little Joe rushed to Martha, but Sister Angelica pulled him away, and told him in English that he was never to approach a girl again.

The boy, who did not understand English, said in Anishinaabemowin, "But Martha is my cousin. She is supposed to care for me."

"Just do as she says," said Martha in the same language. "She'll hit you really hard if you don't."

Sister Angelica, who understood what had been said and did not like it, turned on Martha.

"Stay out of this! I don't need your help to deal with this brat. Remember, it is forbidden to speak your heathen language here at the school. Besides, who do you think you are anyway, talking to a boy and interfering with the duties of a nun?"

She slapped Martha across the face, causing blood to spurt from her nose and down across her blouse, and ordered Little Joe to go to the front of the room. There she started to strap him on his hands and wrists.

As the other children watched in fascinated horror, Martha slipped out of her seat, walked slowly and deliberately to the front, caught hold of the strap and tried to stop the punishment.

"He's just a little boy," she said to the nun. "My aunt asked me to protect him."

"Protect him? Protect him? His mother should be grateful for what we're doing for him."

With the help of another nun, Sister Angelica dragged Martha roughly from the room and down to the basement. There they tied her hands together and attached them with a rope to the overhead hot water pipes. The two of them pulled off her dress and flogged her with electrical cords until her bowels loosened and she fouled her pants. They then untied her, pushed her into the coal cellar and locked the door.

"You dirty savage, never, ever interfere with our work again! Let's hope this teaches you a lesson."

The next morning, they released Martha from her unlit hole but made her stand, stinking and filthy, in front of the student body, and contritely apologize to the nuns.

"Now let this be a lesson to the rest of you. Disobey us and you'll get the same."

The following day, Sister Angelica stopped her after class to say Father Antoine had heard that she had been misbehaving and wanted to see her immediately.

Martha burst into tears, and said she did not want to go.

"You ungrateful animal! You upset the school one day, promise to be good, and refuse to see Father Antoine when he asks for you. I once thought you would have a future in the Church but I was mistaken. From now on I'll be keeping a close eye on you and you'll pay heavily if you don't do as you're told."

She took Martha by the hand and dragged her to Father Antoine's office and knocked on the door. When the priest invited them in, she shoved her inside and left her.

Father Antoine came from behind his desk, took her in his arms and hugged her.

"There, there, *Marthe, ma petite*. I know you have been through a lot of difficulties. You must have missed me over the summer. I missed you. Such a long time. No wonder you have got into trouble with the nuns. Now we are together again and I can help you. You know you are my favourite."

He led the crying little girl to his chair behind his desk and pulled her up on his lap. This time, he went further than ever before.

"I am doing this because I love you," he whispered. "I will now tell the nuns to leave you alone. However, you must stop trying to protect the boy and keep what we do here a secret. If anyone was to learn what we are doing, you would be in great trouble."

He released the sobbing girl who fled back to her dormitory.

Little Joe never adjusted to life at the school. He had learned that first day that Martha was powerless to protect him, and each night he cried himself to sleep and wet his bed. And while crying yourself to sleep was not a punishable offence in the eyes of the nuns, wetting your bed was. Their operating principle was that bed-wetting was anti-social, rebellious behaviour that had to be eradicated by corporal punishment and public humiliation.

The punishment, of course, did not work, since Little Joe had no control over his bladder. Every night, therefore, he wet his bed. Every morning he was beaten by the nuns and forced to stand in front of the other children during breakfast with the urine-soaked sheet over his head. Sometimes he was joined at the front of the dining hall by other boys and girls similarly garbed in wet, stinking sheets, but usually he stood there alone, sobbing quietly.

Martha, cowed into submission when she had tried to intervene and her morale crushed by the ongoing abuse of the priest, gave up trying to help him. Several of the big boys, underfed and always hungry, started bullying him, forcing him to hide food from his plate at meals and give it to them afterwards. If he did not comply, they cornered him in the washroom and beat him.

Martha watched with a sense of resignation as Little Joe grew thin and sickly. Finally one day he did not come to breakfast, did not appear at lunch and was absent from dinner. Martha did not see him alive again.

Several days later, Father Antoine held a funeral mass for him.

"Boys and girls, let us rejoice! The soul of this child has left this vale of tears and gone to a better place! Hallelujah! Praise the Lord!"

Six boys, including several who had been stealing his food, carried Little Joe's tiny wooden coffin out the door to the residential school cemetery. There, he was buried beside the dozens of Native children who had passed away at the school over the years. A wooden cross with his name and date of birth was hammered into the ground at the head of the little heap of earth, and he was forgotten.

Forgotten by everyone, that is, except by Martha and the boy's family at Cat Lake Indian reserve.

When Martha returned home the following June, she did not know that when Native children died at residential schools, often from pneumonia, tuberculosis, malnutrition and heartbreak, school administrators sometimes did not notify their parents. After all, communications with Indian reserves in the north were difficult. Indians, in any case, were ignorant savages, were used to the deaths of their children and probably did not grieve like civilized white people.

There was also the bother of dealing with so many dead children. In the early days, sometimes up to half of all the children in a class died, and it would have taken an inordinate amount of valuable time, better spent on more important matters, like submitting routine reports on the functioning of the school to the bureaucracy in Ottawa, than in informing their next of kin. Why send messages, when their families would learn the news anyway from the other children when they returned home for the summer?

When she emerged from the float plane alone, therefore, Martha assumed that the stricken look on her aunt's face was due to the death of Little Joe. She did not know that her aunt had just realized that her boy was dead.

"I am so sorry, auntie," she said, and walked toward her silent mother who had likewise just guessed what had happened.

In tears, her aunt rushed wildly at Martha, seized her by the arms and began to shake her.

"How could you? You promised me you would protect him! It's your fault!"

Martha's mother intervened. "Don't blame her. She's just a child. You gave her too much responsibility!"

The aunt released Martha and asked, "At least tell me how he died. Did he suffer?"

Martha said nothing, not wanting to cause even greater pain by providing the details. Her aunt, however, mistook her reluctance to speak as an indication of a lack of concern, and after giving her niece a nasty look, returned to her home to break the devastating news to her family. Even later, when the other children told the aunt what had really happened, she never forgave her niece—for she had promised to protect Little Joe and had failed to do so.

When Martha climbed aboard the float plane in late August to return to the residential school, she was accompanied by another six-year-old, this time a girl. In the years that followed, as they turned six, a procession of other children accompanied them on the flight. Humiliated and hopeless after the beating she suffered when she had tried to help her cousin, and embittered by the ongoing sexual abuse from the priest, Martha did nothing when she saw Sister Angelica leading the girls to Father Antoine's office.

As the years went by, the priest became more and more demanding, and Martha coped as best she could by retreating within herself and numbing her emotions. At times she gazed at the photograph on his office wall and wondered who the people were. The young priest in the picture was obviously the son of the happy mother and father who stood on each side of him. But who were the kids in the picture? Were they the brothers and sisters of the priest? Were they cousins or neighbours? Had they just come from church? Had they just had lunch or dinner? What had been served? What had they talked about? Were his brothers and sisters still proud of him? Would the parents have been pleased to know that at this very moment their son was forcing himself upon a helpless child?

One day, however, after she turned twelve, she could take no more. She would kill herself, she told Father Antoine, if he did not leave her alone, and she meant it. The priest, who preferred much younger girls in any case, summoned her no more.

By that time, Martha had become completely disillusioned with life and was desperately lonely, and from time to time would allow a teenage boy to sneak into her bed at night. It was easy to arrange. The nun on duty at her dormitory was hard of hearing and slept soundly from when the lights were turned off until the first bell announcing the start of a new day the next morning. The anxious boy would wait until it was late enough, and slip quietly into the dormitory and join Martha. No one ever reported her, and she was never caught.

Each time she had sex, she thought not of the teenager in bed with her, but of Father Antoine and the nuns. How enraged they would be if they knew she was flouting and undermining their hypocritical moral principles—and under their very noses! She did not even care if she became pregnant, since the worst that could happen would be expulsion from the school—something she would welcome.

In her final years at the school, Martha appeared calm and resigned to serving out her time. She had her moments of laughter and joy, and even if she was not able to forgive Sister Angelica, with the passage of time she came to understand that the nun, like her, was a victim of forces beyond her control. But most of the time, she seethed with pent-up rage, almost weeping when students were punished as she had been by being tied to the overhead steam pipes in the basement, beaten and thrown into solitary confinement in the coal cellar. She could not stand hearing the nuns say, again and again, that the students should be grateful that God had sent emissaries into the middle of nowhere to educate Stone Age savages and to save their souls. She never forgave them for not telling her when her father unexpectedly died of a heart attack.

But it was Father Antoine that she loathed the most. Whenever they passed each other in the halls, he smiled at her and she averted her eyes. Try as she might, she could not shut him out at night when she relived in her nightmares the abuse she had suffered at his hands for so many years. During Sunday mass when he spoke about the love of God, she paid no attention to what he was saying and devised imaginary tortures for him. Sometimes, he was standing in a classroom, his head covered with a urine-drenched sheet as the students jeered. At other times, he was her prisoner and she was lashing him as the nuns once beat her. And if on that Sunday he was preaching about hell, she saw him immersed in fire and brimstone, suffering untold agonies for what he had done to her and to the other girls.

When, a decade after her admission to the residential school, Martha was discharged and sent home, she left with the rudiments of a high school education and with emotional wounds so deep they would never heal. It was no comfort to her that the school closed its doors for good shortly thereafter.

4

Returning Home

WHEN MARTHA RETURNED HOME at the age of sixteen, the chubby six-year-old who had been taken away in a float plane so many years before had become a tall, attractive, physically mature young woman with fine, dark-brown facial features and angry black eyes. Much of this anger she reserved for her mother. For Martha had never forgotten what her mother had told her that summer after her first year at the residential school.

"Stop making up stories," she had said, squeezing her arm and hurting her when her daughter tried to tell her Father Antoine was touching her where he shouldn't. "The government will cut off our family allowance cheques," she had said, "if you don't go back to school."

From that moment Martha believed that her mother valued the money she received from the government over the well-being of her daughter.

Martha never mentioned Father Antoine to her mother again in the years she was away. After the death of her father, who had been the quiet but solid force keeping peace in the family, a gulf opened between mother and daughter that grew more pronounced each time she returned home for the summers. When Martha entered the family cabin in late June 1972 carrying a bag filled with her possessions from the school, her mother sensed veiled hostility.

"So look who's finally made it home," she said, taking the initiative. "I guess we're going to have to find some way to get along. But I can't afford to feed you out of my welfare money and you better get down to the band office and apply for your own."

When Martha responded in what she remembered of her language, her mother laughed at her.

"You know even less Anishinaabemowin than you did last summer. You'd think you'd put a little effort into keeping your language."

When Martha tried to help run the household, her mother was not impressed.

"What sort of person have you become, anyway! You come home spoiled by that school, expecting to be fed the food of the white man. But people like me can't live without country food. You can't shoot a gun, set a net, light a fire, chop wood, clean fish, cook bannock or smoke geese—let alone make moosehide moccasins and gloves. Why, when I was a girl, I could do these things before I was ten!"

Martha's mother was not alone in finding it hard to love a child from whom she had become estranged after years of absence at residential school. Her remarks, however, confirmed her daughter's impression that she belonged neither among the whites nor among her own people.

As the months went by and her relations with her mother remained strained, Martha slipped into a depression. Lacking the energy to get out of bed in the mornings, she sat around doing nothing in the afternoons, abandoned her efforts to learn how to fish and hunt, and no longer tried to help her mother with the cooking and cleaning. From time to time, for no obvious reason, she broke down in tears.

Her mother was appalled when her daughter turned to her for help.

"You're bringing shame on our family! You lie around all day letting your old mother do all the work and expect to be waited on hand and foot. In my day, Anishinabe people never got sick in the head. You're just lazy and spoiled. Pull yourself together and above all don't let the neighbours know what's wrong with you!"

But Martha's condition worsened and she was soon unable to sleep. Matters reached a crisis one night when she was, as usual, lying awake and rigid in bed, her senses on high alert. A cold moonlight flooded in through the open window, casting sinister shadows against the walls, and the normal sounds of the northern community assumed a menacing air. Children running and playing behind her house were making fun of her, the hoot of an owl was a premonition of death, and the distant howling of wolves was a direct threat. The dogs, responsible for protecting their human masters from wild animals, answered them from backyards throughout the reserve with irresolute and fearful barking, as if to say, "If it's Martha you want, just come and get her. We won't stop you."

The wind in the black spruce trees whispered that she came from bad seed, from a flawed, inferior race, doomed to disappear and leave no trace on history. It said the nuns had been right— she and her people were Stone Age accidents of history who had been clothed in the skins of animals when the white man arrived, with no alphabet, no books, no music, no calendar, no domesticated animals, no cities and no monuments. It said the Native gods were inferior to the white gods, had been vanquished and would never return, leaving nature empty and forlorn. It said she was weak, friendless and unwelcome in her mother's house, in her community and in her country. It said she came from a place that no longer existed, was living a life that had no purpose, and ultimately, she and her people would disappear from history without a trace.

Suddenly a gust of wind blew through the open window, lifting the sheets on her bed. A malevolent force, perhaps a bearwalker, perhaps the Wendigo, was coming and was about to attack her. She wanted to seek safety in her mother's arms, but if she tried, her mother would push her away. There was pounding on the door, laughter and the sound of children running.

She heard her mother struggle out of bed, fumble around sleepily and stumble to the door. She heard her open it and mutter: "Those kids. Their parents should teach them better manners. They should be in bed at this time of night."

Martha thought of Father Antoine—how she sometimes secretly welcomed his summons, because he was the only one in all those years who ever displayed any affection for her—even if it was just to abuse her body. A possible exception was Sister Angelica, who had tried to encourage her to conform, not to kick up a fuss, if only for her own sake, since it would do no good. She remembered her sex sessions with the boys and felt dirty. A sense of dread seized her, locking her in an icy grip, a crushing weight squeezed her chest and stomach, feelings of worthlessness and self-hatred overwhelmed her. Her world was now a great black pit from which there was no hope of escape.

Slipping into a fitful sleep, she began to dream. She was a little girl of six again and it was her last summer of innocence before she was shipped away to residential school. Accompanied by her parents, she came from a tent, where there had been feasting, drumming and dancing, to a campfire where the people had gathered to listen to a smiling old man tell the old stories. She edged closer and closer until she was sitting at his feet. There was much laughter and good-natured joking, and the little girl felt safe and secure, surrounded by people who cared for her.

The old man announced that he intended to tell stories about the Wendigo, paused as if lost in thought, and looked down at Martha. His smile was gone and his eyes were no longer friendly but were gleaming like burning coals sunk deep in his head.

"Little girl," he told her, "children are not normally allowed to listen to the stories of the Wendigo. Should you insist, however, you can stay but you must be prepared for the consequences."

The elder was actually a bearwalker but Martha was not afraid. After all, her parents were close by and she could count on them for protection. He shrugged his shoulders and began to tell his tales.

There was a flash of lightning and a distant rumble of thunder. The malicious gleam in the bearwalker's eyes faded and was replaced by a glow of fear. He bent over, thrust his face up close to hers and spoke in a voice only she could hear.

"Little girl, I warned you, but you wouldn't listen. Now, never forget what I tell you tonight as you go through life. The Wendigo can do more than just eat people. It can remove children from their mothers, steal their souls, make them hate themselves and their people, ruin their culture and turn them into soulless devils. Worse, it can change the children of these children into Wendigos. The cycle will continue until a shaman arrives in the form of a raven to break the cycle."

All at once, a smell as foul as the one that used to pollute the dining hall at the residential school filled the air. The earth broke open and a repulsive winged Wendigo, as tall as a tree, emerged and looked around, seeking out its prey. When it spotted Martha, its face turned from devil monster into human beast—assuming the lewd look that Father Antoine used to adopt when he abused her. Seizing her with its claws, it squeezed her chest and stomach until she could hardly breathe. Unable to cry out, she frantically motioned to her parents to save her.

Her mother and father anxiously pulled flaming branches from the fire and ran to the rescue, but as they drew near, their footsteps faltered, and they gave her up without a fight. The Wendigo cried out in triumph, opened its wings, and with a roar that sounded like the engine of a float plane taking off at full throttle, lifted Martha in its talons and flapped away across the lake and up into the sky— vanishing from the view of the small band of people standing help- lessly around the fire.

Night turned to day, and the Wendigo, still clutching the little girl in a tight, icy grip, soared upwards toward black storm clouds that appeared on the horizon in the shape of the residential school where Martha had suffered so much. Other winged Wendigos, dressed in the black habits of nuns, and led by one with the head of Sister Angelica, crawled out from under the eves of the building and launched themselves into the air to escort her back to her prison. But suddenly a raven streaked out of the sun, drove off the Wendigos, and as day reverted to night, returned her to her friends and family.

Martha woke early the next morning shaken and fearful. To her and to most people she knew on the reserve, dreams were not the meaningless activity of cerebral neurons firing randomly during sleep but messages from the other world about the future. She dragged herself from bed and went to the house of Joshua Nanagushkin, a family friend who was home with his wife and young children from Thunder Bay where he had a job teaching school. A serious, good-natured individual in his mid-thirties with kind brown eyes, Joshua had attended the same residential school as Martha two decades earlier and his experience there had been positive. Father Antoine, interested only in little girls, had paid him little attention, and as a pious, well-behaved, astute and intelligent student, he had been a favourite of the nuns.

Over the years, he had become the most respected person in the community, widely admired as someone who had made it on the outside but who had kept his Native language and his love and knowledge of the old wisdom. For years, the elders had been urging him to come home to stay and be chief. He promised that he would, but only after he had retired from his teaching job.

Martha knocked on the door of his family's home and entered without waiting to be invited in, as was the local custom.

Joshua, who was sitting at the kitchen table preparing lesson plans for the coming school year, got up and gave her a hug.

"Look at you," he said, "all grown up and so good-looking! I heard you were back. Was school as bad as everyone says?"

Martha nodded her agreement and said. "I need to talk about it. Do you think you'd be able to spare a few minutes?"

"Of course I can. We go back a long way. I'll never forget when you were just a little girl and you used to come home from the land in the summers. You were always so happy and such a little devil. Let's first have some tea and walk over to the lake. I could use a break anyway."

At the shore, the two friends sat down on a log half-buried in the sand beside a fire pit. The night before, a happy family had gathered around a bonfire at this spot to fry fish and bannock and to talk and to laugh. Before leaving, they had poured water on the fire to put it out and to ensure it did not spread into the nearby tinder-dry bush. A smell of wet ashes and grease lingered in the air, as did wisps of smoke from embers buried deep in the charred sticks of wood that were not completely extinguished.

Neither said anything, hypnotized by the magic of northern Ontario on a summer morning. Off in the distance, high in the sky, they could see eagles and hawks on the hunt. Waves, pushed by an onshore breeze that kept away the bugs, lapped at their feet, and gulls wheeled above calling out to each other. Children were swimming and messing around in canoes. A happy elder walked by, carrying his gear and bait, on his way to his boat and looking forward to a relaxing day of fishing.

Eventually Martha shook off the spell and pointed up at the towering cumulus clouds.

"Do you see that? The clouds that look like the ancestors paddling a canoe? Just like the picture painted by the shamans on the rock wall across the lake? They look so sad. It's as if they know what's happening to us young people today."

Martha went on to tell Joshua that she had been feeling awful since she had returned. Her relations with her mother were bad and there were times when she just wanted to die. She had just had a dream that deeply troubled her. Could he help?

"I'll do my best, Martha," he said. "Tell me what really happened to you at the school and what's been going on since you've been back."

Martha talked and Joshua listened, interrupting only to clarify particular points or to encourage her to continue. Finally when Martha had no more to say, Joshua told her that he had been aware Father Antoine had been preying on the little girls for a long time but this was the first time anyone had ever provided him with the soul-destroying details. She should tell the police, he said. He would go with her to provide moral support if she wanted.

"No! No! Please, no," Martha said. "He'll just say I was lying, the nuns would back him up, the police would take his word over mine and I'd be the one who got into trouble. Besides, I just want to turn the page and move on."

"Are you sure?" Joshua said. "He needs to be stopped."

When Martha once again refused, Joshua said, "It makes me sick to think he's going to get away with his crimes. But I'm not going to try to make you do something you don't want to do."

When Martha did not reply, Joshua did not press her further. The two of them spent the next half hour gazing silently at the ancestors in the clouds until they changed form and disappeared.

"I think I'm now ready to let you know what I think about your dream," Joshua said. "In the old days, the elders liked to tell us stories about bearwalkers casting spells on people and the Wendigo stomping through the bush during the spring thaw, eating trappers and their families. They used to say the bite of a Wendigo would turn someone into another Wendigo. Today, not too many people believe those stories, and they're usually told just to scare the children. They're like the tales everyone tells nowadays about Count Dracula, vampires and werewolves. But there are people, and I'm one of them, who believe there's a lot of truth in tales, especially those about the Wendigo, if they come to us in dreams. Only today, the Wendigo is not the cannibal who eats the flesh of the Anishinabe people. It's an unseen spirit of destruction and death that eventually destroys the person it's inhabiting and that person's kids."

When Martha looked at him in disbelief, Joshua said there was more.

"I don't want to frighten you," he said, "but the part where the bearwalker warns you about the Wendigo inside you is really important. I think the Creator is telling you that Father Antoine is a Wendigo and he turned you into one as well by what he did to you.

He's letting you know that the monster inside you will push you to kill yourself, if not now, at some other time in your life. It also means you will drive someone else, perhaps someone dear to you, to die some day."

"Then even worse things are going to happen to me?" Martha asked.

"Not necessarily," said Joshua. "Because there's a raven in your dream who rescues you. It represents someone who will help you to heal yourself one day, but only if you're willing.

"Now, about your mother," he said. "I've known her all my life and she's a wonderful woman. Sure she's made mistakes. But we all have. Do you think she had any choice about sending you to the school? The Mounties would have come for you. We had no rights as Native people in those days. We don't have too many today for that matter. So don't judge her harshly. I'm sure she loves you in her own way but she's from a different time and doesn't understand today's young people. As for your mental sickness, your mother is right in saying that in the old days people never seemed to feel bad like they do today. If they did, they called it something else and got help from the shaman. In any case, you're not the only one around here who's troubled. Many students return from residential school in rough shape."

When Martha remained silent, Joshua made one final effort to reach her.

"You're only sixteen, Martha. Are you going to spend the rest of your life tormented by the things that happened to you in that school? Maybe you should be asking yourself what you really want out of the rest of your life."

"What I really want," said Martha, "what I want more than anything else, is to get away from my mother and this place and make a fresh start somewhere else."

"Then why don't you go for it?" Joshua said. "You can make a good life for yourself without even leaving the north. Why not try your luck in Sudbury, North Bay or Timmins? If you come to Thunder Bay, my wife and I could put you up. If you're really brave, why not try Toronto?"

Their holidays over, Joshua and his family left for Thunder Bay, leaving Martha deeply frustrated and tired of always having to submit to the will of others, whether her mother, the nuns, Father Antoine or even the Creator himself. The more she thought about it, the more outraged she became, and she decided to defy everybody and everything and leave the reserve for good, as soon as she worked out where to go.

While her relations with her mother did not improve, no longer did she spend her days in tears and her nights reliving the trauma of residential school. Feeling better, she began spending time with other residential school survivors who also had grown apart from their families and the community. With nothing to do, they slept in late and got together in the afternoons and evenings at a secluded spot where they used to play as children. There they lit a campfire and talked until dawn about matters they could never have discussed with their parents.

One night, they organized a party that would change Martha's life. Some time before, the council had authorized modest welfare payments to Martha just as it had to the others returning home for good from the residential school, and she was able to make a contribution to the common pot. After receiving their weekly handouts at the band office earlier in the day, the young people had gone to the Hudson's Bay Company store for cigarettes and to the bootlegger's for wine and gin. Before long, they had built a roaring fire and were having a good time, sharing their cigarettes and passing their bottles around. As always when they got together, they told their war stories about life at the school. As always, the lead was taken by Russell Moonias, a tall, solidly built teenager, a few years older than Martha.

At residential school, although Russell had a reputation for being quick tempered and not to be crossed, the students had looked up to him as someone who had never been afraid to defy the nuns. His reputation was made when, at twelve, he had run away from the school with stolen food and a canoe, paddling upstream more than a hundred miles trying to make it home only to be caught and returned.

Everyone was familiar with the details. How the nuns had summoned the Mounties and they had taken after him in a boat powered by twin thirty-horse Johnson outboard motors, as if he was an axe murderer rather than a homesick kid. How he heard them coming while they were still a long way away off, paddled to shore and hid with his canoe until the Mounties went past. How the Mounties frantically roared up and down the river trying to find him, eventually figuring out how he was evading them. How they went upstream, cut their engines and drifted down silently on the current until they surprised him. How he led them on a wild chase through the bush until they cornered him and took him into custody. How instead of being angry with him, they laughed and said they didn't blame him for wanting to go home, but he would "be in for it" when the nuns got their hands on him.

Thus, even though they had heard his story many times, his friends listened attentively when once again he repeated his account of the adventure that had been the defining incident of his short life.

"Do you remember that time I ran away and the Mounties brought me back and Sister Angelica wanted to make an example of me in front of all the kids? She was giving me the strap and I just smiled at her. That made her mad and she tried to hit me really hard but I pulled my hand away at the last second and she hit herself right on the thigh? Do you remember that? How she howled and started to cry? They beat the shit out of me down in the basement but it was worth it just to see the face of that bitch when she got a taste of her own medicine."

"Yeah, do I ever!" someone said. "I got the strap that time, just for laughing. But I didn't care. Never bothered me. Didn't scare me."

"Who did they think they were anyway!" added Russell. "Coming onto our land and treating us like animals. What a bunch of hypocrites. That fat priest making the little girls see him alone just to feel them up and do even worse things to them. The nuns knew what he was doing and did nothing about it."

Like young people everywhere, they also talked about what they wanted to do with their lives. Some wanted to return to the land.

"I'm gonna get married and go live in my father's cabin on the old trapline," one person said. "I don't have an outboard, but I know where I can get a canoe to get there. There's lots of game over there and plenty of good fishing. Since no one has trapped there for years, I should get a good haul."

"You gotta be dreaming," was the comment of another. "There's nobody on the land any more. It's a lot easier to live on the reserve, collect welfare and maybe get a little work in the summers fighting bushfires for the government. You hardly know how to paddle a canoe. And who taught you to trap and skin animals? Where you gonna get money for a grubstake? If you brought back furs, where do you think you'd sell them? The market collapsed years ago."

"Better watch out or the Wendigo will get you!" someone else said. "It'd love eating tender young Injuns even if they were raised on residential school slop."

Others could hardly wait to leave to take their chances in the big city.

"My uncle Amos went off to Toronto years ago. He's back for a holiday. He says there's lots to see and do in the big city and lots of work if you want it. Says it sure beats lying around doing nothing here. But it's a long way. It takes about twenty-four hours by bus to get there. Every two or three hours, it stops to pick up new passengers and to let you buy something to eat if you want. The drivers change every now and then but you can stay on board till you reach Toronto."

"I heard the same thing. All you gotta do is bum a ride out on one of the float planes to Pickle Lake. There are buses going south every day from there and tickets are cheap."

At that moment, Martha decided that she would make Toronto her future home.

But as the night wore on, Russell, who had not paid any attention to Martha during the years they had known each other on the reserve and at the school, seemed to notice her for the first time.

"Hey," he said, twisting off the top of a bottle of gin and holding it out to her. "Why dontcha take a little swig. It'll cheer you up."

Martha had taken the occasional drink since she had started hanging out with the other survivors, but she had confined herself to wine and had not enjoyed the taste. She took the bottle of hard liquor and held it in her hands, uncertain whether to accept Russell's invitation. Seeing her hesitate, he egged her on.

"Go on," he said. "It won't kill you. We're all drinking. Whatsamatter? All of a sudden you're better'n the rest of us?"

Martha tipped the bottle back and took a deep swallow. Russell was good-looking and someone, unlike herself, who had not been afraid to stand up to the nuns.

Gasping and choking, her throat on fire, she wanted to throw up but a deep, warm and exhilarating feeling such as she had never before experienced started in her stomach and mounted to her head, driving away her anxieties, making her deliriously happy and transforming the world around her into a place where everyone was her friend.

"Good, that was really good," she stammered.

"See, I told you," he said. "If one drink can make you feel like that, two'll make you feel even better."

Smiling goofily, Martha seized the bottle and took an even longer drink. This time, she became dizzy and her head began to spin. Finding it hard to focus and to stand, she stumbled and fell to the ground.

Russell helped her to her feet, and led her away. "I know a quiet place not far from here where we can have some fun in peace," he said.

The two lurched along in the dark, hand in hand, laughing, talking and drinking until they came to a little moss-covered moonlit clearing. Russell drew Martha to him and kissed her and told her that he loved her, had always loved her and wanted her to be his girlfriend. He dropped to his knees drawing her down beside him. Martha reached over and loosened his belt and he rolled to one side and removed his clothes. He then pulled her down backwards on top of him and kissed her, repeating again and again that he loved her, that she was beautiful and that he wanted her to be his girlfriend.

But while Martha moaned with pleasure, she grew irritated when Russell continued to insist that he loved her. Through the alcoholic fog that befuddled her mind, she heard herself telling him, "You don't mean it. You're just like Father Antoine saying nice things to me to get your way."

That was the last thing she remembered before waking up alone early the next morning, naked, covered in mosquito and blackfly bites, with the sun in her eyes and a throbbing headache.

When Martha discovered she was pregnant, she told Russell. To her surprise, he was happy. "That's great news," he said. "I've always wanted to have my own family. Let's get married and raise the kid together."

For Martha, however, marriage was out of the question since she suspected their lovemaking had meant no more to him than it had to her. She knew, however, that many of the girls who returned home from residential school were becoming pregnant and moving in with the fathers of their babies as unwed mothers. She decided to do the same thing. She would have to put her plans to leave for Toronto on hold until after she had the baby, but at least she would be able to get out of her mother's house.

She thus told Russell that although not ready for marriage, she would live with him on condition he found them a house. The band council, however, had no funds to provide accommodation to anyone, let alone young couples, who were expected to move into the cabins of their parents and live with them until they built their own log homes. Most of the young people returning from residential school were prepared to do just that, even if it meant a dozen or more men, women and children had to squeeze into homes suited to families of four or five.

Russell, however, managed to obtain possession of the house of a distant relation, an old bachelor, who had recently died. In fact, their new home was just a one-room tarpaper shack. On one side of the room along a wall was an ancient cast iron bed with sagging springs and a filthy mouse-hole-riddled, yellow-stained mattress that smelled of mildew and urine. In the middle of the room, a makeshift stove cut out of a fifty-five-gallon oil drum squatted on legs of empty bean cans, and a column of rusty stovepipes reached up from an opening on the top to the exposed roof, emerging on the other side as a rudimentary chimney. A battered table made of rough lumber with a handmade chair pushed up against it leaned against another wall. A jumble of mouldy, picked-over men's clothing had been tossed into one corner, and in another was a dipper and an empty galvanized steel pail used to carry water from the lake.

The only other piece of furniture in the room was a tattered couch that reeked of old, unwashed men and their billy-goat smell. There were mouse droppings on the mattress, table, chair and couch, and dirt and debris littered the floor. The front door was off its hinges, and water-stained pieces of cardboard covered windowpanes broken by children with nothing better to do. Strategically placed throughout the house were empty lard buckets to catch the water that dripped through holes in the tarpaper roof when it rained.

The new couple made no effort to clean up the shack and to find more furniture. Their friends did not care. The gang of survivors now dropped by every day, sitting on the floor and talking, laughing and arguing late into the night. As before, they celebrated welfare days with bootleg wine and liquor. When they ran out of money, they made a potent homebrew from dry raisins, yeast, water and sugar and kept on drinking.

Martha's mother was overjoyed that her daughter was expecting but shocked at the behaviour of her daughter.

"This is no way to live," she said, when she went to the shack one morning. "There's a baby on the way. Grow up. I didn't raise you to live like a pig."

"But you didn't raise me," Martha said. "Remember? You sent me away when I was little and let the nuns do the job. So why don't you leave me alone? I know what I want. I've got more in common with the kids who were with me at that school than with you!"

After her mother left, Martha celebrated by filling a glass with homebrew and drinking to freedom and to the revenge she was exacting against her mother. But her angry words masked another truth. While resigned to having the baby, she did not want it, afraid to bring into the world someone whose lot in life would probably be as miserable as hers. Besides, she had no idea how a child should be raised, and had not the slightest wish to learn.

Perhaps unconsciously passing a message of rejection to her unborn baby, she abused her body by drinking heavily for a month before it was born and was drunk during its delivery. When she sobered up, however, and saw her baby, a boy, for the first time, her maternal instincts kicked in, and she was overjoyed, convinced that her child was absolutely the most beautiful, the most intelligent and the most lovable infant that had ever existed.

That opinion was naturally enough shared by her mother who took pride in assuming the role of Nokomis, or grandmother, to the little one. The two women, united in their common love for the little boy, put their differences aside, at least for a while, and Martha left Russell to move back home to occupy her old room. Her mother took out of storage the *tikinagan* that Martha had used when she was a baby, and gave it to her daughter for the baby. Shuffling around her cabin, she fussed over Martha and took great pride in her grandchild.

Martha liked being spoiled and had big plans for her baby. His name, she decided, would be Spider, after a prominent web-shaped birthmark on his forehead. He would have an easier life, she was determined, than she had had. Thankfully, the last residential school in the province had just closed its doors for good, and Spider would not face the prospect of being torn from her at the age of six to be raised by white people in an institution devoid of love.

Several months later, however, after a fierce quarrel that started when Martha's mother made a disparaging comment on the quality of her daughter's housekeeping that escalated into a full-blown verbal battle in which both women dredged up past real and imaginary wrongs, Martha strapped Spider into the *tikinagan* and returned in a huff with him to the shack. Russell had prepared the way by coming every day to her mother's home to plead that she come back to him. He loved her, and parents should live together, he said. Their friends were wondering if she thought she was better than they were. And Martha, even if she would not admit it, was now in love with him.

Her broken-hearted mother went to the shack in a final attempt to reason with her.

"You're making a big mistake. If your father was still alive, he'd tell you the same thing. Just think of the well-being of Spider. Your roof leaks, your house is dirty, full of empty beer bottles and cigarette butts and the windows are broken. All the drunks and good-for-nothings hang out here. You can't raise a child in such conditions."

"Look who's talking," said Martha. "There you go preaching to me about how to be a good mother, and yet you sent me away at the age of six to that school. You wouldn't even believe me when I told you I was being molested. You're a hypocrite and I hate hypocrites. Now go away and leave me alone!"

Martha's mother was only in her early forties but like many Native people of her generation who had spent years on the land, looked much older, with a deeply lined face and sunken mouth filled with the blackened stumps of diseased teeth. When her daughter unleashed her torrent of recriminations, she bowed her head and bit her lip.

Once Martha had finished, she tried to make amends. "I can't deny I let you down and wasn't there when you needed me. I'm also bad tempered and hurt your feelings. But I can help you with Spider now. I'm his Nokomis and I love my little grandson. Can't you let bygones be bygones and forgive me?"

Martha slammed the door in her face

Martha and Russell reverted to their old ways, welcoming their friends back to their shack and drinking heavily. When she was sober, Martha made an effort to feed Spider, to play with him and to keep him clean. More often than not, she drank too much and forgot he was even there. Other unwed mothers moved in with their babies and they, like Martha, let their infants go hungry and left them in soiled clothing while they drank, smoked and partied.

One day, officials of the Ontario Children's Aid Society, responsible for the welfare of children in Canada's most populous province, arrived on their doorstep.

"We regret," they said after inspecting the living conditions of the babies, "but the infants in this house are being neglected. It is in their interest that we take them away and put them up for adoption to couples in Canada and the United States who will give them the love and care they deserve. The new mothers and fathers will not be told of the origins of the children and the children will never know the names of their biological parents. To protect them, you will never be told where they are being placed, and you will never see them again. Our decision is final and you have no recourse under the law."

The officials took the babies, including Spider, and departed.

5

Change Comes to the Reserve

IN SHOCK OVER THE REMOVAL OF SPIDER, Martha did not fully grasp the extent of her loss for some time. At first, she blamed white people in positions of authority for trying to force her and the mothers of the other children taken away by the Children's Aid Society to conform to the standards of the outside world. Then the full weight of what had happened hit her. How could she live without her little Spider? How would he be able to cope without his mother? She could not bear the thought she would never see her baby again.

To make it worse, she knew deep down inside that her mother and the Children's Aid Society had been right. She should have been a better mother. She had not taken care of Spider's basic needs and had been a drunk. Her friends lived aimless lives and neglected their kids. She deserved what she got. However, perhaps all was not lost.

"I've decided to quit drinking," she told Russell. "Why don't you do the same and we head off to Toronto and make a new life for ourselves. There's no future here. We could look for Spider. Maybe we could get him back if we show Children's Aid we've cleaned up our act."

"I didn't know you believed all that stuff they fed us at school about the wonderful life we would have if only we lived like white people," he said. "You stop drinking and take off if you want. I like it here and am not going nowhere."

"I wouldn't leave without you," was Martha's answer. "I'll wait as long as it takes for you to change your mind."

Russell's answer was to take the *tikinagum* and throw it out the door, shoving Martha out after it.

"Now go home to your mother if you know what's good for you."

He returned to drink and to brood sullenly as the other couples who had lost their children to the Children's Aid Society partied. Several hours later, by now blind drunk and belligerent, he ordered everyone out, angrily telling his guests not to come back. He then seized an axe and in a wild fury chopped great chunks of wood out of the walls and broke up the furniture. Hurling the axe to one side, he kicked over the stove, stomped on the stovepipes and smashed with his fists the shack's few remaining unbroken windows. His rage spent, he settled down on the floor, his back against the wall, a bucket of homebrew and a dipper beside him, and drank until he passed out.

When he came to and saw Martha standing in front of him, he lurched to his feet, knocked her down and kicked her repeatedly in the ribs, howling drunkenly, "I warned you. I warned you. I warned you not to come back." He then took a gallon of coal oil, sloshed it on the floor, set it alight, and as Martha crawled out the door of the burning shack, slipped away into the bush.

"You're lucky to be rid of that maniac," Martha's mother told her as she recovered at home from her injuries. "He could have killed you. But now you can get on with your life. You're only eighteen and whatever you decide to do, I'll be there for you."

"I'm going to go to Toronto," Martha told her. "I'm going to Toronto to find Spider as soon as I'm back on my feet."

But as time passed, Martha thought less and less about leaving for the big city, and when the government decided to give more authority to Native people across the country to manage their local affairs, she obtained one of the low-level administrative positions that became available at the band office and settled down into a comfortable life with her mother. Although the two headstrong women continued to clash, their relationship improved as the years went by, particularly after Martha learned to speak proper Anishinaabemowin and they began spending their summers together at the old trapping cabin, fishing, picking blueberries and experiencing some of the life they had enjoyed in the old days on the land.

Well aware that her mother preferred country to white man's food, Martha ensured there was always game and fish in the house. She took up a position on the shore of Cat Lake, shooting migrating geese by the hundreds, smoking and curing them for later use in a small traditional birchbark wigwam beside the house. Throughout the winter, she set snares for rabbits that her mother made into stews and roasts, tanning the skins to transform into blankets, coats and mitt liners. Every fall she joined one of the hunting gangs who went after big game deep in the bush, gaining a reputation as a crack shot who brought down her share of moose and deer, and as an expert butcher who could more than hold her own in dressing and quartering animal carcasses.

Her mother could now barely suppress her pride in the hunting prowess of her daughter, and the two women were now able to joke about how green Martha had been when she returned from residential school. And each year, Martha would tell her mother that she would be leaving for Toronto "as soon as I get myself organized," but she never did.

Meanwhile, as the 1970s became the 1980s, the outside world came to the community. The bureaucrats with the money in Ottawa issued contracts to white entrepreneurs to push through a rough but serviceable winter road that would connect Cat Lake with the small, white town of Pickle Lake one hundred miles due east, and the all-weather highway to the south. After freeze-up, workers mounted bulldozers to cut a track through the bush and over the frozen muskeg, pushing aside trees and boulders, shoving sand and gravel into ravines and building causeways to gain access to the lakes and rivers. After the arrival of the first heavy snows, they used modified snow groomers of the type used to prepare hills for skiing farther south to pack the snow down into a drivable road. And from December to March, they kept the road open through the bush and across the lakes by regular snowploughing with graders.

The opening of a road, if only for a few short winter months each year, allowed other contractors to haul in building supplies, prefabricated buildings and everything else needed to erect a new school, a nursing station, jail, and an airport with a one-room terminal building and all-season runway. The band council began replacing the old log cabins with bungalows complete with electricity and indoor plumbing. A co-op came in to take over from the Hudson's Bay store. Satellite dishes appeared on the sides of homes, and the residents were soon watching the same programs as the people in the south.

The people lost no time in using the winter roads to drive out to visit relatives in neighbouring reserves and to make expeditions to the south. Everyone looked forward to the excitement of the trip to Pickle Lake. Those who could cobble together the money would continue on to even more distant places like Sioux Lookout and

Thunder Bay where there were shopping centres and movie theatres. Wives wanted to stock up on detergent, toilet paper and pasta that cost a fraction of what was charged locally. Husbands were interested in cars and trucks, even if they could only admire rather than buy the latest models. Some visited used car lots and bought old clunkers that they nursed back home. When the wrecks fell apart, they put them up on blocks in front of their homes and cannibalized them for spare parts. The young men made for the topless dance bars to ogle the women, sometimes drinking too much and getting themselves into trouble. Children nagged their parents to take them to McDonald's and Burger King and to the movies to see scary films and to let them hang out at the malls, just like the white kids. Everyone relished the chance to catch up on the latest news from friends and relatives who had moved to the city, and who were expected, by aboriginal custom, to invite them to stay in their homes, as their guests, for the duration of their visits.

And just as matters seemed to be going their way, the young people began to kill themselves, and not just at Cat Lake First Nation. In other remote fly-in Anishinabe, Oje-Cree and Cree communities throughout the north, at places no one in the south had ever heard of—Pikangikum, Poplar Hill, Slate Falls, Sandy Lake, Deer Lake, Kee-Way-Win, Sachigo Lake, Bearskin Lake, Big Trout Lake, Weagamow Lake, Muskrat Dam, Webeque, Wapekeka, Kasabonika Lake, Neskantaga, Kashechewan, Nibinamik, Fort Severn, Weenusk, Fort Albany, Attawapiskat, Marten Falls, and Eabametoong—the youth started to die.

Children as young as twelve were doing it. Girls as well as boys were involved. They joined together in suicide pacts, they copied the actions of friends who had killed themselves and they deliberately overdosed on drugs before doing themselves in. More often than not, they hanged themselves, making a statement in the extreme manner of their deaths that they considered themselves to be fundamentally worthless and to merit suffering as they left this world. In the farewell messages, many said they had no other way to escape pain and almost all of them said life was not worth living.

Across the vast northern wilderness, families were shattered emotionally and communities were left deeply scarred and in a state of shock. Schools and band offices closed and there were wakes and funeral services. People, many of them strangers, alerted to the tragedy by the Native-language radio station, Wawatay, broadcasting from Sioux Lookout, came from reserves across northern Ontario to demonstrate solidarity with the bereaved in the face of the incomprehensible suicide of one of their children.

If the death was in the winter, the people would mount their old broken-down vehicles and travel great distances by winter road to the home of the grieving family. In summer, a few would come by boat, but most arrived by air, somehow finding the money for the fare. They would be met either at the shore or at the airport by volunteers in pickup trucks who would drive them to the home of the deceased. There they would take their place outside in the lineup of friends, neighbours and other visitors from far away, and wait patiently to go in to express their condolences.

When their turn came, they would mount the steps of the stoop, push the door open, enter the house, grasp the hands of the family members waiting solemnly inside, averting their eyes in accordance with their custom, and express their sorrow over and over again in the soft, measured tones of their language: *Nin kashkendam, nin kashkendam, nin kashkendam.*

After handing over simple gifts of food—a loaf of bread, a small bag of flour or sugar, a fish, a smoked goose, a piece of venison or moosemeat— they would stand silently and respectfully in front of the simple wooden coffin holding the body of the young person in the living room. And later that evening, they would return to sit throughout the night, weeping and keening and singing the heart-felt, comforting old hymns in Anishinaabemowin with the families of the bereaved.

After the formal church funeral service, usually held in the school auditorium or hockey arena to accommodate the press of numbers, the people would go home and life on the reserve would slowly return to normal.

Another teenager would then be found dead, lying in the underbrush by the side of the road from a drug overdose, dangling from a cord attached to a hook in a closet, or hanging from a rope tied to a tree branch outside a school as the other children pro-ceeded to class in the morning. The cycle of grief, mourning and incomprehension would begin again.

Why? Why? Parents, chiefs, religious leaders, teachers and the staff at the nursing stations all wanted to know why.

Having thought of suicide during her darkest nights, Martha believed she knew at least part of the answer. Despite the signs of material progress, many of the communities were sick in their collective souls. In many families, the parents, grandparents and great-grandparents had spent their childhoods and much of their teenage years in residen-tial schools where no one ever hugged them, unless it was to molest them. No one ever said "I love you," unless it was a prelude to sexual assault. Dysfunction had cascaded down through the generations with survivors neglecting their children as they had been neglected. Or worse, they sexually abused them as they had been abused.

But the main reason the young people were killing themselves, Martha suspected, was because they had lost their culture and had found nothing to replace it. When Martha was a child, families had spent winters on the land and summers in their cabins around the trading post, and there had always been enough people around to help out the lost generations who returned home broken in spirit. There had always been a few younger people who had managed to avoid attending residential school and were able to befriend the ones who had suffered, and elders who knew the old ways and could help survivors reconnect with their language and culture. However, in far too many places, the experience of the residential schools had inflicted too much damage, destroying the restorative power of the healers.

To be sure, the Native leadership did what it could to cope. The sign at the airport had been changed from Cat Lake Indian Reserve to Cat Lake First Nation in accordance with a practice being adopted by Native communities elsewhere. The chief had said that it would inspire the people to have greater pride and confidence in themselves, but Martha doubted whether symbolic gestures would stop the rot. For the sense of purpose of the communities in her part of the Anishinabe homeland continued to die. The removal of so many children by the Children's Aid Society had shaken them to the core. The people were angry, but they were also ashamed that so many of them had been poor parents. Few of them now had the heart to keep up the annual summer feasting, drumming and dancing celebrations. Even fewer sat around their campfires listening to the elders tell the old stories.

More and more people were now attending services at new churches and accepting what they were told on Sunday mornings as the literal truth. The old view that the land was sacred and that there was mystic power and current running through and uniting all things was being quietly abandoned. The objective of life, they came to believe, was to love God, to fear the devil, to suffer stoically through their earthly existence and to rejoice in death that led to heaven.

If anyone mentioned the shamans, the people would look at each other uneasily. At Cat Lake First Nation, only the elders and a few members of Martha's generation who took an interest in the old ways knew what the reddish-brown pictograph of the ancestors paddling a canoe on the cliff face on the other side of the lake really represented.

Although they had embraced the ways of the white man, the people felt betrayed. The bureaucrats in Ottawa, who were supposed to protect their interests, had spent enormous sums of money to change their communities into modern towns. But less than a decade later, the houses, band offices and schools, often constructed by shady contractors with shoddy materials, were falling apart. The drinking water from the new pumping stations and treatment plants was more often than not unfit to drink, and the sewage lagoons were leaking effluent into the lakes and rivers, killing the fish and poisoning the water supply.

What future did the young people have, other than sitting around at home and collecting welfare cheques? They could not turn to their parents for advice since they had none to offer. So why not just give up and end it all?

When she was feeling down, Martha would wonder whether Native youth were more prone to suicide than white youth. That would lead her to think about Spider, since he was the same age as many of the young people in the north who were dying. Had he been able to resist the temptation? Perhaps he was already dead. If he was not dead, maybe he was alone on the streets of Toronto, hungry and sick after being abandoned by his adoptive parents who had treated him as badly as she had been by the nuns.

At these moments, she would feel bad and blame herself for not having had the will to tear herself away from the reserve to look for him in the big city when there was still time.

———

One morning shortly after Christmas in 1989, Russell, his face scarred and bloated, his eyes cold and hard, his beer-belly hanging down over his belt, and his pants clinging precariously to his hips, pushed open the front door of the family home and came in unannounced.

"Fifteen years," Martha said, "fifteen years and you wander in as if it was just yesterday!"

"Was just in the neighbourhood," Russell said cautiously. "Thought I'd drop in and see you. No hard feelings about our little misunderstanding so long ago?"

"I guess not," said Martha. "A lot of water has gone under the bridge since those days. Have a seat and I'll fix you something to eat."

Martha and her mother busied themselves preparing fresh bannock and tea and Russell made himself at home, stretching out on the couch and talking non-stop about what he had been up to since he had left the community.

"You know, am I ever glad I got out of this dump when I did. To think I used to be satisfied living in that old shack. After I torched it, I headed off cross country to Mishkeegogamang where I know lots of people. I'd always been at home in the bush and it only took me a week to get there. A couple of Native guys came by selling drugs. They were from Thunder Bay and were peddling smokes, dope, coke and prescription drugs to Native high school students across the north. They had more business than they could handle, they said, and they asked me help out. In no time at all, I was rolling in cash. Had a nice car, nice apartment, the girls thought I was something. Then the cops got me," he said, ignoring Martha's mother's look of disapproval.

"But I was lucky. My lawyer told the judge I'd been mistreated in residential school and that was why I had turned to a life of crime. It wasn't my fault, he said. The judge bought the story, hook, line and sinker, and let me off, telling me to behave myself in the future."

"And you followed his advice, I suppose?" said Martha.

"I tried, but I had bad luck. Got into a fight when I was drunk and stabbed someone and the bastard died. Got two years less a day in the Sudbury jail for manslaughter. Was never able to get it together after that. In and out of jail, on the streets, in halfway houses. Got to see the inside of jails in Timmins, Thunder Bay, Parry Sound and who knows where else. But I wasn't to blame. It was the booze. I've been dry for six months now. That's why I'm here."

Martha offered to put him up until he got settled. "But remember, things are different now and if you drink, out you go!"

"Don't worry," he said, "I've learned my lesson. Tomorrow I'm going over to the band office to apply for welfare, and I'll look up the old gang and try to talk someone into taking me hunting and fishing."

The first several days went well. Russell's return had brought back memories to Martha about how much she had loved him when they lived together in the old shack and how terribly upset he had been when the Children's Aid had come for Spider. Thus, although she should have known better, she did not push him away when he joined her one night in bed.

A few evenings afterwards, he was in a bad mood because the chief and council had turned down his request for welfare.

"I really need a drink," he told Martha. "C'mon with me to the bootlegger's and help me drown my sorrows."

But Martha had no sympathy for him. "Listen," she said, "I told you long ago my days as a drinker were over. And don't think you can stay here if you come back drunk!"

"Look whose playing the goody-goody now," he said. "You were a slut in residential school and a drunk when you came home!

Such a rotten mother the Children's Aid took away our son. I'll never forgive you for that."

He stormed out, returning in the early hours of the morning, drunk and in a foul mood, to kick open the front door and scream for Martha. Emerging from their bedrooms, the two women found him staggering around the living room. When Martha's mother told him he had to leave, he became enraged and pushed her to the floor before collapsing beside her in a stupor.

Martha helped her mother to her feet, settled her in a chair and went to her bedroom where she kept the rifle she used to hunt moose and deer. After opening a box of shells, she slid a cartridge into the chamber, slammed home the bolt, returned to the living room and prodded Russell in the belly again and again with the barrel until he groaned and opened his eyes. She then aimed at the space between his eyes, released the safety catch with her thumb, placed her index finger on the trigger and told him to get up and get out.

"If you don't, I'll shoot you, you son of a bitch!"

The next day, the police came across Russell sleeping on the side of the road and took him into custody. Since Martha's mother was not injured, the women did not press charges and he soon left to resume his life on the streets. They never saw him again, but Martha was pregnant.

Mother and daughter were delighted and looked forward to the birth of the baby. But as time went on and winter turned to spring, Martha began to worry. Was she bringing into the world a child who would drop out of school in grade nine like most of the kids on the reserve and drift into a life of alcohol, drugs, welfare and despair? Would Child Welfare come and take away her new baby?

Her mother, however, told her no one in authority would bother her.

"You've learned your lesson," she said, "and you'll be a good mother now. But don't you think it's time you decided what you want to do with the rest of your life? You're not getting any younger and you'll soon be in your mid-thirties. You've never left this place, not even to go out to Pickle Lake for a visit—You've always wanted to go to Toronto," she added. "So why don't you just go and get yourself a good job. In the old days, daughters would often hand over a child for the grandmother to take care of or maybe raise. Why don't you do the same?"

Martha was immediately suspicious. Did her mother want to steal her child? All the old anger suppressed for so many years boiled to the surface. Afraid of losing control of herself and saying something she would regret, she left the house and made her way to a secluded place on the shore of Cat Lake where she often went when she wanted to be alone and do some quiet thinking. Sitting down on a piece of driftwood, she looked up, and to her delight saw high in the clouds the ancestors, this time joyously paddling their canoe across the sky. Without knowing why, Martha felt reassured. Her mother had only the best interests of her family at heart and she could trust her.

"I'll go," she told her mother on returning home. "You'll do a good job looking after the baby and I'll be able to keep an eye out for Spider. As soon as I get a job, I'll send money to support you and the little one. But remember, once I'm established, I intend to return home and bring my baby back to Toronto to raise."

A daughter was born at the time of the Flight Moon, when birds that were hatched in summer begin to fly. Martha named her Raven, because ravens were instruments of deliverance in her dreams. And in January of 1991, she kept just enough money out of her savings to pay for her bus fare and a few nights in a hotel, gave her mother the rest, and prepared to leave for Toronto.

PART TWO

The Big City

~

1991–2003

6

Leaving for Toronto

THE MONTHS BEFORE HER DEPARTURE were not easy for Martha because, immediately after the birth of Raven, Nokomis insisted on assuming total responsibility for the care of her grandchild.

"If you develop close ties with your baby," she told her daughter, "you'll never leave for Toronto, or you'd miss her unbearably when you're gone."

Nokomis convinced Martha not to breast-feed Raven and used her pension money to buy expensive ready-made baby formula from the co-op. When Martha tried to feed and change her baby, Nokomis elbowed her out of the way. Martha persuaded her mother, however, to let her do the night shift.

"I have to get up anyway to put wood on the fire," she said. "It just makes sense for me to take care of her at that time."

Fortunately, Raven was a calm, well-behaved baby who cried only when she was hungry. Martha would get out of bed and carry the *tikinagan* holding her daughter from her bedroom into the living room and prop it up in an armchair. As she walked to the woodbox, she would talk to her quietly and the infant would solemnly follow her mother with her eyes.

"I'm first going to feed the fire, my daughter, and then I'll feed you. Is that okay? Do you agree? Because if I don't, the house will become cold and we'll all freeze. You wouldn't want that, would you? Nokomis would be unhappy and we wouldn't want to upset her, would we? Even though she loves us, she can sometimes get really grumpy!"

Raven would look at her mother gravely with her enormous bright black eyes as if she understood what she was saying.

Martha would open the lid on top of the stove, pick up the poker and stir the embers until they glowed red.

"Now, my daughter, I'm going to give the stove something it loves to eat—some nice, black spruce. I cut it myself last spring in the bush, left it to dry over the summer and hauled it home in the fall. You were there with me, keeping me company, in such a hurry to be born, kicking me all the time to make sure I didn't forget you were there, and I was so happy!"

The fire would crackle after Martha loaded it with wood and she would say, "See, my daughter, the stove is thanking us for its supper and telling us it'll keep us warm for a while yet."

Martha would place a bottle of formula in a pot of water on the stove to warm.

"Now it's your turn to eat. But first I must change your diaper."

After changing and feeding Raven, Martha would rock her gently in her arms, and quietly sing an old Anishinabe lullaby to her, repeating over and over, "Rock, little baby, go to sleep, mommy is watching."

> *We we we we we we we we we we*
> *Nbaa bebiins mamaaamasaa*
> *Nbaa bebiins mamaaamasaa*

The night before her departure, Martha got up around four in the morning, tended to the fire and changed and fed her daughter for the last time. She pulled a chair up and sat beside the stove, rocking her and listening to the sound of the burning wood as she reflected on what the future held for her and her family.

Would she be able to find work in the big city? Were the stories others told about racism against Natives true? Would she find Spider? Toronto was far away and she would miss her daughter. But with any luck, their separation would not last long and she would be able to raise her in a place where there were good schools and a job for her when she grew up.

When Raven closed her eyes, Martha gently put her back into the *tikinagan*, carried it into her bedroom, sat down and watched her sleep. Startled by the rifle crack of a tree exploding from expanding ice in its bark, she went to a window, scraped a peep-hole in the frost covering the glass and looked out. Wawatay, the Northern Lights, had turned night to day. Wanting to experience their beauty and power one last time before leaving the north, she pulled on her boots, donned her parka, opened the door and went outside. Green and red lights swirled down from the heavens to mingle with the smoke that rose straight up from chimneys throughout the community in the subzero temperatures before dancing off across the snow. Gitche Manitou was saying goodbye.

After going back inside, Martha sat up for the rest of the night beside the stove, watching the flames through gaps in the metal and savouring the peace and tranquillity of her mother's home in winter. In the morning, she looked on as Nokomis took care of Raven. Neither woman spoke as they shared their final meal, since it was so hard to say goodbye. Martha dressed warmly, picked up the small backpack she had prepared the night before, kissed Raven one last time and prepared to leave.

Her mother took her in her arms and hugged her.

"I don't want you to go before I say something I should have said years ago. I never told you, but I missed you terribly all those years you were away at residential school. Your father felt the same way and I think he died of a broken heart. I'm going to miss you again, even if I now have Raven to keep me company."

Martha stepped out into the dark of the subarctic morning and wiped away the tears freezing on her face. The morning star, hanging low in the sky, had by now replaced the Northern Lights, and the snow crunched underfoot as she made her way down the road. Dogs lay curled up in the snow in the front yards of their owners, their noses buried under their tails for warmth. Most houses were in darkness, their occupants still in bed after watching televison until the early hours of the morning.

The evening before, she had dropped by the community hotel, a building with three bedrooms, a living room, a common bathroom and a self-serve kitchen used by contractors, truckers and other visitors to the community, to see if there was anyone there who could give her a ride out to Pickle Lake. The driver of a tanker truck, who had just delivered a load of diesel to the generating plant, promised to give her a lift, but told her she had to be ready to leave by seven.

Now as Martha drew close to the hotel, she saw that he had kept his word. A truck, its motor throbbing and enveloped in a great cloud of gasoline fumes and frozen water vapour, was waiting. Grasping the handle to the door of the cab, Martha turned it, pulled it open and hoisted herself up onto the seat beside the grizzled old driver sitting behind the steering wheel.

"Morning! Welcome aboard," he shouted over the roar of the motor. "I was afraid you weren't coming. It'll be nice to have some company. It's a long and boring ride out to Pickle Lake."

The driver turned on the headlights, put his rig in gear and moved it through the community, shifting from first to second, and to third as he picked up speed. Talkative and friendly by nature, he sought to engage Martha in conversation.

"My name's Olavi. That's Finnish. What's yours? Where are you going after Pickle Lake? Off to Thunder Bay? Got relatives there? Taking a winter break? Looking for a job? You lived all your life on the reserve? Do you think it'll be hard to adjust on the outside?"

Martha told him her name and said nothing further. It was difficult to hear what he was saying over the sound of the motor and transmission, and she found his English with its heavy Finnish accent hard to understand. And as her thoughts turned to the life she was leaving behind, his words simply did not register. When she did not respond, Olavi resorted to the radio for company, turning it on and scrolling through the dial until he picked up the local one-watt community FM station operated by a volunteer speaking in Anishinaabemowin.

"*Bojo*. Good morning, everybody in beautiful Cat Lake First Nation. It's seven o'clock and time to get up. It's a cold one this morning. Minus fifty without the wind chill. Sunrise at nine, sunset at three. A sunny day ahead. Mothers, be sure to bundle up your kids before you send them to school. Those of you heading out to Pickle Lake, remember to take spare cans of gas, blankets, shovels, sand and food in case you break down. You might have a long wait. Conditions are good but count on eight hours of hard driving. Now a little gospel singing in our very own language to get you ready for the day."

Olavi was happy when he heard the music. Although he did not understand Anishinaabemowin, he loved listening to the old-time favourites sung with passion whether in Finnish, English, Anishinaabemowin or Cree. In a few minutes, they reached the shore of Cat Lake, and Olavi shifted to first and eased his truck carefully down the embankment onto the ice. Ahead, illuminated by the headlights, was the start of the winter road, marked on each side by black spruce branches stuck in the snow.

"Now the fun begins," said Olavi. "There's only six feet of ice between us and freezing water one hundred and fifty feet deep! I've lost plenty of friends driving on these lakes in winter. Problem is the weight of the truck bends the ice and we push a wave of water ahead of us as we go. Sometimes the wave bounces back off the shoreline and ice just explodes ahead of you from the pressure and down you go. But I'm an old hand. I respect the ice and never go too fast. I keep my door unlocked and am always ready to jump, and you'd be wise to do the same thing."

Martha did not respond and Olavi listened to the gospel music until they were out of range of the station. He then tuned in to the CBC Northern Service broadcasting from Thunder Bay but turned off the radio when he heard classical music playing.

"I like that kind of music but am not in the mood for it today. How about you, Martha?"

Martha said nothing and Olavi tried again. "I've lived in Pickle Lake for more than forty years now. Ever since the end of the war. I'd been called up when I was just a kid to fight the Russians in 1939. Everything went well at the beginning. We pushed those Ruskies back almost to Leningrad and were winning. But our mistake was to have the Germans on our side. When they lost, we lost, and the Russians took their revenge. It was terrible. They stole half the country and times were really tough."

Martha stared impassively out the window as Olavi glanced at her, uncertain how to interpret her apparent indifference. He had seen things as a young man that he would never forget: hand-to-hand combat in the snow, advancing through artillery barrages to engage the enemy as comrades fell beside him, retreating with his unit through burnt-out villages, and long lines of refugees fleeing advancing Red Army troops. Faced with death, he had been more alive than he ever had or would be in peacetime. Perhaps it was too much to expect that someone who had spent her life in the bush would understand the importance of his story.

"That's when the bride and me decided to clear out and take our chances in Canada," he said, feeling compelled to go on. "We came up here because we'd heard there were lots of Finns working in the mines and logging camps. Best thing we ever did. We were already used to the cold and there was always work if you weren't afraid to get your hands dirty. The kids did well. Went to university in Thunder Bay. Became professional people. The bride and me are really proud of them. Just wish they'd come home more often. We miss our grandchildren."

By now Martha was uncomfortable, not understanding what this white man, one of the few she had met since her days at residential school, wanted from her. Why was he telling her about his life before he came to Canada? Who were the Ruskies anyway? What point was he trying to make when he talked about his kids? Was he saying white kids were smarter than Native kids? Was he talking down to her? She wasn't sure. In any case, his words were barely intelligible and he seemed too friendly to be sincere. Perhaps he was just like Father Antoine, saying nice things but just wanting to have sex with her. It was better just to ignore him even if it made her look rude.

Olavi shrugged his shoulders and muttered to himself in frustration.

"What disrespect. I give her a lift and she won't even talk to me. Never understand these Indians if I live to be a hundred! Never open their mouths. Don't even know if she speaks English. Don't understand them. In Finland there were aboriginal people—Lapps.

Raised reindeer and paid their way. Why can't these Indians do the same? I belong in the north just as much as they do. I come from Finland after all. How come I can come to Canada and get a good job—they live here and they can't. How come my kids go to school and become teachers and lawyers and theirs don't? Are these people lazy? Yes, that's probably the answer. They want something for nothing."

As the truck moved eastward, the stars faded in the night sky and were replaced by a crimson glow that lit up the horizon ahead of them. The sun came up, a red ball in a warm orange-cream sky that soon turned lemon yellow and cobalt blue. On the lakes, the sunlight reflected off the snow in a harsh glare, but in the bush, a soft light filtered through openings in the black spruce, hemlock and cedars, colouring the snow green and turquoise. Other than the occasional crow and raven, there was no wildlife to be seen.

From time to time, they met trucks and cars going in the opposite direction, and Olavi would pull over, exchange information on road conditions, tell a joke or two and have a good laugh before continuing on. After each encounter, he would turn to Martha, make a comment or two in the hope she would respond, but she remained silent.

At noon, Martha opened her backpack, removed a cardboard box and gestured to her companion to share her lunch. Olavi brought his rig to a halt and they ate cold smoked Canada goose, bannock, boiled whole potatoes and blueberry pie accompanied by cups of hot tea from Martha's Thermos. While Martha remained as taciturn as ever, the mood in the cab was much improved when they resumed their journey.

By mid-afternoon, a shadow began to run ahead of the truck, the sun turned red and set in the west behind them, the light of the short northern day vanished, and by the time they reached Pickle Lake, the stars had reappeared. When Olavi dropped Martha off at the entrance to the restaurant that doubled as the bus terminal, he gave her a big, friendly smile and wished her a sincere "Good luck."

Martha pushed open the door, went in and sat down at the counter beside two Native men from Mishkeegogamang who were eating fish-and-chip dinners. They were speaking to each other in Anishinaabemowin when one of them, responding to a joke, burst out laughing. The other grinned and made a quick comeback that provoked an even heartier guffaw from his friend. Martha wanted to join in as they carried on with their bantering, but she was too shy and said nothing.

However, a half-dozen white men and women, waiting for the bus to Toronto at a nearby table, exchanged worried looks. Were the Indians talking about them? Were they drunk? Were they dangerous? Would they have to share the bus with them? Would they smell? Did they have lice?

One of them got up, went over to a woman behind the till who doubled as waitress and ticket agent, and whose name, "Yvette," was embroidered on the blouse of her uniform.

"Yvette," he said, squinting first at her name and smiling at her with an air of complicity.

"Yeah," said Yvette. "What can I do for you?"

"It's about those Indians," the man said in a low voice, indicating with a nod of his head the two Native men who continued to chortle and talk rapidly.

"What about them?" Yvette replied, putting her hands on her ample, matronly hips.

"Look, don't get me wrong, I've got nothing against Indians but I sure hope you haven't sold those two any tickets on the next bus south. My friends and me are worried. They're laughing and carrying on in here and we think they've been drinking. Drunk Indians are dangerous, especially on buses. Don't you think you should call the police?"

But if the white man expected a sympathetic response, he was mistaken. For Yvette, with her blue eyes and blond hair, had come north one summer at the beginning of the 1980s from her small Franco-Ontarian hometown of Hearst to work as a maid at a local fishing lodge. Shortly thereafter, she had met and married a Native guide, and they settled down to raise their family at Pickle Lake. Life would have been perfect had it not been for the racist names their two brown-skinned children were sometimes called in the schoolyard.

"What's it to you if they're going on the bus?" she said, raising her voice until she was almost shouting, and drawing the attention of everyone in the room. "You call the cops if you've got a problem, but you damn well better have some good reasons for bothering them because those two men are behaving themselves just as good as you."

"Okay, okay. Forget I asked," the man said. He returned to his seat, shrugging his shoulders to his companions as if to indicate that he had done his best but this hick waitress obviously wasn't prepared to listen.

After witnessing the exchange, the two Native men glanced at each other and at Martha, paid their bills, pulled on their parkas and went out into the cold. Afraid the white people would try to prevent her from taking the bus since she was Native, Martha wanted to follow them. But Yvette had been watching her and went over to provide reassurance.

"Now don't you worry about those yahoos. You've as much right to be in here and to take the bus as them. Now what can I do for you, dear?"

"I'd like a one-way ticket to Toronto please."

"My, my, you are burning your bridges. I hope you know what you're doing. That'll be fifty bucks. The next bus is in two hours."

With her ticket in one hand, and her backpack over her shoulder, Martha went outside to wait, preferring to stand alone with her thoughts in the snow and cold rather than to share the restaurant with the white travellers who had something against her people.

Eventually, the Greyhound from Toronto pulled up and with a sucking pneumatic hiss, the door opened to let out a handful of passengers. The white people, led by the man who had clashed with Yvette, emerged from the terminal and lined up to present their tickets to be punched and to have their luggage stowed in the exterior compartments before climbing on board. Martha was the last one to enter, clutching her backpack tightly as she took a seat by herself at the rear, as far away from the others as she could get.

For the first three hundred miles, the bus went south and there was little to see from the light of its headlights other than high snowbanks, utility poles, poorly marked roads leading into the bush to far-off reserves, signs indicating they were passing through provincial parks, and billboards advertising fishing and hunting lodges with scenes of moose and giant northern pike and muskellunge leaping into the air.

After reaching the Trans-Canada highway at the Franco-Ontarian community of Ignace, the bus made its way through the light traffic of the winter night southeast toward Thunder Bay. The driver by then had turned off the interior lights, and the only visibility within was provided by the tips of cigarettes glowing in the dark and the illumination of the dashboard dials. One after another, the passengers extinguished their cigarettes, pushed their seats back into the recline position and slumped over asleep until Martha and the driver were the only ones left awake.

From time to time, someone would cough, wake up, stumble half-asleep to the rear, push open the thin aluminum door to the toilet and go in. After a few minutes, there would be the sounds of flushing and water running, and if the person was a man, he would usually lurch out the door still zipping up his fly, and if a woman, she would be adjusting her clothing. Male or female, they brought with them the stench of the toilet mixed with the smell of cheap air fresheners and stale cigarettes.

Eventually, Martha grew angry. She would not allow her fear of the white passengers to keep her confined to the back of the bus! She was a human being too and deserved respect! She would stand up for her rights and not allow anyone to push her around!

She struggled out of her seat and moved forward to join the others, taking possession of an empty seat just behind the driver and defiantly placing her backpack beside her to keep other passengers away. All the way to Toronto she protected her place, not allowing anyone to sit beside her.

As the bus made its way through the northern Ontario night, Martha leaned forward, peering over the driver's shoulder out the front window and wondering if her decision to leave home had been the right one. She felt ill at ease, for she had entered a world that was unfamiliar and vaguely unsettling and menacing.

Each time the headlights of oncoming traffic lit up the interior of the bus, she recoiled and shielded her face with her hands. Whenever the driver accelerated and changed lanes to overtake slow-moving snowploughs and sanders with their ominously flashing blue lights, she seized the arms of her seat and hung on, terrified the bus would skid off the road. When tractor-trailers and trucks, loaded with pulpwood, logs and lumber, went roaring by in the opposite direction, mudguards flapping, spraying sand, salt and water over the front windshield, she held her breath until the over-taxed wipers cleared the view ahead.

In the middle of the night, the driver pulled into the terminal at Thunder Bay and the passengers got off, some to go to their homes and others to stretch their legs and have something quick to eat before climbing on board again. New passengers joined those who were continuing on, and another driver took over to navigate the next leg of the journey—the seven-hundred-mile swing along the arc of the north shore of Lake Superior to Sudbury.

When the bus entered the small towns and villages strung out along the highway, Martha could not help comparing them to her reserve. At Cat Lake First Nation there were no restaurants, no strip malls and no movie theatres—only a rudimentary outdoor rink with natural ice for recreation. These communities with their Italian, German and Finnish clubs, Chinese eateries, McDonald's, Burger Kings, Zellers, Shoppers Drug Marts, hockey arenas, bingo halls, video rental outlets, beer and liquor stores, used car lots, snowmobile sales outlets, topless dancing bars and churches, attracted and repelled her at the same time.

There was obviously so much more to do in these places than back home. Yet would she be accepted if some day she wanted to settle in one of them? That was not at all certain. As at Pickle Lake, each one was served by a combined bus terminal and restaurant. And as at Pickle Lake, although they were still in the north, she had the impression the white people looked at her with barely con-cealed fear, distrust and suspicion when she left the bus to buy coffee and sandwiches. What would they think of her in the south? She wouldn't live anywhere she wasn't welcome.

In the mid-afternoon the bus made a stop at Sudbury and headed south, leaving the sparsely settled north to begin its final run through central Ontario to the provincial capital. No longer did Martha spend her time looking at the passing panorama. Instead she stared out the window with unseeing eyes trying to make sense of what she had experienced in her life to date.

She thought of the years she had spent listening to people in authority at the residential school telling her that Natives were primitive and inferior to whites. She thought of the spirit of resignation that had infected the people of her own community, most of whom had already relinquished their old self-sufficient ways to subsist on government handouts. She thought of the two Native men in the restaurant in Pickle Lake, the racist comments of the white customers, and Yvette, the waitress who had been nice to her. She thought about Spider, now well into his mid-teens, and wondered if she would see him again. But most of all, she thought of Raven and missed her terribly.

It was all too difficult to sort out. But by the time the bus pulled into the Bay Street terminal, Martha had decided that she had only one life to live and had no intention of spending it brooding over past wrongs, real or imaginary.

But first she had to survive her initial night in Toronto. Knowing nobody and with no idea where to go for accommodation, she set off walking aimlessly through the alien world of Toronto's downtown core. It was early evening, and the rush hour was at its peak. Cars, trucks and buses clogged the streets, spitting out wet, foul-smelling fumes from exhaust pipes, befouling the air and making her queasy. Police cars, ambulances, fire engines and streetcars, pushing their way through the traffic, assaulted her ears with wailing sirens, honking horns and clanging bells. More people than she could ever have imagined poured out of subway exits to gather on corners and stare at traffic lights, as if waiting for permission from some unseen power buried deep within their mechanical guts to cross the streets. A giant flashing electronic sign high up on the side of a building displayed a happy family drinking Coca-Cola under the slogan Can't Beat the Real Thing. In the well-lit window of a clothing store, elegantly dressed individuals stood motionless, staring straight ahead with their arms extended. Martha paused and waited for them to grow tired and to leave. She moved on, smiling when she realized she was looking at mannequins of the type she had seen in Eaton's mail-order catalogues back on the reserve.

When she saw through the street-level window of a restaurant a young couple holding hands and talking, she paused to look at them. They were so lucky to be in love and to be so happy. But she was embarrassed and moved on when they turned to stare back at her.

In front of a construction site with a large illuminated billboard advertising luxury condominiums, panhandlers held up pieces of cardboard on which they had crudely scrawled messages telling the world that they were unemployed, they needed help to return home, they were sick or they were hungry—and asking for handouts. Others walked out into the stalled traffic to wash windshields, soliciting change. Teenagers with orange and purple hair, with rings piercing their eyebrows and lips, and dressed in ripped jeans and studded leather jackets stood in doorways begging for money.

On sidewalk hot-air vents, the homeless were already settling down for the night, wrapped in old blankets, with their possessions in dirty plastic bags at their feet. Other unfortunates, the collars of their coats pulled up high against the cold, were lining up for hot meals and beds at hostels run by the Salvation Army and the Shepherds of Good Hope.

As she crossed the downtown area, Martha felt ever more fearful and discouraged. The snowbanks were black and dirty, not pristine white like they were back home. The temperature on the reserve was much lower than what she was now experiencing, but the cold did not ooze through her parka and underclothing to penetrate deep into her bones like it did in the big city. Most unsettling of all, to someone used to the comforting silence and darkness of the northern night, was the relentless background rumble of street traffic: the noise and the harsh glare of streetlights and headlights that lit up the night sky accompanied her like an aching toothache no matter where she walked.

From time to time, Martha saw people she thought were Native. Some wore their hair in braids and were dressed in buckskin jackets proclaiming pride in their heritage. Others, who seemed completely demoralized and adrift, were dressed in cast-off clothing and were trying to wheedle money from people walking past their refuges in doorways and alleys.

Martha looked at them carefully, hoping she would see a well-dressed young aboriginal teenager with a birthmark in the form of a spider's web. But if she did, what would she do? Perhaps she would go up to him? But what could she say?

"Hello, my name is Martha and I used to have a baby boy with a birthmark on his forehead just like yours. The Children's Aid Society took him away because I didn't look after him properly. You wouldn't happen to be that boy, would you? If you are, could we pick up where we left off so many years ago? I've missed you so much. I assure you I've changed! I'd be a good mother now."

A Native woman stepped out of a dark alley and brought Martha's fantasy to an end.

"Hey, I bet you're Indian," she said, slurring her words. "New in town? Wanna drink? I got plenty of wine."

Martha stopped to talk to her. After only a few hours in

Toronto, she was already homesick and wondering if her decision to leave the reserve had been a good one. Overwhelming loneliness hit her. She had been lonely at residential school, and she had been lonely when she had returned home. She had succeeded in making a life for herself back on the reserve following Spider's removal. But now, in her ambition to fulfil an old dream, it seemed she had come to the most desolate place on earth—the big impersonal city filled with people who ignored the misery in their midst and who seemed to care only for themselves.

"C'mon sister, let's be pals. I may be a drunk but I'm your kind of people."

The woman, who was holding a half-empty bottle of wine, grinned mirthlessly at Martha through broken teeth. Her thin face was dirty, and long, unkempt black hair dangled down in front of her empty black eyes.

Behind her, someone wrapped in a blanket and sitting on the snow-covered ground among a pile of green garbage bags, muttered, "Wuz goin' on? Is it the food van? Get me some hot soup, will ya?"

Martha was tempted to join them. She would be living among bums and winos and would be looked down upon by everyone, but she would no longer be lonely. She could learn to beg. She could start drinking again. Perhaps it would even help her forget Father Antoine and her failures as a mother.

What choice did she have anyway? She had hardly slept in two days and didn't know the city. With few skills and without a high school diploma, her chances of getting a decent job were bleak. She sensed, however, that if she stepped into the alley, she would spend the rest of her life on the streets.

7

Spider

THE CHILDREN'S AID SOCIETY put Spider up for adoption soon after he was taken away from his mother in 1974. In the same way that the Society for the Protection of Animals today advertises "cute puppies and kittens free to a good home," the officials responsible for such matters in Ontario's child welfare system placed an advertisement in a number of Toronto newspapers with a photograph of Spider lying on his back, smiling at the camera and attempting to suck his toes—with his birthmark conveniently obscured.

> New arrival from northern Ontario. Adorable baby boy, eleven months old, excellent health. Make an unfortunate Indian child a part of your family. Your reward will be a lifetime of love.

Shortly thereafter, a middle-class couple in the suburbs of Toronto, who had been trying without success for years to have children, saw the notice, were enchanted by the child's appearance and made an appointment to see him. When they saw the baby drooling and cooing and holding on to the side of his crib, they ignored his birthmark so certain were they that he was the answer to their pent-up longings to establish a family and to lavish love and attention on a child of their own.

The adorable baby would grow up to be a noble, fully assimilated Native Canadian and a source of joy to them for the rest of their lives. The wife would bake cookies for him, just as her mother had done for her when she was a child, and her new son would help his new mother mix sugar, raisins, butter, eggs and oatmeal in a casserole, and lick the spoon when the preparations were done. The husband would take him fishing, and the son being Native, and thus instinctively understanding the ways of nature, would become the teacher and not the student of the father.

The husband would show him how to skate, take him to hockey practice and look on with pride as his son displayed exceptional talent, rise through the ranks, play for the national team at the World Junior Hockey Championships and score the winning goal as Canada defeated the Soviet Union to take gold. The Toronto Maple Leafs would recruit him and he would become a National Hockey League star, like the great Native hockey player George Armstrong, captain of the Leafs when they won the Stanley Cup in 1967.

He would excel in elementary and secondary school, win a scholarship to university, be a track star, editor of the university newspaper, president of the student council, graduate at the top of his class, become a schoolteacher like his parents, live close by, get married, spend the summers at the family cottage and come home with his wife and children for Sunday dinners. And when his parents became old, their son and his wife would be there for them, building an addition on to their house and insisting that they move in to spend their last days with them in peace, security and loving care.

———

The young couple said of course they wanted to adopt him. In fact, they insisted on doing so as soon as possible so that their dream might begin and their lives be fulfilled. After the paperwork was submitted, the background checks completed and the obligatory domicile inspections made to ensure their house was fit for a baby to inhabit, the Children's Aid handed him over.

The new parents could not have been happier—at least for the first several years. They gave him a new name, Edward, which they shortened to Eddy, and undertook to raise him in their cultural tradition—white, Anglo-Saxon, Protestant. When they took him to church, everyone seemed to know other families who had adopted Native children who had turned out well, and they praised the wisdom of their decision.

"My. My. You are doing such a wonderful thing. Saving a poor child from a life of deprivation."

"You are true Christians. Practising what others preach."

"I never could understand why so many people are trying to adopt babies from Bangladesh and China when there are plenty of Indian children right here who could use a good home. After all, we stole the land of their people and put them on reserves. By adopting their children, we can help put things right between our peoples."

Their happiness grew even greater when the wife became pregnant and gave birth to the cutest imaginable baby boy whom they named Robert. Two years later, a daughter, Amanda, came along. Naturally, the parents treated all three children the same. They became concerned, however, when Eddy became obsessively jealous of his younger brother and sister, going so far as to hit them in blind, uncontrollable rages. They became really worried when he did not talk until he was four.

After he started school, his teachers reported that his "work habits left much to be desired" and that he had "difficulty paying attention in the classroom," which was their way of saying that he was disruptive and lagging behind his peers. His parents' suspicion that he had a deep-seated learning problem was confirmed when they took him for thorough physical, developmental and psychological testing. The diagnosis was fetal alcohol syndrome, acquired when Martha drank during pregnancy and alcohol penetrated the wall of the placenta to poison and damage her son's brain.

The years that followed were difficult for everyone. The younger brother and sister did their best to include Eddy in their lives, but they sensed he was different, not just in skin colour but in emotional stability. His parents lavished love and attention on him, and at times he was a dutiful, well-behaved son. More often, however, he was unpredictable, lashing out at his parents and reproaching them for taking him from his "real" mother. And as he grew older, he began to steal money from his mother's purse, skip school and bully his brother and sister.

At the age of fifteen, Eddy ran away from home for the first time. By the time he was sixteen, his heartbroken, deeply disappointed and secretly relieved parents had given him up to the streets. By the time he was seventeen, he had become a fixture of the Toronto punk scene.

In contrast to Martha, who saw a hostile urban jungle as she walked the streets of Toronto in search of shelter that night in January 1991, her son felt secure in the big city. He may have been unwashed, he may have been wearing cast-off jeans with a big rip in the seat strategically situated to show off his purple underwear, he may have been coiffed with a Mohawk haircut dyed purple with spikes on top, and he may have had safety pins stuck through his ears, nose and lips, but that was his style: he was a punk and proud of it.

His new friends accepted and respected Spider for what he was, warts and all. For the punks never asked personal questions. Most of them had been judged by others all their lives and found wanting, and were not about to do the same thing to their fellow punks. They didn't care, for example, that Spider was of Native origin and was affected by fetal alcohol syndrome.

Like him, they had been square pegs in round holes. Like him, they were angry, were full of unanswered questions, did not want anyone telling them what to do and were looked down upon by society and by the police. Like him, a number were Native kids taken from parents who had been residential school survivors and had been unsuccessfully adopted out to people who had never heard of fetal alcohol syndrome. Unlike him, some came from homes where they had been physically and sexually abused, and they felt safer on the streets than with their parents.

The punks coexisted uneasily with the other species of the harmless marginalized—the bag men and bag women, muttering to themselves and pushing shopping carts filled with their possessions through the downtown crowds, the down-on-their-luck unemployed who spent their days looking for work and their nights sleeping in shelters, the older winos who panhandled and drank and gossiped together by day and slept rough by night, the mentally ill, off their meds, who wandered around in worlds of their own, and the hookers, male and female, old and young, who stood on street corners in the evenings, trying to make eye contact with prospective johns.

Others who shared the margins of society, the ethnic gangs and the skinheads, were not so benign. The Jamaicans, Tamils, Vietnamese, Latinos and Russians, busy doing their thing extorting money from their own communities, selling drugs, feuding among themselves and occasionally carrying out some nasty piece of work for the bikers, usually paid no attention to the punks, so low were they in the pecking order.

The skinheads, however, were a different matter. *A Clockwork Orange* was their cult movie of choice. They revelled in its celebration of violence and mindless aggression, and modelled themselves on its psychopathic anti-hero, Alex Delarge. Self-appointed guardians of racial purity, they behaved like jackals seeking defenceless animals to devour; they preyed on the weak, and the punks were their raw meat of choice. With their shaved heads, rolled-up pant legs, red suspenders, Nazi tattoos and steel-toed Doc Marten boots, they swaggered down Yonge Street at night in search of victims to attack with baseball bats, chains and brass knuckles. If punks were unavailable, holed up in their squats or attending concerts, the skinheads attacked the homeless asleep and helpless on their park benches. When from time to time, someone, ravaged by alcohol, weakened by poor nutrition and undermined by mental illness, died in the course of a beating, the skinheads considered they had rendered a service to society.

Spider knew that life as a punk was for him when he first ran away from home one September day two years before. He had been in a special education class with children much younger than himself and felt humiliated. When his adoptive mother kept insisting that he needed an education to succeed in life, he walked out and took the subway to downtown Toronto.

Emerging from the Yonge and College street exit, he saw a punk with long purple hair and a safety pin through his nose begging for spare change. He asked him where he could get something to eat, and the punk took him in hand, accompanying him to a drop-in centre for a meal and to meet other kids in situations like his.

Life, they told him, was good, but you had to be organized.

"When you get up in the morning, you gotta get out to pick a good spot to bum spare change. Subway stops and entrances to shopping centres and restaurants are good places. In front of Maple Leaf Gardens is always good. You sit on the ground with a cap in your hand and beg. Takes some getting used to. Some people shell out without saying anything. But there's always some jerk saying 'get a job,' 'get a haircut,' or 'go home.' Stupid stuff like that.

"We normally just try to get enough for breakfast at Burger King or McDo. Sometimes the staff won't serve you, even when you have the money. But that's no problem. You can always get a free meal at the Evergreen Drop-in Centre on Yonge. The staff there are cool. That's where you meet up with the others and find out what's going on, who got jumped by skinheads and who was given a hard time by the cops the night before. You then go out and bum some more change, share your take with the others to buy a case of barley sandwiches and go to a park to drink it."

The punks took Spider back to their squat in a derelict warehouse in Kensington Market. He was accepted without fuss and he loved it. A dozen or more young people were lounging around, sharing beer and dope on a floor littered with cigarette wrappers, empty food cans, old newspapers, soiled clothing, beer bottles, stained mattresses, used tissues and candy wrappers. No one seemed to mind the smell of feces and urine that wafted in from the hallway, one corner of which served as a makeshift communal toilet. On the walls, barely visible in the candlelight, were graffiti art depictions of their idols: the Sex Pistols, the Dirty Rotten Imbeciles, Black Flag, the Ramones, DOA, Bad Brains and the Misfits.

Spider drank his first beers and smoked his first pipe that night, and resolved never to return to life in suburbia. The next day, however, as he was leaving with the others from the warehouse, a policeman in a parked scout car got out and came over.

"Kid, you're awfully young to be hanging out with these degenerates. You should be in school."

He took him back to his vehicle and punched in the data Spider gave him.

"Just like I thought. You're a runaway. Only fifteen. It says here your parents are worried. Let's go."

Now, two years later, that first foray into the life of the streets and his embrace of his new punk identity seemed an eternity ago. He was already seventeen years old, and a tall, dark brown, heavily muscled teenager. His birthmark was as visible as ever, but he had long forgotten it was there, even though his nickname on the streets was Spider. He was happy because the past twenty-four hours had been good ones.

It had all started the previous evening when Spider and his friends realized they were short of toilet paper, candles, Kraft Dinner and other essentials. They had long since blown on beer and dope the monthly welfare payments handed out by the city to the homeless, and it was out of the question that they would spend the money they had earned bumming change that day on such boring things when they needed it to buy beer and entrance tickets to a punk show that night.

Thus the punks did what they usually did when they needed supplies: they went out to swarm a convenience store. With the hoods of their sweatshirts pulled over their heads to avoid identification by the security cameras, they gathered in the light snow outside the modest business establishment of a recent immigrant from South Asia. He kept his store open around the clock and was trying to make a living selling milk, newspapers, magazines, lottery tickets, "freshly brewed" coffee, cold cuts, shrivelled-up apples and other items to neighbourhood clients.

After checking to see that there were no customers inside and no police vehicles on the street, the punks rushed through the door a dozen strong and began stuffing cans of pop, loaves of bread, cold cuts, relish, margarine, toilet paper and tissues, porno and music industry magazines, flashlights and batteries under their clothes. They paid no attention to the owner, who yelled out from behind the counter.

"What are you doing? Stop! Stop! I am calling the police. Please! Please! I work hard for my money. You are destroying me!"

Like a flock of crows taking flight, the punks ran for the door, loaded down with their stolen goods. When the owner came around the counter and tried to stop them, they pushed him aside and fled into the night. Everyone, that is, except for a new member of the group, a skinny girl with a bad complexion who was being initiated into the fine art of shoplifting, punk-style. She was the last one out the door and the owner caught her on the sidewalk outside, seized her by the arms and began shaking her.

"Why? Why? Why are you doing this to me? I work so hard. I work day and night. I have a family to support back home, and yet you come to steal! Have you no shame? Have your parents not taught you right from wrong?"

Although he knew the police would be on their way, Spider returned to push the owner to one side, free the girl and run with her laughing to catch up with the others.

Later on, she came to say thank you.

"No one in my real family would've done what you did for me tonight."

After their raid, the punks sat around back at the squat, sleeping bags and blankets over their legs in an unheated room lit with stolen candles, eating cold Chef Boyardee spaghetti and Campbell's soup from cans, drinking beer and rehashing the events of the evening.

"Did you see the face of that sucker when we burst in. I thought he'd shit his pants."

"That capitalist bastard, squealing like a pig over a few cans of pop and spaghetti. He makes plenty overcharging the public and yet complains when we make him share a little of his profits with us. He's lucky we didn't trash his dump."

"Hey, Spider. You're the man."

"To the rescue just like last summer."

"You showed him."

The previous summer, Spider had earned the group's gratitude when a gang of skinheads had attacked them. It was after midnight on a hot July night in a poorly lit park. The punks were lying on the grass, enjoying the weather, talking about the events of the day, drinking beer from a case of twenty-four, smoking dope and, when the mood struck them, slipping away for a little quiet sex.

A dozen skinheads emerged from the shadows to spoil their night.

"Whatavwe here. A bunch of creeps! Shoulda known from the smell, you dirty rotten sponging bastards!"

"Why dontcha take baths? Afraid a little water will wash off those fake tattoos!"

"Why don't you guys just bugger off?" replied one of the punks, who scrambled to his feet to confront the intruders.

"Okay, okay, calm down. We're not going to attack you," the skinhead who appeared to be the leader said. "To show our good faith, let's shake on it," he added, extending his hand and smiling.

But as the punk put out his hand in friendship, in one movement the skinhead withdrew his and kneed him in the groin, and as his victim bent over in pain, hit him with an uppercut to the head, knocking him to the ground. The others whipped out chains and moved in, indiscriminately beating and kicking the other punks, male and female, with their steel-toed boots. Spider, who had done nothing up to that point, pulled out a hunting knife with a ten-inch blade that he kept strapped to his calf under a pant leg. With a mad cry he went wild, slashing and stabbing the skinheads in such a frenzy that they turned and ran.

A member of the group that had robbed the convenience store limped into the squat, his face bloody and bruised.

"Cops picked me up and took me on the Cherry Beach Express," was his explanation, and everyone understood what he meant.

The police of 51 Division were responsible for one of Toronto's poorest and toughest downtown neighbourhoods. Sometimes, to help keep order, rogue officers administered summary justice in the form of beatings to people not considered worth their while to take to jail—punks, skinheads and criminals caught in the act of committing petty crimes—at a desolate part of the waterfront, called Cherry Beach.

The victims never complained. What judge would take the word of someone living on the margins of the law over that of a policeman? There were never any witnesses, for even in summer, few people frequented the area, filled as it was with abandoned warehouses and factories. In winter, it was even more deserted and sinister.

"Was just heading back here with the goods when this cruiser pulls up and the cops tell me to come over.

"'Whatcha got under your coat, you green-haired little prick?' one of them says.

"'Do you kiss your mother with that mouth?' I says to him. 'Go screw yourself.'

"I didn't like their attitude and told them they couldn't stop and search me. I was minding my own business. I knew my rights. Didn't they have something better to do? That was sure the wrong thing to say.

"The two pigs got out, slapped me around, cuffed my hands behind my back and searched me. They threw the loot away and pushed me into the back.

"They told me it was time for a little attitude adjustment. The sunsabitches took me on the Express. On the way down Yonge to Lakeshore, I told them what I thought of them. But once we turned down Cherry Street, they played their little game—speeding up and slamming on the brakes, pitching me headfirst against the wire cage in the backseat. They thought that was funny.

"At Cherry Beach, they hauled me out, dragged me into the bushes and put the boots to me.

"'Let this teach you not to rob convenience stores and to give us lip in our part of town,' they said. 'If we have to take you down here again you won't get off so easy.'"

If the aggrieved punk was expecting sympathy from his friends, he was mistaken. They were at a stage in their drinking when almost anything would send them into peals of hysterical laughter. They were all used to being hassled by the police, and they knew the best thing to do when pulled aside was to say as little as possible. Their buddy had been asking for trouble.

"You stupid jerk. Why didn't you keep your mouth shut?"

"I woulda loved to have seen the face of that cop when you told him to screw off."

"At least you didn't get arrested when they found the stuff from the store."

———

An hour later, the punks wandered off to attend a show being held at a club on the corner of Yonge and Dundas. It was only nine o'clock but raucous music could be heard a block away. An enormous, unsmiling bouncer looked them over, opened the steel door and motioned for them to enter. Inside, they quickly paid the three-dollar cover charge and joined hundreds of people slam dancing in the mosh pit in front of the stage.

The musicians, bare to the chest and lathered in sweat, bobbed and weaved, downed beer, smoked weed, hammered drums and attacked guitars as they spit into the microphones the incoherent in-your-face slogans of the outsider—self-hatred and loathing, disgust and revolt, reckless abandon and delirium. Spider and his friends hurled themselves at each other and at the others on the floor, chest against chest, shoulder against shoulder, elbow against face and knee against groin, under flashing red, green and blue lights to the sound of pulsing, throbbing, off-key, jarring electric guitar music and frenetic drumming. Dancers, overcome with emotion or stupid drunk, climbed up onto the stage and dove recklessly into the churning mass below, blindly trusting members of the crowd to catch them before they hit the floor. A blue cloud of marijuana and cigarette smoke hung over the room.

Spider could not have been happier. He was caught up in the hysteria and thrived on the physical contact, and each time he slammed someone or was smashed hard he was filled with physical and mental release. He loved the chaos and the crowd of tattooed, pierced, leather-jacketed, metal-studded bodies, and was at one with the anarchistic, broken lyrics of revolt. He sucked in with voluptuous pleasure the smell of raw sex, sweat, adrenaline, body odour, dope, smoke, blood and beer. He felt a profound sense of existential joy, was alive in the moment and would not have cared if he were to die the second the music stopped.

And if he had known that Martha was at that time making her way to Toronto, he would not have cared. He loved the punks and they loved him. To Spider it was the punks, not his birth mother or his adoptive parents, who were his real family.

8

New Beginnings

AT THE ENTRANCE TO THE ALLEY, Martha was replying in Anishinaabemowin to the offer made to her by the homeless woman.

"I'm from way up north from a reserve called Cat Lake First Nation. It's so small you've probably never heard of it. I just came out on the winter road and took the bus from Pickle Lake. I don't know anyone here."

The woman, speaking hesitantly, replied in the same language.

"I don't speak Anishinaabemowin no good no more. Lost most of it when I was sent away to school but I still understand okay.

"Never heard of your place," she said, carrying on in English, "but that don't mean nothing. My reserve is back in the bush near the Quebec border. We knew nothing about the people who lived to the west of us when I was a kid."

Happy to have a Native person to talk to, Martha told her how she had been raised on the land as a little girl, been sent off to residential school, had returned home, had a hard time fitting in, and had two children, and how her son had been taken from her. One of the main reasons she had come to the city was to find her son.

"He has a big birthmark in the shape of a spider's web on his forehead, and would be about seventeen now. You haven't seen him, have you?"

"No, I don't think so," the woman said, after thinking about the question for a minute. "I've seen a lot of Indian kids on the streets, but they usually stick to themselves.

"My story's a bit like yours," she said. "Raised in the bush. Taken away when I was ten and sent to residential school. But I guess I was lucky 'cause the nuns and priests were really good to me. None of those beatings and sexual things you hear about that happened at other schools. My family didn't want me so I stayed at the school in the summers until I was sixteen. When I went back to the reserve to stay, my family still didn't want me. I started running around. Got pregnant. Got pregnant again and again until I had half a dozen kids. I guess I wasn't the greatest mom and the Children's Aid stepped in and took them away. Don't know where they are—never tried to find them. I got fed up and took the bus to Toronto. Just like you.

"Been here about two years, all of them on the street. Met up with a guy from up north and we've been together ever since. So whadyasay? Gonna join us?"

Martha did not reply.

"Our life's pretty good," the woman said. "We get welfare just like back home. Some days we make good money bumming change. When we buy booze we can go into any liquor or beer store and pay the normal price. No big bootlegger prices here. And if you like Indians, there's lots of us here.

"Didya know Toronto's Canada's biggest reserve? There's Indians around here from up north, from down south and from the States. Even some who call themselves Indians from Mexico. People who were once rich and important. Everyone's got lots of stories to tell, even if most of it's lies."

"But isn't your life dangerous? Where do you sleep? What do you eat?" asked Martha.

"I'm not gonna shit ya," the woman replied after a pause. "It's a hard life just the same. Sooner or later you go from booze to rubbing alcohol, to mouthwash, to aftershave, to shoe polish and eventually to Lysol. Didya know you could go blind if you're not careful? Before ya know it you're having the shakes, you know, the DTs—the seizures and craziness when you think you're being chased by pink elephants and monsters—and that's it for you. But it's always the other guy who's gonna get it. Won't never happen to me 'cause I'm too smart."

"But it's cold. Where do you sleep?" insisted Martha.

"It's a secret, but since we're such good friends, I'm gonna tell ya."

In a theatrical whisper, the woman said, "Under the overpass at the bottom of Spadina Avenue. Right where it goes onto the Gardiner—not much of a secret, eh?" She laughed. "It's actually not so bad. We gotta big pile of sleepin' bags and blankets. We crawl into them and drink to our heart's content. We don't even hear the traffic no more. And do you know something? I actually like the smell of exhaust fumes—reminds me of nights back home when I came back from residential school and a bunch of us used to do a little sniffing. Not too fussy, though, about the water that drips on us when it rains."

" And your food?" Martha asked.

"That's easy," she replied. "We get breakfast in bed. The Sally Ann comes by every morning with their Welcome Wagon and gives us hot coffee, soup and sandwiches. We don't even have to get up—all we gotta do is pretend we're interested when they ask us to pray with them."

"Sometimes we go to the Council Fire over on Dundas for a meal. That's an outfit that's run by Indians for people like us. Every night the Indian guys who run the Anishinabe Street Patrol bring more soup and sandwiches. Plus sleeping bags, socks, gloves and blankets if you need them. If you get sick, someone will call 911 for you. Everything's all taken care of."

Martha hesitated.

"Look," the woman said, "I came to the city not so long ago just like you. It was a tough place. But I made real good friends with people just like me who liked drinking. We're heading back now to finish off our booze and you're welcome. And that's an offer you won't get around here every day. It seems to me," she added, "that we gotta lot in common. I bet we're even the same age. Come on, guess how old I am."

Martha thought that she looked to be in her fifties or sixties, but to be polite, told her she was about forty. The woman laughed and said she was only twenty-six.

Martha shivered, this time not from the cold. She had been growing increasingly uneasy as the woman described her life. Why did this person assume that just because she was Native she would want to live on the streets? It was true that she was lonely and wanted friends but not at the cost of losing her self-respect and dignity. She would rather die than live under an overpass exposed to the elements like an animal and have to rely on the handouts of the Salvation Army and the Anishinabe Street Patrol to survive.

Surely there was more to life than spending her days with people who appeared determined to drink themselves to death. What about her mother and Raven? She had to find a job to make money to support them. There was Spider to think about. Now, to her horror, she discovered that the woman she was talking to was actually eight years younger than she was. Looking at her more closely, she saw herself in two years if she opted for life on the streets—sick and woebegone and waiting to die. There had to be a better way.

The woman cut in. "Well, what's it to be? You coming or not?"

But before Martha could reply, she saw a sign blinking out of the dark. "Kwawag Andwad, Native Women's Shelter."

Martha knew that *kwawag andwad* meant "our home" in Anishinaabemowin. Perhaps the people there could help her.

"*Meegwetch*," said Martha, "but I think I'll try that place down the street."

The woman shrugged her shoulders. And as Martha walked away, she called out, "No skin off my ass!"

After Martha rang the doorbell, it did not take long before a Native woman in her mid-thirties, short, round-faced, with dark brown skin and alert, friendly black eyes, opened the door. Seeing Martha standing there silently in the dark with her pack on her back, she guessed she had just arrived in the city.

"Looks like you've come a long way. My name's Nora Simcoe and I won't bite you. C'mon in and make yourself at home."

Martha entered saying in a low voice, "Mine's Martha. I saw your sign."

Nora motioned to the closet and said, "Hang your coat up and stow your pack in there. Do you want to visit the washroom? It's just down the hall. Then let's get together in the kitchen."

The two women sat together around the kitchen table drinking instant coffee.

"Looks like you've had a tough day," Nora said.

When Martha did not reply but fixed her eyes on the table, Nora did not press her. She was Anishinabe herself from Chippewas of Rama First Nation on Lake Couchiching, one hundred miles north of Toronto. Although the Anishinabe of southern and northwestern

Ontario were separated geographically by great distances, their culture and language were similar and they had no problem understanding each other. In their tradition, long silences in conversations were the norm, and Nora did not interpret Martha's lack of response as a sign of indifference or rudeness.

Nora also had years of experience in dealing with women who came to the city with high hopes, but who had neither the life skills nor the training to survive in a tough urban environment. She had graduated from the University of Toronto as a social worker and had devoted her life to helping Native women who had left their reserves and were in a state of cultural shock.

It was critical, she knew, to help them as soon as possible after they arrived in the city and before they drifted into a life on the streets, or before pimps in search of gullible girls to exploit as prostitutes took control of their lives. All too often, she knew, these women joined the ranks of the thousands of Native women who had simply "disappeared" over the years across Canada, murdered by their pimps or their johns and dumped like roadkill in places where they would never be found. Since they were street women, the police just went through the motions in looking for them and society did not seem to care.

Eventually, in a soft voice, Martha asked Nora in Anishinaabemowin if she spoke her Native language: *"Gdi nesh naabem nah?"*

Nora answered her in the affirmative: *"Aanish gonna."*

Martha smiled and remarked that Nora sure talked in a funny way: *"Gdi pkan gdi nwaam."*

Nora shot back saying she could say the same thing about Martha's accent: *"Maa dash wiin miigoo Naasaab! En weeyagng ma north."*

The two women laughed and the ice was broken.

"I was about to make myself a snack. We don't have any country food here but I make real good grilled cheese sandwiches. Want one?"

Martha nodded her agreement, and soon they were eating and talking quietly.

"So where do you come from and what are you doing in the big city?" asked Nora.

"I'm from way up north," said Martha. "It was time to make a new start in my life and I thought I'd try my luck in Toronto. But this is a scary place and I don't know if I can handle it."

"Sure you can," said Nora. "You just have to get used to it and make some friends. I can help you."

"Could you put me up for tonight?" asked Martha. "I have some money."

"Of course," said Nora. "You can stay as long as you want, and if you run short, you don't have to pay.

"What about your family. Are you married? Any children? Are they coming down to join you?"

At the mention of children, Martha began to sob. Nora got up and put her arms around her shoulders and it was not necessary to say anything. When Martha stopped crying, she returned to her seat and waited for Martha to speak.

Although used to keeping her feelings and thoughts to herself, Martha was comfortable with Nora and felt she could confide in her. She thus told her about Spider and Raven and how bad she felt for not being there for them when they needed her. When Nora said she shouldn't be so hard on herself, and there were surely reasons for acting as she did, Martha opened up and told her everything: her residential school experience, Father Antoine, the death of her little cousin Little Joe, her depression, the circumstances of Spider's birth and removal, the life she made for herself in the community afterwards, Raven's birth and her departure for Toronto. By the time she had finished, it was one in the morning and both women were crying.

———

With the help of Nora and the other staff members of Kwawag Andwad, Martha adjusted to life in the city. For the first six months, she lived at the shelter, taking her meals there and sharing her room with other women who likewise had come to Toronto knowing no one and trying to make a fresh start in life. The staff helped her prepare the paperwork to receive temporary welfare assistance, to register for medical care at the Anishinabe Health Centre, and to begin classes to finish her high school diploma. When Nora noticed that Martha sometimes appeared troubled, she invited her to join their weekly healing circle.

"You will never be well, Martha, if you don't share your feelings with others."

But Martha refused. She had been prepared to talk privately with Nora about her past—and that had helped—but it was a different thing to air her problems in public with strangers.

As the years went by, Martha lived a modest version of the Canadian dream, moving to her own apartment and finding work as a waitress to pay for evening studies to obtain her high school certificate. She took courses to become a bookkeeper, obtained a well-paying job at the Native Friendship Centre and was even able to buy a car.

Life would have been good were it not for the poor state of her relations with her mother and daughter. In the years she was away, even though Martha had the money to do so, she took no trips home. It was not that she did not want to see her family. She did, and after she had put some money aside, she told Nokomis in a letter that she would be returning home for the summer holidays. But the reply, drafted for Nokomis, who did not know how to read or write, by a clerk at the co-op, was a great disappointment.

My daughter, I would like nothing better than to see you here at
home again. But as much as it hurts me to say so, a visit at this
time would upset Raven, even though she is still very young and
I think it best you stay away awhile yet.

Afterwards, Martha wrote often to her mother enclosing money to
help her with living expenses and asking about Raven. In her letters
back, Nokomis enclosed photos of her daughter that Martha framed
and kept on her bedside table, but she gave no news of the little girl
other than to say she was well. When Martha wrote some time
later to say that she was now well established in Toronto and
wanted to bring her daughter to live with her, her mother replied
that she would be ever so lonely if her granddaughter were not with
her to keep her company.

Down there in the big city everyone looks down on the Anishinabe
people. We may have our problems on the reserve but at least up
here she would be among her own. What would you do with her
when you go to work? You've no husband or family to help you
and she'd eventually get into trouble. Remember what happened
to Spider when you didn't follow my advice on how to raise him?
Don't make the same mistake again.

Filled with guilt at the memory of how terrible a mother she
had been to her baby boy so many years before, Martha did not
have the heart to contradict her mother and agreed to leave her
daughter with her to raise. But when she was old enough, Raven
began sending her own letters, initially with a child's scrawl, and
later more assertively, but always ending with, "I love you, mommy.
When are you coming home?"

Martha hated receiving her letters since she could not tell

Raven the real reason she was staying away. From time to time, she would put a twenty-dollar bill in an envelope and send it off with a note telling her to buy herself a present at the co-op. Eventually, Raven sent her a terse note saying she didn't want money, she wanted her mother. The next time Martha sent her twenty dollars, Raven sent it back without comment.

Meanwhile, Martha got on with life, wearing her hair in braids and buying stylish clothes including a beautiful buckskin jacket with fringes and a traditional floral motif that she wore everywhere to proclaim her pride in her heritage. In addition to becoming close friends with Nora she became a regular volunteer at the shelter, helping women from remote reserves who arrived in the big city knowing no one.

Then one day in the summer of 2002, Martha asked Nora whether she had liked attending university. "I've lived in Toronto far too long stuck in a comfortable rut. Maybe it's time I exercised my brain. I've got the grades to get into the University of Toronto but don't know if it's for me. What do you think?"

"I loved it," said Nora. "But it's not for everyone. I knew what I wanted to get out of it when I went in, to be a social worker and help Native people. Some go because they just want to learn about other cultures and religions and generally to improve their minds. How about you? Looking to upgrade yourself to get a better job?"

"Not at all," said Martha. "I like being a bookkeeper. I'm just curious about things and I like reading and books even if I'm no expert."

"Why not take an evening course and see if you like it?"

Martha decided she would start off by studying nineteenth-century Canadian authors, and if all went well, she would move on and study the great writers of Canada of the twentieth century. Thus early one September evening, Martha joined several hundred other extramural students filing into a classroom for the first lecture of the fall semester on *The Poets of Confederation*. At seven o'clock, exactly on schedule, Professor Marshall, noted authority on the subject, entered the room and began his lecture.

"Poetry," said the professor, "bridges the gap between the prosaic and the sublime. It is like music in having the ability to convey an emotion and meaning that prose cannot."

Martha was not certain what Marshall was talking about, but listened attentively as he went on to say that the greatest of all the early Canadian poets, in his opinion, was Duncan Campbell Scott.

"Scott," he said, "was born into a modest family in the small town of Smiths Falls in eastern Ontario. He was a man of deep artistic sensibility and humanity, and he became a poet who would have no equal in the pantheon of early Canadian authors. But remember, all poetry is personal. You may prefer someone else—that's your right. But Scott touches me. I find it hard to read his poems without becoming emotional."

His voice breaking, Professor Marshall read from a selection of Scott's poems. Those in which Scott described Indians were his favourites, particularly one called "Indian Place-Names."

> The race has waned and left but tales of ghosts,
> That hover in the world like fading smoke
> About the lodges: gone are the dusky folk
> That once were cunning with the thong and snare
> Mighty with the paddle and the bow . . .

The professor carried on, but Martha had stopped listening. Why was this poet writing about her people in such a superior way? Perhaps she didn't understand what he was saying. After all, Scott was Marshall's favourite poet, and as a professor he obviously would know more than she did about what was good poetry. When she picked a topic for a term paper, therefore, she decided to do hers on Scott to uncover his "deep artistic sensibility and humanity."

But what she discovered when she visited the university library was frightening. The books confirmed that he was considered one of Canada's most famous early poets, widely admired for his disciplined and intense diction, for his depiction of Canada's wilderness at the turn of the twentieth century and for his portrayal of Native people.

So far, so good. But then Martha read his poem, "The Onondaga Madonna."

> She stands full-throated and with careless pose,
> This woman of a weird and waning race,
> The tragic savage lurking in her face,
> Where all her pagan passion burns and glows,
> Her blood is mingled with her ancient foes,
> And thrills with war and wildness in her veins
> Her rebel lips are dabbled with the stains
> Of feuds and forays and her father's woes.

Martha shuddered. Scott was speaking about her. She read other poems in which he described Indians as being on their way to extinction, inherently bloodthirsty, lacking in principles, dark and wild. In some of them, the offspring of an Indian and a white person was depicted as being even more degenerate and savage than his Indian parent.

There was more. She learned that Scott had been an influential member of the Department of Indian Affairs for some fifty years. He had been one of the government commissioners who had arrived in her community wearing a pith helmet and imposed the unequal treaty on her people so long ago. Most damaging of all, he was one of the architects of the Indian residential school system.

Martha discovered that Scott believed Native people did not fit into the new Canadian identity that was coming into being as the twentieth century arrived. In his view, Indians should be assimilated, and the best way to do this was to send them to residential schools, to forbid them to speak their language and to force-feed them the values of the white man. The drastic measures were needed to ensure "there is not a single Indian in Canada that has not been absorbed into the body politic." And it was on his watch that thousands of children, like her little cousin, deprived of proper food and medical care, died of malnutrition and disease in their lonely barracks.

Martha was puzzled. How could someone who had done such terrible things go down in history as a man of great humanity? What was she missing? She then read that his only child, a daughter, had died at the age of twelve, and his wife had passed away some years later. She thought of Little Joe and remembered how hard her aunt had taken it when she learned of his death. Scott would have felt just as bad, she was sure. How then was it possible for someone who had suffered so much in his own life to have inflicted so much harm on so many Native people? He must not have understood that they were fully human.

In her term paper, Martha said Scott's poems about Natives were racist. If that meant Scott should go down in history as a racist poet, then so be it. And if anyone said that he was just a man of his time, then the people of that era—the church leaders, the politicians who supported his evil policies, and the Canadian public who found the government's policies acceptable—were racists as well.

Some time later at the beginning of a class, the professor asked a student to hand out the corrected term papers. When Martha received hers, she saw that she had received a failing grade. Worse was to follow.

"Today," the professor said, "I want to address the issue of political correctness in my classroom. One student, whom I will not name, in her paper on Duncan Campbell Scott, sought to mix political considerations with literary criticism. You should know that type of approach has been popular on university campuses for the past decade. Faculty members in some universities cannot even put *The Adventures of Huckleberry Finn* on the syllabus without being called racist since Mark Twain uses the 'N-word' in his remarkable novel.

"Well, let me tell all of you today that I will not stand for such nonsense in my class. Duncan Campbell Scott has been unfairly maligned for opinions and views he expressed that were accepted in his time. This student even had the nerve to condemn him for what he did in his day job. This I will not accept. We cannot judge Scott for not conforming to the politically correct standards of today."

Martha said nothing during class but went to see him afterwards. Marshall's face turned red when Martha, dressed in her buckskin jacket, entered his office and sat down in a chair facing his desk. Although he had never spoken to her in class, he had taken note of her, and had assumed she was Indian from her name, brown skin and facial features.

"I half-expected you would show up here, Ms Whiteduck. But I'm afraid I won't be changing my mind about your mark."

Martha looked at the professor for a moment, the term paper in her hand. When he began to look uncomfortable, she spoke. "I'm proud to be Indian," she said. "I'm also a residential school survivor and personally suffered a lot from the policy Duncan Campbell Scott did so much to put in place. I haven't come looking for a better grade. I've come to talk to you person to person. I want to understand how you can admire someone who did so much harm to my people for so long." Marshall looked at Martha more closely, noting for the first time that while she was older than most of the other students in his class, she possessed a type of sensuality that was more appealing to him than the fresh-faced beauty of women much younger that he normally cultivated.

"I hope I haven't hurt your feelings," he said, in a more understanding manner. "I'm so used to students trying to use my class to promote fashionable political causes that I sometimes become angry and overreact. To tell the truth, I know next to nothing about your people and what you've lived through. Why don't you wait until my office hours are over and join me for a coffee to talk things over?"

An hour later, professor and student were deep in conversation in a neighbourhood coffee shop. While by nature Martha was shy, the professor displayed such an interest in her story, she opened up and told him about her life on the land as a little girl and her time at residential school and in Toronto.

Marshall pressed her for greater detail. He had frankly been disturbed by what Martha had said about the schools in her term report. But had these schools not prepared Indian children for life in the twentieth century? Had the children not been taught to read and write? Had they not returned home every summer to their families? Had the teachers not served as role models for the students? Were there not reasons other than the residential school experience to account for the problems Indian communities were dealing with today?

"I want to tell you about what happened to me and let you judge for yourself," said Martha. After she told him about Father Antoine and Little Joe, Marshall looked away.

"I had no idea," he said. "I had no idea such things were still going on during my lifetime in Canada. I've always believed, and

I guess I still do feel, that we should judge literature on the standards of literature and not on the political views or behaviour of the author. But you've really shaken me and given me lots to think about. Now let me have that paper back and I'll give you a better grade."

But Martha refused. "I told you, Professor Marshall, I didn't come to see you to get a better mark. Besides I've learned a lot from our discussion tonight."

"Well, at least let me buy you dinner. I owe you that much for giving you such a hard time. And please call me Linden. Professor Marshall is for use only in class."

9

Different Worlds

THE NEXT MORNING, Martha woke up in a strange room to the sounds of Linden puttering around somewhere in the house. She got out of bed, turned on the light and saw her clothes neatly laid out on an armchair, just as she had left them the previous night.

As the memories of what had taken place came back, she wondered what had come over her. Since her arrival in Toronto, she had found it hard to establish relationships with men. It was not that they did not pursue her. They did, drawn by her natural elegance, good looks and intelligence, but after her experience at the hands of Father Antoine and Russsell, none of her relationships had lasted for long. Now she had allowed someone who was almost a stranger to talk her into returning home with him "for a quiet nightcap" and into his bed.

But without knowing why, she trusted Linden. Perhaps it was because he was so knowledgeable about things she knew nothing about and had an excellent sense of humour. Perhaps it was because he had been so forthcoming about his marital situation, telling her he had once been married but was now happily single. Whatever the reason, she was flattered that such a cultivated person would take an interest in her.

Linden opened the door and came in. "I see you're up. Welcome to my home in the daylight. I'm cooking up a great English breakfast for the two of us. How do you like your eggs?"

"Sunny side up would be great. But I've got to rush. I'm due at work at eight-thirty."

"Don't worry. It's only seven and I'll drop you off in my car in plenty of time."

Twenty minutes later, Martha joined Linden in the breakfast nook overlooking a carefully groomed lawn, well-tended rock gardens and birdbath surrounded by mature maple and oak trees.

"I love this house," said Linden, as he served breakfast and joined her at the table. "I've lived here all my life. My parents were professors at the University of Toronto and bought it when house prices were low. They left it to me when they passed on. I certainly wouldn't be able to afford such a place on my salary today. It's filled with good memories and its location is great, in the heart of Forest Hill, a step away from good shopping and restaurants, plenty of walking trails and lots of friends nearby that I've known since I attended Upper Canada College as a kid."

Afterwards, Linden took Martha on a brief tour. Everywhere she looked, in the living room, in the family room, in the hallways and even in the washrooms there were books.

"Have you read all of them?" she asked. He proudly told her that he had. "Because, "he added, "they're the central passion of my life. I couldn't live without them."

That evening, Linden telephoned and proposed that they get together for a drink once again. Martha, who was hoping he would call, agreed and soon they began to see each on a regular basis. Martha would often stay at Linden's from Friday night to

Sunday evening and they would get together once or twice a week for a meal, conversation and perhaps a movie. Then Linden made a suggestion.

"Let's have an old-fashioned dinner party. My friends are dying to meet you. No more than a dozen people altogether to keep it intimate. It'll be a chance to put on the dog, bring out the family silver. I know an excellent caterer who'll do all the work. All we have to do is to sit back and enjoy ourselves. What do you say?"

Martha was uncertain whether she would fit into Linden's world but he brushed aside her concerns, saying there was no need for her to be intimidated by a few ageing profs.

Martha reluctantly agreed and sought Nora's help in getting ready. The two friends visited several department stores looking for something appropriate to wear before settling on a little black dress on sale at The Bay. The black colour of the dress, the two women agreed, would go well with a discreet beaten silver Haida brooch Martha had bought some time before and had not yet had an opportunity to wear.

The morning of the dinner, Nora took her to a beauty salon where a hairdresser undid her braids, washed and dried her hair and did it up in a chignon. And that evening, after dabbing some perfume behind her ears and looking into the mirror before leaving her apartment, Martha was sure Linden would be proud of her.

At eight o'clock, Linden and Martha greeted the guests as they arrived. The door would open, there would be little squeals of greeting and delight, and Linden would shake hands with the husband and bestow a discreet kiss on the cheek of the spouse.

Almost every time he introduced Martha, the guests said the same thing.

"So this is who you've been hiding from us."

During drinks, they bombarded her with questions and comments.

"Linden tells us you come from somewhere up in northwestern Ontario. From the land of snow and blackflies, eh?"

"Do you speak your Native language? I saw that movie, *Dancing with Wolves*, I think it was. Have you seen it? It was supposed to be authentic. They used real Indians in some of the lead roles instead of the usual heavily made-up Italian- or Greek-Americans, and they spoke Indian dialects—or at least that's what I heard."

"What are you planning to do after your undergrad degree? Law school? Medicine? Going home to help your people afterwards?"

Martha was flustered, not knowing how to respond to such an outpouring of good will, and retreated within herself and said little. Linden came to her rescue, laughing. "Don't everyone jump on her at once. You'll get your chance to grill her when we sit down to eat."

But matters did not improve over dinner. Never before had Martha seen such an elegantly laid-out table. The overhead lights had been dimmed, and candlelight from a pair of three-branched candelabras glistened off crystal wine and water glasses and highly polished sterling silverware. Between the candles was a magnificent silver centrepiece, holding a selection of leaves in all their autumnal glory—scarlet maple, silver birch and russet oak—on a bed of Spanish moss.

Linden and Martha took their places at each end of the table, and five guests sat down on each side. Linden had told Martha beforehand that he would entertain the guests close to him. Perhaps she could keep those near her amused? She had agreed, not fully understanding what he meant until the moment arrived.

The waiters, poker-faced and dressed in tuxedo jackets with starched white shirts and black bow ties, entered with the first course, lobster tails with lukewarm garlic butter sauce. They exited and returned with bottles of Sauvignon blanc, and everyone looked to the host to take the lead. A waiter opened a bottle and poured some wine into Linden's glass. He carefully sampled it, pronounced it fit to drink, unfolded his napkin, placed it on his lap, picked up his knife and fork, nodded to Martha to do the same, and the dinner began.

Martha stared at the cutlery arrayed in front of her, not knowing which knife and fork to select, worried she might make the wrong choice and expose herself as someone who did not belong at Linden's sophisticated party. She solved the problem by following the example of the person across the table. In the meantime, the person on her right was doing his best to get her attention.

"I understand from Linden," he was saying, "that you went to a residential school and had a really bad time with a priest up there on James Bay."

Martha, preoccupied with trying to master her silverware, apologized and asked him to repeat his remark. He did so and added, "I'm sorry. Perhaps you don't like to talk about it?"

Martha was embarrassed. She had not expected Linden to share her confidences about Father Antoine with anyone else, even with a friend. Annoyed, she said nothing and concentrated on eating her dinner.

"I don't mean to pry," the guest continued, in between a bite of food and a sip of wine, "but the press are full of stories about the terrible things that were supposed to have gone on at those schools. On the other hand," he said, hoping Martha would laugh at his wit, "there's always the bright side. Maybe you could make yourself some money suing the Church?"

When Martha still did not respond, he tried another approach. "Have you heard of an author called Vladimir Nabokov?"

"No, I haven't," Martha said, relieved that her neighbour had apparently given up prying into her personal life. "What sort of writer is he? Can you recommend any of his books?"

The guest was happy and looked forward to imparting his insights on the iconic Russian émigré writer to someone obviously in need of enlightenment.

"Nabokov," he told her, "was one of the giants of twentieth-century literature. The book I recommend you read is called *Lolita*. It's about a middle-aged pedophile by the name of Humbert Humbert who becomes obsessed with a twelve-year-old girl and takes advantage of her over a two-year period. On the face of it, it's a repugnant story of rape and exploitation. But on a deeper level, literary critics and professors of literature, like those of us around this table, have long considered it to be a wonderful and moving love story, full of passion, tenderness and social and political satire."

Martha put down her fork, her dinner ruined. Why couldn't he just drop the subject? What kind of a person wouldn't know the difference between love and rape? Obviously he had never met Father Antoine. Did everything he knew about life come from books? But before she could tell him what she thought, the guest on her right spoke up.

"I've always been fascinated by the north," he said. "In contrast to the ignoramuses in this room, I've been up there. Way up there! When I was a boy, I used to spend my summers at a wilderness camp on Lake Temagami. We used to go by canoe all the way down the Moose River to James Bay and take the train back from Moosonee to Cochrane. It made me feel like a real Canadian."

Martha, deeply offended by the remarks on *Lolita* by the first guest, took out her anger on the second.

"Why do you think that's such a big deal?" she said. "A lot of us from up there don't believe people down here think Natives are real Canadians. At least we're not treated like we are."

"You're probably right," he said, surprised at the vehemence of her reaction. "We pretend we're better than the Americans who slaughtered their Indians in the nineteenth century but look how we deal with ours today."

Martha said nothing and a stony silence prevailed among the guests at her end of the table in contrast to an animated discussion led by Linden with those around him. They were hotly disputing the merits of the various authors short-listed for Canada's most prestigious literary award, the Giller Prize. The award ceremony was scheduled to be held in the coming days and everyone had an opinion on who should win. Those in favour of Austin Clarke's *The Polished Hoe* were squaring off with others who thought the award should go to Wayne Johnston for *The Navigator of New York*, and there was much good-natured arguing and laughter.

There was a pause as the waiters served the second course—rack of lamb, potatoes, green beans and caramelized small carrots—and filled the glasses with a red Merlot. The discussion resumed, this time with the people from Martha's end of the table entering into a completely new debate with those from Linden's side, this time happily and inconclusively on the relative merits of Canadian and French wines. During a lull in the conversation over dessert, however, as they ate their *crème brûlée* and drank their ice wine, the guests turned their attention back to Martha.

"I teach English literature," a woman sitting beside Linden said, peering down the table at her, "and have always been struck by the role the north and Indians play in our literature. Which author, in your view, most accurately depicts that reality?"

By this time, Martha was frustrated at not being able to hold her own in the discussion. None of the people she knew talked about literary prizes or authors or fine wines. The only author she had studied in any depth who wrote about Indians was Duncan

Campbell Scott, and she had no intention of starting an argument over him with a group of people who probably shared Linden's view that he was a poet of "deep artistic sensitivity and humanity."

"I'm sorry," she said. "But I just don't know enough about the subject to say anything sensible."

"Now since you're Indian, I bet you know a lot about Native art," another woman said. "It's the big fashion here in Toronto. Norval Morrisseau? Does he ring a bell?"

Martha was now thoroughly irritated. The woman was obviously talking down to her since Morrisseau was the best-known of all the Native artists of the Woodland School that had come into its own in the previous thirty years. But she knew something about him the other people in the room did not. Morrisseau came from Sandy Lake First Nation, not far from her home reserve, and the legends he portrayed in his paintings were ones she was familiar with from her childhood. When she had first come to Toronto, she had been surprised that he would dare reveal the sacred teachings of the elders, apparently claiming that he was a modern-day shaman using art to share his heritage with the wider world. But after reading that he was an alcoholic, she had concluded that he was a fraud, just churning out artwork that betrayed his culture to buy booze to feed his addiction.

Then one day, out for a lunchtime walk in Yorkville, one of Toronto's most elegant shopping districts, she saw on display in an art gallery a Morrisseau painting depicting the Wendigo. To her horror, it was the Wendigo with the lewd face of Father Antoine as it had appeared to her in her nightmare after she returned home from residential school and had haunted her nights repeatedly in the ensuing years. She had rushed away in a panic, pushing her way frantically through the tourists crowding the sidewalks, afraid the monster would float free from its canvas prison and come chasing after her. And from that moment, although rationally it made no sense, she could not help thinking that Morrisseau, if not a shaman, was a bearwalker and someone to be feared.

Not wanting to be negative in everything she said, Martha searched for some way to sum up her mixed feelings about Morrisseau that would not provoke the laughter of a group of strangers. But before she could provide her views, someone else, a man this time, broke in.

"I've always thought the paintings of the Woodland School have an uncanny resemblance to the early Picasso. The *Demoiselles d'Avignon* in particular, with its primitive African mask influence. There's also a brutal primitivism and raw emotion in Stravinsky's *Rite of Spring* ballet. What do you think, Martha?"

Martha was confused. She had not heard of Picasso or Stravinsky. Was her questioner trying to humiliate her by deliberately asking her a question he knew in advance she could not answer? Had he really just insinuated that the art of her people was primitive? Primitive meant savage, did it not? At residential school, the nuns had said Indians were Stone Age savages. Surely this individual was not calling her people Stone Age savages? Her feelings were hurt.

"I'm afraid I haven't the slightest idea of what you're talking about," she said.

The dinner guests exchanged puzzled looks and the conversation around the table came to a halt. The farewells after dinner were less enthusiastic than the greetings had been at the beginning, and Linden looked relieved when Martha told him she wanted to sleep in her own bed and went home.

Martha did not sleep well that night, tossing and turning and reliving the events of the evening. The dinner had been a failure and she suspected Linden blamed her. He was probably right about that. She had been thin-skinned when she should have been diplomatic, and if she was to keep him, she would have to learn to hold her tongue. She would have a frank discussion with him to put matters right.

The next morning, therefore, she called him to propose they get together at the same coffee shop near the university where they had first met socially two months before. She wanted to have a "heart-to-heart" talk, she said. When Linden did not reply, Martha asked him if he was still there.

"I'm still here," he said. "You've just taken me by surprise. I'll meet you there in half an hour."

Martha arrived first, and after ordering a black coffee, waited at a table next to a window streaked by raindrops for the arrival of Linden. It was a dreary, rainy, late-November Toronto Sunday morning. A happy chocolate Lab went by dragging through the puddles a laughing teenage girl in a yellow raincoat. A few minutes later, a grey-haired, expressionless middle-aged woman, a dirty-brown kerchief around her head and wearing a loose, heavy once-fashionable coat, shuffled along, leaning into the wind and pushing a shopping cart filled with plastic bags stuffed with old clothes and empty beer and liquor bottles. From time to time, a gust of wind tore wet leaves from the nearby trees and slapped them against the window.

His hair wet, Linden pushed open the door and went over to join Martha. After kissing her on the cheek, he removed his coat and sat down.

"Now what have you got to tell me that's so important you wanted to meet me here rather than over at my place," he said, leaning forward and smiling confidently. "I hope I'm not in trouble."

"Of course not," said Martha. "We've really hit it off in the short time we've known each other and I thought it would be a good idea to see where we're going, especially after last night. But first why don't you order a coffee and let's talk about something else for a while."

For the next hour, Martha and Linden drank coffee and leisurely rehashed the events of the previous evening. They both laughed when they remembered the earnest seriousness of the guest who wanted Martha to provide an expert opinion on the links between Picasso and the Woodland School.

When Martha thought the moment was right, she broached the issue of their long-term future, confident that Linden would want their relationship to continue and become stronger. If that were not the case, surely he would not have insisted on holding a dinner party in her honour.

"You're really special to me, Linden," she said. "But our backgrounds are so different. Do you think we can have a future together just the same?"

But Linden's reaction was not what she expected.

"Martha, Martha, my dear, adorable Martha from the north," he said. "This is a surprise. I've always tried to be honest with you. I really like you, but I'm a little worried when you mention a future together. When I had my divorce, I concluded I'd never be the sort of person who would ever want to be tied down. We're friends. Why not leave it at that? If at any time, either of us want to see someone else, we should feel free to do so."

"Then maybe it would be better," Martha said, "that we didn't see each other again."

Once again, Linden said she was being ridiculous, but he said it in such a way that Martha knew the relationship was over.

Martha's heart was pounding as she trudged back to her apartment in the rain from the coffee shop. How could she have misinterpreted the signals coming from Linden so badly? She now regretted being overeager and pushing him to commit himself. Perhaps if she had given their ties more time to mature, he would have come to care for her as much as she did for him. But now that was too late. Now all she had left were regrets.

But by the time she met Nora for lunch several days later, Martha had come to a different conclusion. After describing in detail the events of the dinner party, she told her astonished friend that she and Linden would not be seeing each other again.

"I was naive and it wouldn't have worked out anyway. But what makes me so mad is that I now think he used that stupid dinner to put me on display like an exotic animal. It was some sort of exam to see how I'd perform with his friends and I failed. Just like I flunked his term paper on Duncan Campbell Scott. The more I think about it the madder I get, and the happier I am to be rid of him."

"Men are all the same," Nora said. "I can tell you from personal experience they just want to get you in bed and when they get tired of you they drop you."

"You're probably right, at least as far as Linden's concerned," said Martha. "He's shallow-minded and manipulative. But the sad part is I liked him and will miss him despite everything. The next man I fall for will be different."

"That's what they all say," said Nora. And the two women burst into laughter.

"Okay, okay," Nora said. "Let's drop the subject and do something really interesting. I always go to the big powwow that takes place every year at this time at the Skydome. Why not come along and keep me company?"

Reconnecting

MARTHA'S EXPECTATIONS WERE NOT HIGH when ten days later she met Nora at the entrance to the Skydome, the covered stadium where the Toronto Blue Jays play their home games. Pow wows were not part of the cultural life of Cat Lake First Nation and most other remote fly-in reserves of Ontario's far north, looked upon by many people as being somehow anti-Christian and the work of the devil. Despite her years in Toronto, Martha had never attended one, assuming they were put on for the entertainment and amusement of the general public.

After paying their entrance fees, the two women joined the throngs of people heading for the bleachers. From on high, they looked down on a reviewing stand framed by banners, standards, flags and pennants. Around the reviewing stand was a carefully raked circle and around the circle were vendors selling Native crafts, music, books and clothing, and kiosks serving bannock, corn soup and other Native foods. Martha liked the carnival atmosphere and enjoyed seeing people of all ages, white and Native alike, having a good time.

The pow wow when it started, however, was not the

Hollywood-style commercial show that she expected. The master of ceremonies, an expert on Native dancing from a Blackfoot First Nation in Western Canada, began to speak from his place on the reviewing stand. "What you are about to witness," he told the crowd, "is a celebration of Native culture by Native people for Native people. Non-Natives are welcome to participate in the inter-tribal dancing. Please show respect for the dancers, drummers and singers, and remember, alcohol and drugs are strictly forbidden."

Then in one thunderous drumbeat, one hundred and fifty drummers smashed their batons down on two dozen big drums signalling to one thousand dancers, led by war veterans and elders bearing Canadian and American flags and carrying eagle staffs, to make the ceremonial grand entry. Everyone in the bleachers rose as a demonstration of respect, as the drumming, this time accompanied by high-pitched wailing, carried on. The master of ceremonies informed the crowd that the dancers were coming from the east entrance, the direction of the rising sun, and like the sun in its daily course, would move clockwise around the circle.

A voice sang out raising goosebumps on Martha's skin. The words were not intelligible but she understood their meaning. They were a lament—melancholic, mournful and heavy-hearted, full of yearning for lost glories. They were a cry of defiance—fierce and raw, challenging those who had despoiled the world of the ancestors. They were a howl of the wild—wolf-like in their wails of loneliness and echo of the primeval. They were prayers to Gitche Manitou and the spirits of the departed shamans, appealing to them to return from their places of banishment to nurture their people.

Martha was transported back almost forty years to the Treaty Day celebrations on the shore of Cat Lake. The people of her childhood were singing, chanting and crying out. The chief was pounding on a water drum and it was echoing out across the waters

summoning the spirits to come join the festivities. Friends and relatives were shuffling around the inside of the tent in the direction of
the sun on its daily travels. Outside, it was dark and a campfire
blazed on the beach waiting for the community to arrive for an
evening of storytelling.

A chief in full ceremonial dress stepped up to the microphone,
breaking the spell, and asked the dancers to align themselves in
formation in front of the reviewing stand. Another, the chief of the
Mississaugas of New Credit First Nation, the people on whose land
the pow wow was being held, welcomed everyone to his traditional
territory. An elder stepped up to the microphone, lifted an eagle
feather up high and intoned a prayer to the Great Spirit.

*Today at this pow wow and each time we gather together, we
form a circle, from infants to youth, from adults to grandparents.
We are mindful that the circle represents life and the circle never
ends. Gitche Manitou is master of the circle and his power runs
through all things, even here in Canada's biggest city. We thank
him for the light of Grandfather Sun, the illumination of Grandfather Moon and for the animals, the fishes and insects and for
the spirits in the wind.*

After lighting a smudge of sweetgrass in a bowl, the elder drew
the sacred smoke toward her with the feather to purify her body,
and blessed the dancers, drummers and members of the public.
There was a moment of silence and Martha and Nora joined the
crowd pouring out of the bleachers to join the dancers on the floor.
Soon five thousand people, First Nation, Métis, Inuit and white,
were travelling around the floor in time with the beat.

All of a sudden, the drumming and dancing stopped and the
master of ceremonies announced that an eagle feather had fallen to

the ground from an eagle staff. Everyone waited patiently, aware that the eagle feather represented a fallen warrior and could not be touched until a special ceremony was performed. Four war veterans drew near and addressed to it a special song of respect. They bent over and touched it in turn, symbolically communicating with the spirit of the dead warrior before the oldest veteran picked it up in his left hand, the hand closest to his heart, and handed it to the owner.

That was the cue for the drummers once again to smash their batons against the drums with hammer blows and to join their voices together in a celebration of pride, affirming that Natives were the equal of the people from other continents who had come onto their lands over the centuries. The dancing picked up where it had left off. Jingle dancers circled, hopping from foot to foot; others, wearing masks adorned with eagle feathers and animal horns, whooped, crouched and leaped into the air. Some moved like grass blown by the wind and waved their shawls to represent butterflies flitting from flower to flower. Men, women and children inched ahead, holding their bodies erect, turning in circles and twirling hoops around their waists, necks and arms.

Martha shuffled forward in a world of her own, her feet close to the ground, feeling the pull of Mother Earth. She was no longer in the tent at Cat Lake and no longer at the Skydome. She no longer knew who she was, where she had come from and where she was going. She forgot her happy years on the land as a child, the abuse at the Indian residential school, the men who had treated her badly and her deep and painful yearning for the children she had not seen in years.

Hypnotized by the repetitive beating of the big drums, the cries and chanting of the singers, the swaying of the dancers and the contagious energy of the crowd, she hoped the dance would never end. She was as lost in the magic of the pow wow as Spider had been in the music of the punks that first night she spent in Toronto so many years ago.

When Martha left the Skydome that night with Nora, she was quietly jubilant, feeling connected to her aboriginal roots with an intensity and sense of belonging that she had not experienced since she was a girl. But before she could become further involved in the Native life of the city, she received a telephone call from Joshua, the friend who had helped her when she was in distress so many years before. Joshua had retired from his position as a teacher in Thunder Bay and had returned home with his wife to be a respected elder and chief of Cat Lake First Nation. He now had bad news to tell her. Her mother, Nokomis, had died and he wanted to express his condolences.

Martha burst into tears and hung up. After regaining her composure, she called him back apologizing for cutting him off. Joshua told her he completely understood her distress, for he too had loved her mother and already missed her. He told her there were practical matters to deal with. The funeral would be in three days. Could she make it back in time?

And what did Martha want to do about Raven? She was now living at his house, but a long-term solution was needed. Martha could send for her daughter and raise her in the big city. He recommended, however, that she return home and be a mother to her there in familiar surroundings. If she wanted a job, he could always use another bookkeeper at the band office.

"Of course, I'll come home," Martha told him. "I can't make it back in time for the funeral since it'll take a month or so to wind up things here, but I'll be there by the end of January for sure. Could I ask you as an old friend to look after the funeral arrangements and take care of Raven until I return?"

"You can count on me, Martha," he said. "I'll stay in touch and work out the details on the phone. Don't forget, a job in the band office will be waiting for you when you get home."

With great reluctance, Martha began her preparations to depart. She would at last be reunited with her daughter but was worried that after so many years of separation, they would be strangers to each other. She was also dismayed at having to give up the job she had become so attached to over the years, the comfortable apartment she had called home for so long and the friends she had made in Toronto.

To make matters worse, the sensational stories constantly being carried in the press on the hardships being suffered by the people on Ontario's northern reserves made her wonder whether she would have the strength to pick up her life where she had left it.

"Children at Pikangikum First Nation Burn Down School"; "Four Dead in Youth Suicide Pact at Webeque First Nation"; "House Fire Kills Family of Six at North Spirit Lake First Nation"; "Two Thousand at Kashechewan First Nation Evacuated Due to Flooding"; "United Nations Condemns Canadian Government for Neglect of Native Children"; "Government Slashes Expenditures for Native People"; "Water Supplies in Remote Native Communities in Ontario Polluted"; "Literacy Levels Among Native Children in Northern Ontario a National Disgrace"; "One in Five Native Children on Reserves across Canada in Care."

Even though Martha had long ago lost hope of finding Spider, she deeply regretted having to leave Toronto as ignorant about his fate as she had been when she arrived in the provincial capital. Until one day when she passed a tall, emaciated dark-skinned person of uncertain age panhandling for change at the Yonge Street entrance to the

Eaton Centre. Martha had often seen him at this spot as she made her way to work but had always taken him to be just another jittery, prematurely ageing alcoholic on his last legs begging for money to buy booze.

Later that morning, however, as she sat at her desk during a lull in her work, her thoughts, as they often did at such moments, turned to Spider and the memory of the derelict came to her. He looked Native; he even looked like Russell. Could there have been a web-shaped birthmark on his forehead? She should have paid more attention to him. Maybe it was Spider. It was a long shot but she was not about to take any chances. She hurried back, but he was gone.

The next morning, however, he was there at his usual spot.

"Any spare change, lady? I'm hungry and need something to eat."

Martha pulled out a toonie and dropped it into his hand, trying not to be obvious as she stared at his forehead. The birthmark was there under a layer of grime. Afraid she might scare him away if she was to blurt out her discovery, Martha invited him to have breakfast with her at a nearby Tim Hortons.

"Their coffee's good and they serve a great breakfast sandwich."

"Okay, why not. As long as you're paying."

A short while later sitting at a booth drinking coffee, Martha took a closer look at her unsuspecting son as he ate his breakfast. His eyes were dull, his clothes were torn and dirty, he smelled strongly of wet garbage and skunky beer, his hair hung down over his face in discoloured strands, and his lips and eyebrows were pierced with rings. She had found her son but he was a wino on the streets! She had to fight to keep from crying.

Spider grew uneasy as the strange woman stared relentlessly at him.

"Why don't you take a picture while you're at it?" he said. "Never seen an Injun before?"

"I didn't intend to be rude," said Martha. "It's just that I'm Indian too, from a reserve way up north and always feel bad when I see one of our people down on their luck. What's your story?"

"I've no idea where I come from and couldn't care less," was Spider's answer. "My mother gave me up for adoption when I was a baby. Probably too ugly to keep. No complaints though. You wouldn't have another toonie, would you?"

Martha looked at him carefully and said, "I bet your mother really misses you."

"Yeah, I guess. How about that toonie?"

Martha handed him his coin. "When I was only seventeen," she continued, "my boyfriend and I had a baby boy who was taken away and put up for adoption. He'd be about your age now if he was still alive. He had a birthmark in the form of a spider's web on his forehead just like yours, and we called him Spider."

Spider looked at Martha, not believing for a minute she could be his mother, even though she had guessed his nickname. Perhaps he could play along and mooch more than just a toonie or two from her. She was, after all, well-dressed and probably had a good job.

"Well, what do you know! Maybe I'm your long lost son. Hi, Mom! What took you so long to find me!"

When Martha's eyes filled with tears and she began to sob, Spider had second thoughts.

"Look, lady, I'm Indian but I'm not your son. I'm just a bum on the streets on the lookout for spare change to buy some booze. Do you know where I live? Under the overpass at the bottom of Spadina where it hits the Gardiner. Would any son of yours live in a place like that?

"Now leave me alone if you know what's good for you. I don't need no mother and I'm poison."

He got up and left, but not before taking the twenty-dollar bill Martha thrust at him.

Spider was not at the entrance to the Eaton Centre when Martha went looking for him the next morning, and she took a cab to the underpass where he said he lived, determined to bring him home with her. It was raining, and a raw, wet wind off Lake Ontario was scattering torn sheets of old newspapers, plastic bags, empty shoe polish boxes and discarded toilet paper around the concrete abutments. There was no one to be seen and Martha at first thought no one lived there. But then she noticed the little shacks thrown together from pieces of discarded lumber, the piles of clothing, blankets and sleeping bags, the sleeping platforms built high up among the girders and a smouldering, rusted, fire-blackened barrel.

Martha went to the shacks, hammering on the doors, one after the other, calling out Spider's name, half expecting to meet the street person she had run into the night of her arrival in Toronto.

In some places, there was no reply and she assumed the occupants were already out on the streets doing their thing, begging for money, buying booze and socializing with their friends. In others, her efforts were greeted by sleepy voices calling out: "Who's there?" "Leave me alone, will you." "Let me sleep."

Finally someone told her to check out a pile of old clothes close to the burn barrel. There she found her son, in a sleeping bag buried under a pile of rags.

"It's me, Spider," she said, shaking him. "I'm really your mother. It's true. I want to help you. Let's go for breakfast and talk."

Spider was curled up and asleep. When he did not respond, Martha shook him until he moaned and slowly opened his eyes and stared with bloodshot eyes at the frantic woman hovering above him.

"Spider, it's me. It's your mother. Remember we had breakfast together yesterday. We need to talk."

Spider, however, had a crushing headache and was furious that anyone would dare violate his privacy when he needed peace and quiet to sleep off his drunk of the previous night.

"Screw off, lady. Can't you see I'm sick? This mother stuff is no longer funny. Go away and let me sleep."

Martha left to buy a mickey of whisky and returned. She sat beside her sleeping son until the afternoon, when he woke up.

"Not you again! Go find someone else to mother! You're becoming a real pain in the ass!"

When Martha showed him the mickey, Spider seized it and took a big slug.

"That sure was good. Now it's your turn, Mom," he said, holding the bottle out to her with a smile. "As they say, a family that drinks together stays together."

When Martha declined, Spider became angry.

"What's the matter? You too good to drink with me? Piss off why don't you and leave me alone!"

Martha took the bottle and drank.

"Now that's more like it. You can be Mom again. I'm hungry. What are you going to feed your son for dinner?"

"Why don't you come home with me? You don't think I'm your mother but that's all right. I've got a spare bedroom, and I'll give you good meals as well as something to drink if that will help you. Just don't expect me to drink with you."

"Now that's the first time anyone's ever made me an offer like that. I'll come and call you Mom if that makes you happy, as long as you keep me in booze."

Martha hailed a cab and brought Spider back to her apartment. Once inside, Martha showed him his room and told him to make himself at home.

"There's the bathroom," she said, "complete with a fresh towel, razor, toothbrush and a change of clothing. I don't imagine you've had too many chances to get cleaned up under the Gardiner."

Spider stayed in the bathroom for over an hour and when he came out, he looked ten years younger. He had removed the rings from his lips and eyebrows, his hair was washed and tied behind his head in a neat ponytail, his scraggly beard was gone and he had put on the new clothes Martha had laid out for him.

Over dinner and after a drink, Spider surprised Martha once again by opening up and revealing a thoughtful side to his nature.

"You know, this is the first time in years that I've been inside a normal house. I used to have okay adoptive parents but I was a jerk and left to be a punk. For years, I lived in squats and thought I was really cool. Then I got older, started to drink too much, got too violent for the punks, and they wanted nothing to do with me and I ended up under the Gardiner. Can't tell you how much I hate that life. Doing really stupid things, begging for money for booze and worse, living with a bunch of losers, and having no hope whatso- ever. I'd do anything to turn my life around."

"Well, maybe you can," said Martha. "I want you to look at this photo."

She handed a photo of a group of laughing people with bottles of beer in their hands standing in front of an old shack.

"Now, do you recognize anyone? Take your time."

"That must be you," said Spider, pointing to a much younger Martha.

"Who's that standing beside me?"

Spider looked carefully at the young man beside Martha for some time before quietly saying, "Looks like me even if it's not."

"It's your father," said Martha. "I loved him but we didn't get along. You were our first child but, I'm ashamed to say, we were poor parents and the Children's Aid took you away. I hope someday you'll be able to forgive me."

Spider looked intently at the photo and said, "Is that really you? Is that my father?"

"It is," said Martha. "But I haven't seen him in years and have no idea where he is, or even if he's still alive. You also have a sister called Raven. She's now twelve and lives back on the reserve."

"You must have had your reasons for letting them take me, but what happened?" said Spider. "Didn't you want me? Did you give me away? Did you ever look for me?"

"It's a long story, Spider, and I'm not proud of what happened. Come back to the reserve with me and I'll tell you all about it. Your sister needs me and she'll be happy to see the brother she thought was gone for good. Once we're back home, I'll help you shake your drinking problem."

PART THREE

~

The Healing Circle

2003

II

Back to the Reserve

ONE EARLY AFTERNOON IN JANUARY 2003, after spending the morning delivering her furniture, rugs and appliances to Nora to use at the shelter, Martha packed her clothes, books and mementos into her car and set off with Spider on the long drive to the reserve.

As she pulled out of the heavy Toronto traffic on to Highway 400 north to Sudbury, she thought back to how unprepared she had been to cope with life in the big city when she had made this same journey by bus in the other direction. So much had changed. Now a woman in her mid-forties with a hint of grey in her hair, she had her failures but was happy with what she had accomplished during her time in Toronto in acquiring an education and a profession.

It had come as a surprise, but she had discovered that she had felt as much at home, if not more so, in the city as she had back on the reserve. Tens of thousands of Native people, many of them middle class, now lived in the big city. If so inclined, she could have attended Native dance, theatre and music productions every night of the week. Moreover, as a dark brown Native Canadian, she had been at ease in the crowds of new Canadians from Asia, Africa and

Latin America who had made migrated to Ontario's capital in the years since she had left home.

But to the west of Sudbury on the Trans-Canada Highway in search of a room for the night, she discovered that even though a new millennium had begun, some things remained the same in her Canada. She pulled up before a motel with vacancies flashing out in front on a neon sign, and accompanied by Spider, pushed open the front door and went in.

The overweight, balding, middle-aged night duty manager watching the local evening news from a television set suspended from the ceiling over the reception desk was a self-proclaimed expert on Indians, and he did not like them. In the 1960s, when Martha was still a child at residential school, he had been a pimply-faced, long-haired high school dropout with bad teeth and clunky glasses stocking shelves at a grocery store. He had but two interests in life: cars and girls. The purchase for three hundred dollars of a used, rusted, two-tone black and yellow 1953 Pontiac hardtop convertible, with two hundred thousand miles on the odometer, power steering, power windows, power brakes, leather seats and push-button radio, had satisfied his craving for the perfect automobile.

But when he tried to entice the white girls of his town to climb into his Pontiac and drink bootleg gin and make out, they laughed at him. He then took to roaming the back roads of the surrounding reserves that dotted Manitoulin Island and the northern shores of Georgian Bay and Lake Huron in search of an Indian girl who would be so impressed with his car that she would be willing to hop into the back seat and have sex with him. But every Indian girl he met told him to get lost.

At hockey games, he would sit with his friends and utter war whoops and yell out "Wagon burners!" whenever Indian players stepped onto the ice. Then one night after a game, a group of Indian teenagers trashed his beloved Pontiac and gave him a beating he hadn't forgotten forty years later when Martha and Spider came in from the winter cold in search of accommodation for the night.

"You gotta pay with a credit card if you want to stay here," the manager told them, eyeing Spider's ponytail as he turned off the sound of the television.

"No problem," said Martha, and she reached into her bag, extracted a card and handed it over.

"Two rooms please."

Without looking at it, he placed the card on the desk and slid it back.

"We're full up. Try somewhere else."

"What do you mean full? Your sign says you have vacancies."

"So it does," he said, "but I'll soon fix that."

He reached under the desk and pushed a button to turn off the illuminated sign. Sitting down, he picked up the remote, turned on the sound of the television and resumed watching the news.

Martha watched him quietly until he looked up.

"Look, lady, gimme a break. I got nothing personal against you but I've got a living to make. I never to rent rooms to Indians. They're nothing but trouble—drinking and fighting and disturbing the other guests. So why don't you do me a favour and let me watch television in peace. And while you're at it," he said, raising his voice, "go somewhere where you'll be welcome. There's at least a dozen reserves around here. Try your luck at one of them. You'll be with your own kind."

Martha protested. "But we have our rights. The Charter says you have to treat us fairly. I could take you to court."

"Then sue me. Canada's a free country."

It was a kick in the stomach and a return to the racism Martha had experienced at the residential school and seen on her way south. Defeated, she picked up her credit card and beckoned to Spider to follow her back to the car.

It was not in Spider's nature, however, to walk away from a fight. "So you want us to sue you," he said and walked over to the desk. With one sweep of his arm, he brushed everything—a rack of brochures on local tourist attractions, pens, papers, registration book, plaques declaring that the motel accepted Visa and MasterCard and was a member in good standing of the Canadian Automobile Association, the Better Business Bureau and the Canadian Chamber of Commerce—to the floor.

Raising his arm to protect himself from the flying papers and bric-a-brac, the manager jumped from his seat and backed away saying, "You've had your fun, now get out or I'll call the cops."

"On what charge? I haven't hurt you—not yet anyhow. Now give us keys to two rooms if you know what's good for you!"

But Martha just wanted to get away. "Come on, Spider, I wouldn't stay here now even if he were to get down on his knees and beg us."

She marched out the door followed by her son and drove off into the night. Two hours later, unable to keep her eyes open any longer, she tried her luck at a motel near Blind River. This time, she trembled when she asked for accommodations, afraid the woman behind the desk would refuse them, and was angry with herself for feeling grateful when the keys were handed over with a cheery "Enjoy your stay."

The next day, Martha grew moody, and paid no attention to Spider who quietly sipped his whisky and did his best to cheer her up as they continued their journey home. At Pickle Lake, they took rooms at a motel for the night, but, anxious to be on her way,

Martha woke Spider at two in the morning and in the moonlight retraced in reverse the trip she had made on the winter road with Olavi. And when the next morning she saw the reserve from afar across the sweep of ice-covered Cat Lake, a host of bitter memories engulfed her: her departure by float plane for the residential school forty years before, the birth and removal of her son, the years of separation from her daughter and the death of Nokomis.

Trying hard to keep herself under control, Martha drove directly to the band office to see Joshua and pulled up alongside a collection of pick-up trucks and snowmobiles scattered across the parking area. After telling Spider to wait in the car, she left it running to keep him warm and got out. A stray dog, its ribs showing, greeted her tentatively, wagging its tail in the hope she would have a scrap of food to share. Three children, who should have been at school at that time of day, leaned against a large graffiti-splattered black and yellow sign bolted to the building wall that said: If the Parents Drink, the Children will Sniff. Hatless, without mittens, and wearing lightweight running shoes in the minus-thirty-degree temperatures, they stared at her blankly, wisps of smoke seeping from their half-open mouths and cigarettes dangling from their fingers.

Martha climbed the steps to the landing, opened the battered steel door and stepped into the foyer. A hand-written notice in English and in Anishinabe syllabics politely invited visitors to remove their boots before entering the main part of the building. After adding hers to the others lined up neatly on old newspapers along the wall, she took off her coat and carried it into the reception area. A dozen reserve residents, many of them friends and relatives, were sitting on plastic chairs, their parkas across their knees, gossiping animatedly. Some were there simply to pass the time of day. Others were waiting to see the chief or one of the band councillors to lobby for better housing, jobs or band funds to send one of their children out to Thunder Bay, Sudbury or North Bay for post-secondary education.

A well-swaddled four-month-old baby girl peeped out from a *tikinagan* propped up on a chair beside her grandmother. Two five-year-olds played hide-and-seek on the clean but heavily worn linoleum floor behind the garbage bin. Colourful posters on one wall warned expectant mothers about the dangers of fetal alcohol syndrome, overweight people about the risks of Type 2 diabetes and young people about the hazards of drug use. On another wall, there were blown-up photographs of Native hockey players and coaches who had made it big in the National Hockey League: Jonathan Cheechoo, Reggie Leach, Bryan Trottier and Ted Nolan.

On another wall, above a large-scale map of the community and its traditional territory, a sign proclaimed:

Homeland of the People of Cat Lake First Nation
Developers must check in at the band office

"Hey, it's Martha. Welcome home, everyone's been expecting you."

"How was the big city? Back to stay?"

"You gonna work here in the band office again?"

"What a nice outfit!"

"You must feel awful about your mother. Too bad you couldn't make it back for the funeral."

Martha was overwhelmed by the warmth of the greetings and the babble of friendly voices, and went around the room shaking hands.

"*Bojo! Bojo!* News sure travels fast. It's great to see you. I'm back to stay and will have plenty of time later on to catch up on the news."

Just then Joshua came down the hall. Now in his mid-sixties, he looked exactly like the grandfather he had become, with white hair, comfortable paunch, friendly wrinkled face and with a pair of reading glasses dangling from a chain around his neck.

"Welcome home, Martha," he said, kissing her on the cheek. "Come on down to my office. We've got lots to talk about."

Joshua led the way down a narrow hallway past offices marked Housing, Education, Health Services, Child Welfare Services, Employment, Economic Development, and Accounts.

"We are now self-governing," he said. "At least, that's the theory. Ottawa has given us responsibility to manage more of our own affairs and we do the best we can. But for reasons best known to itself, the government provides less money to us for education and child welfare than it does to white people for similar services in their jurisdictions. It's unfair and frankly racist."

Joshua invited her into his office, closed the door, told her to take a chair and settled into his creaky seat behind a desk piled high with papers.

"It's been a long time since I've seen you, Martha. You really look good. My wife and I have often talked about you over the years, wondering how you were making out in Toronto. Now that you're home, I want you to know you can count on me to do anything I can to help you, just like in the old days."

Martha nodded but said nothing and Joshua carried on talking, bringing her up to date on her mother's funeral and the latest local news. Raven, he then said, had taken time off from school and was at his house.

"Let's go get her."

Martha did not move. What if Raven was to reproach her for not coming home for so long? Should she tell her that her beloved Nokomis was the one at fault? Or should she say nothing and just shoulder the blame?

Joshua asked Martha what was wrong.

"I'm sorry if I haven't been paying attention," she said. "It's just that I'm worried about how I'm going to be able to face Raven."

"I can't deny you're going to be in for a rough time," said Joshua, "since she thinks you abandoned her. I don't know what advice to give you. For what it's worth, Raven is an extraordinarily sensitive twelve-year-old filled with a great love of life. Someone who's stayed away from the lost kids wandering around here at night getting into trouble. My wife and I've got a soft spot for her since our kids have long since grown up and are making lives of their own in Thunder Bay. She's also a born leader, speaks fluent Anishinaabemowin and knows all the stories about Nanabush, Gitche Manitou and the Thunderbird by heart.

Martha stared at Joshua wide-eyed, his words not registering.

"Nokomis taught Raven the traditional ways and when she was able," Joshua went on to say. "She even took her out in the summers to the old trapping cabin. And in Nokomis's last years, Raven took care of her all by herself and did a real good job. I just wish the other kids in the community were as well brought up."

"And there's another thing," Martha said, interrupting Joshua. "I've brought Spider home with me and he's now a man of thirty with big problems. He was living on the streets of Toronto and is an alcoholic, just like Russell was, and he can't go a day without drinking. It's going to be a handful to look after both of them."

"You really have bitten off a lot," was Joshua's response. "But that's great news. Spider and all those kids who were taken away so many years ago belong with their own people, not with the whites in the city."

Putting off the time she would have to see Raven, Martha asked when she could start her new job.

"As soon as you can. We're swamped with work and the demands keep coming. Everyone wants a better house but no one makes an effort to keep what they've got in good repair, the water treatment plant keeps breaking down, people don't even try to feed themselves with country food, prices are high at the co-op, almost everyone's on welfare, the bootlegger's the only one who's making any money around here, and there's no work except at the band office."

Joshua sighed. "Everybody, especially my own relatives, are at my door day and night, complaining and looking for something for nothing. And I'm only human."

Three months earlier, Raven had prepared a letter to her mother to tell her Nokomis had been suffering from diabetes for many years but had managed to keep it under control with medication and by watching her weight. Recently, however, her vision had blurred until she could hardly see, her blood pressure had shot up and she suffered from pains in her heart. During one of his periodic visits, the doctor recommended that she be evacuated by air for treatment at a hospital in Thunder Bay, but Nokomis had said no, saying she would rather end her days at home rather than go to a big, impersonal hospital on the outside.

Raven had ended her letter by asking her mother to come home when there was still time. But she tore it up at the request of Nokomis. "I would rather end my days with my granddaughter than with a daughter I have not seen in years," she said.

Thus when she met her mother at Joshua's, Raven was torn between joy at seeing her and anger at being abandoned when she was just a baby. Uncertain, not knowing how to respond, she lashed out, giving vent to years of frustration. "Who are you?" she said. "I've never seen you before. What do you want from me?"

Disappointed, but not surprised at her daughter's greeting, Martha took a seat on the couch. She decided to say nothing about the real reason she had not returned home, not wanting to tarnish the memory of Nokomis in the eyes of her daughter, and left it to Spider to take the lead.

"Hi, sis. I'm the big bad brother you've probably never heard of. Everyone calls me Spider after this mark on my forehead. I just met Mom a week or so ago and don't know her much better than you do. I decided to come up here to reconnect and sort out my life."

"I've heard of you," said Raven. "Nokomis told me about you. How that woman did such a rotten job raising you, the Children's Aid came and took you away for your own protection. She treated me no better. She abandoned me when I was a baby and wouldn't even come to the funeral of her own mother. I don't know why she's bothered to come back now that it's too late."

"Now, look, Raven," said Martha, "I understand how you feel but I'm your mother and I'm responsible for you. Joshua phoned and told me about the death of Nokomis. I've wanted to come home to see you many times over the years but it just wasn't possible. I've got a lot of catching up to do but I intend to be as good a mother to you as I can. Get your things together and let's go home."

In the months following Martha's return, mother and daughter ignored each other, and the atmosphere in the family house was glacial. Martha coped by leaving home early each morning for the band office, immersing herself in her work and coming home as late as she could. After making supper for her family, she would wash the dishes and retreat to her bedroom, leaving Raven and Spider alone in front of the television. Spider would go out and spend his evenings at the home of Lester Weasel, the community bootlegger, using an allowance given to him by Martha to buy drinks. When he ran short of money, he had only to ask and his mother gave him more.

One night in late spring several months later, he returned

home in the early hours of the morning in a foul mood. A group of drunks at Lester's had taunted him, calling him a "city Indian" who didn't speak his own language and a failure who didn't belong in their community.

"Look who's talking," Spider had answered. "You guys are just a bunch of hillbilly Injuns who think modern music is the Grand Ole Opry. I bet you think Elvis is still alive and haven't ever heard of Mick Jagger, Kurt Cobain or even John Lennon."

"You know it all, I suppose," a tall, middle-aged regular with an enormous beer belly told him. "You're just a skid-row drunk from the streets of Toronto. Someone whose mother used to put out for all the guys when she was at residential school. I speak from personal experience, since I was there."

As an enraged Spider moved toward him, the regular winked broadly at the others, and said, "I also heard she was away for so long in the big city because she was making a good living down there on the streets as a hooker."

Spider buried his fist in his stomach and shut him up but was soon fighting everyone in the room. The battle was unequal and the patrons gave him a drubbing, dragged him to the door and pushed him down the steps face-first into the ground. Humiliated, he picked himself up and limped home, bloody and drunk, to kick in the front door—just as his father had done thirteen years earlier when the house was owned by Martha's mother.

"You dirty whore!" he screamed, when Martha came out of her bedroom. "You ruined my life once and are doing it all over again by bringing me to this goddamn reserve! Why didn't you leave me in peace under the Gardiner!"

He smashed his fist into her face, blackening an eye and knocking her down before sinking into an armchair, blubbering, his eyes full of tears.

"I'm really sorry, Mom. I didn't mean to hurt you. Don't know why I do things like that. Tell me you forgive me!"

By this time, Raven had emerged from her room.

"Look what you've done to Martha, you creep! Hitting your own mother! Get your drunken butt out of this house and don't come back."

"No! No! Please don't go," said Martha. "Raven, it's just a mistake. He didn't mean it. He's had a hard life."

"He's not the only one," said Raven, and she went to the gun rack, removed the family hunting rifle from its place and drove her brother away into the night—just as her mother had done to their father so many years before.

The next morning, Spider could not be found and Martha was upset.

"If anything has happened to your brother, it'll be your fault," she told Raven. "He was right when he said I'd ruined his life. He'd calmed down by the time you came out of the bedroom with that rifle. There was no need to chase him off and you could've shot him by mistake. He probably feels abandoned and who knows what he might do? Maybe he'll even kill himself!"

Raven did not answer but it did not take her long to guess what had become of her brother. A canoe was missing from the beach.

"He's run off to hide down the river," she told her mother.

Joshua, who had joined in the hunt for Spider, agreed with Raven.

"Over at Lester's he's been telling people that he'd like to live on the land the way we used to in the old days. Some of the elders told him how they fished and hunted in those days. That's what he's done."

"Let's go find him and bring him back," said Martha.

"Do you think that'll do anyone any good?" said Joshua. "If we brought him back he'd just start drinking and getting into trouble again. There's no better way to deal with a drinking problem than to go cold turkey in the bush. I say leave him alone. That way, maybe he'll find himself. I'll have a word with the people who own the canoe he took to explain what happened so they won't report it stolen."

12

Spider and the River

WHEN SPIDER STUMBLED OUT THE DOOR, he wandered to the
beach and sat down on a log half-buried in the sand and held his
face in his hands. Why was he always so self-destructive? Was he
wired differently from other people? He had turned his back on his
adoptive parents who'd tried so hard to love and help him. The
punks had accepted him into their lives but he had frightened them
with his violent ways and drunken rages until even they avoided
him, and he had ended up under the Gardiner. Now he had hit the
only person who had displayed any love for him in years.

There was only one thing to do—he would kill himself. But
how? He had no rope, no gun, no knife and no drugs. But there in
front of him was Cat Lake. He would take one of the canoes drawn
up along the shore into the centre of the lake and upset it! Not
knowing how to swim, he would drown, and then maybe people
would be sorry.

Grabbing hold of one of the canoes, he pushed it into the water,
scrambled aboard and sat down on the floor in the centre, his back
against a thwart. Although there was a paddle at his feet, he did not

know how to use it, and he decided to wait for the canoe to drift out into deep water before making his move. It would be humiliating to set out to drown yourself and fail because you were in shallow water. The sound of the waves lapping against the side of the canoe, however, combined with the alcohol he had consumed, made him drowsy and his head drooped until his chin rested on his chest. Forgetting where he was, he snorted sleepily, eased himself down onto the floorboards, made himself comfortable and dropped off into a deep and drunken slumber.

And as he slept, a fast-moving current swept the canoe downstream toward the rapids.

It was about noon the next day when Spider slowly returned to life. At first he thought he was sleeping rough under the Gardiner as a convoy of heavy tractor-trailer trucks rumbled by over his head. But when he opened his eyes, rather than the familiar rough, grey concrete underbelly of the overpass, he saw a sky such as he could never have imagined, so deep and blue and cloudless it seemed to have no end and no beginning.

For a moment, he was encased in silence. A spray of cold water from over the bow then slapped him in the face and he found himself lying flat on his back in the bottom of a canoe taking him on a deafening roller-coaster ride to some place unknown. When he pulled himself up into a sitting position, he saw to his astonishment that the canoe was plunging downwards past semi-submerged boulders and logs. Certain that he was about to be thrown into the water, he seized hold of the gunnels, eased himself back onto the floor, closed his eyes and waited for the end.

But only a few seconds later, the roaring and buffeting stopped and he was still in the canoe and still alive. He heaved himself back up into a sitting position, soaked and shivering, and looked around.

The canoe was now being carried by the current down a deserted river half a mile wide and framed by heavy bush on each side.

It all came back—the beating at Lester's, the run-in with his mother and sister, and his plan to do himself in by drowning. But he now had absolutely no intention whatsoever of ending his life. Shrugging off the pain of the cuts and bruises sustained in the brawl, he just wanted to get back to the reserve to bum money off Martha to buy booze to quench his now-urgent need for a drink. To do that, however, he would have to turn the canoe around and return to the reserve, even if that meant forcing his way back up through the rapids.

He leaned forward and picked up the paddle. Now what? He had no idea how to use it. For that matter, he had never been in a canoe before. But, he told himself, it couldn't be all that hard. He had seen little kids handling canoes with great ease back on Cat Lake. And he was an adult. He was also an Indian—even if just a city Indian. Paddling was probably in his blood.

Leaning to one side and sensing that he needed to stay low in the canoe to keep it from tipping over, he dipped the paddle in the water and pulled back hard. Nothing happened. He repeated the manoeuvre, this time pulling back even harder.

The canoe turned ever so slightly and his spirits rose. Increasing the pace, he stabbed the water and pulled, stabbed the water and pulled, stabbed the water and pulled. The canoe slowly turned in a half circle. He was on his way.

His triumph was short lived. The current took over once again and swept the canoe and its occupant sideways downstream. He paddled desperately to impose his will on the rushing water, but to no avail. The river was laughing at him.

"Do your worst!" it seemed to be saying. "It won't help you. I'm in charge here and you're coming with me whether you want to or not."

Exhausted, Spider stopped fighting, let the canoe be carried along, and used the paddle only to keep the bow aligned as he drifted throughout the afternoon and into the long summer evening past dense stands of black spruce, balsam fir, tamarack, poplar and birch. In some places, spring floods had eaten into the mud banks and littered the shores with tangles of uprooted trees and broken branches. In others, vast swamps, crowded with the black trunks of drowned trees, stretched away as far as the eye could see. In still others, encroaching walls of rock squeezed and hastened the river through narrow channels, launching the canoe on further wild rides downstream through the rapids.

Meanwhile, Spider thought only of whisky, beer, wine and gin, anything that could satisfy his now all-consuming need for an alcohol fix. The tea-coloured water that he scooped out of the river with his hands to drink was refreshing but gave him no satisfaction. He hoped against hope that he would meet other people, campers or fishermen, who would have a bottle to give him. If not, he knew what was in store for him.

All too often under the Gardiner he had seen winos, when they had been unable to bum enough change to buy booze, mouthwash or Lysol, screaming out in terror from the shakes—the seizures and hallucinations that beset alcoholics when they were deprived of alcohol. Sometimes other winos would come to the rescue, sharing their bottles, and they would survive. But other times they went into shock and convulsions and died before they could be taken to the hospital.

Then from overhead he heard the shrill, heart-rending cry of a baby in distress, frantically calling out to its mother. A red-tailed hawk was winging its way at low attitude down the river, clutching in its talons a panicked rabbit shrieking in pain and anguish, as if it already knew the fate that lay in store when the great bird reached its nest.

Just before darkness settled in, Spider steered for shore and pulled the canoe up on a sandy beach that ran along the base of a cliff. By this time, he was sweating despite the cool night air, and when he fell asleep, the first vision came.

The skinheads he had attacked with his knife when defending his punk friends years ago were back, and had surrounded him on the sidewalk outside the Eaton Centre.

"Who's the tough guy now?" they said. "You're gonna beg for mercy before we're done with you."

He screamed for help and a group of purple-haired punks approached. They were friends from the old days, but they looked on, chanting, "Break his wrists, break his wrists, he needs to die, he needs to die!"

Spider reached for his knife but it was not there. To the applause of the punks, the skinheads began lashing him across his feet, legs, torso and head with steel chains.

The pain was unbearable and he woke up shrieking. "Stop! Just stop. Just tell me what I did wrong and I'll never do it again. I promise, I promise, I'll be good. Pity, please have pity on me. I'm all alone, no one loves me, just stop, I can't take any more!"

The muscles in Spider's legs were contracting and cramps were working their way up from the soles of his feet to his legs, his groin, his chest, his back; they attacked his arms, his neck, his jaws, his cheeks, even his forehead and scalp, until he was one convulsing mass of flesh. He trembled, he struggled for air, he choked, he shit, he farted, he pissed, he puked, his head throbbed and his heart pounded until he was carried away once more by another vision.

This time, he was the one administering the beating. Robert and Amanda looked on with resignation as he kicked his adoptive parents with his steel-toed Doc Marten boots. On their knees and calmly accepting the punishment, they were telling him, "We tried, we really did. We loved you but you were damaged goods when you arrived and an ungrateful punk when you left. Don't come to us for help now. We stopped loving you long ago and don't want you back."

It was then Martha's turn and he was hitting her with his fists. "Why did you abandon me. Didn't you love me?"

Martha was pleading for her life, saying, "I've always loved you and I missed you so much. I'm doing my best, please believe me, I'm doing my best. Just give me a chance!"

As the image of Martha faded, the monsters appeared. A seven-foot 51 Division cop in a pink rabbit costume morphed into a South Asian convenience store owner, who pursued him from his snug burrow in a jumble of old clothes under the Gardiner, chasing him northwards, ever northwards, past a motel with a giant neon sign flashing No Injuns Allowed, to Cat Lake First Nation where once again he found himself surrounded by enemies, this time at Lester's, where ten-foot slobbering devils whose breath smelled of rotting flesh were beating him to the tune of Johnny Cash singing "I Walk the Line" at the Grand Ole Opry.

Just when his anguish could get no worse, he heard the voice of the river. "This will pass. Everything eventually passes, and so will your torment."

The next morning, Spider woke up covered in vomit and diarrhoea. The monsters were gone, but he knew they would return if he did not appease them with alcohol. Too tired to rise to his feet, he rolled into the shallow water along the shore, sprawled out on his back half submerged on the sand bottom and let the waves wash over him, cleansing and reviving him. After resting for a while, he struggled to his feet and made off upstream, determined to make it back to Lester's.

His way, however, was blocked by a swamp. No matter, he would go around it. But hours of climbing over a heavy matted tangle of fallen trees and rotting stumps, of tripping over roots and rocks, and of forcing his way through a mesh of dead interlocking branches of hemlock and black spruce trees, brought him no closer to his goal, and the swamp still stretched off deep into the interior.

In desperation, he plunged into the tepid murky water, stirring up the deep muck of the bottom and releasing the putrid smells of rotting vegetation, and fought his way through the densely packed cattails and tag alders in an attempt to reach the other side. The water became deeper and deeper until it reached his neck. One more step would bring it over his head, but he did not want to die.

He made his way back to high ground and crawled out of the mire with bloodsuckers clinging to his skin, with his arms, legs and torso raw and scratched, and his head and neck covered in mosquito and blackfly bites. After an hour's rest, he got up and stumbled back to the canoe to await the return of the visions.

When night fell, he once again underwent the horrors of alcohol withdrawal. Once again, when he thought he could no longer bear the suffering, the river spoke to him, and told him not to give up.

In the coming days, Spider drew on an inner toughness he did not know he had and threw everything into the fight to survive. He would not last long, he knew, unless he managed to find something to eat. In between seizures, he scoured the lower slope of the cliff in search of berries, but those he found were green and inedible. He began to climb, hoping he would find ripe ones on the top. As he worked his way upwards, a cloud of angry, screaming gulls flew into his face and battered him with their wings, trying to stop him from going any farther.

At the summit, he found a white, excrement-splattered, rocky platform covered with nests filled with chicks and unhatched eggs. Ignoring the frantic attempts of the gulls to drive him away, he helped himself to the eggs, cracking them open one after another, greedily sucking back the liquid whites and choking down the dark orange yolks with their strong taste of carrion and the wild. For a minute, he felt wonderful, but his stomach revolted, and in one explosive convulsion, expelled the strange food. After resting for a while to give his body time to adjust, he tried another egg, and this time he kept it down.

Each day he returned to the rookery to fight off the gulls and to feast on their eggs, and each day the intensity of his seizures diminished. One morning, he woke with a soft, warm summer rain on his face and he felt at peace. The river, enveloped in a heavy mist, was not visible, but he could hear it murmuring at his side, telling him that he had won his battle and it was time to continue his journey.

From across the water came the cry of a loon—a strange and haunting sound unlike anything he could have imagined in his years in the city—rising and fading, rising and fading. Shortly thereafter came an answering song, and another and another.

"Do as the river tells you," they seemed to be saying. "We are the voices of your ancestors and know what is best for you."

After the rain ended and the mist lifted, revealing a world lush and washed clean of impurities, he pushed the canoe into the water, climbed aboard and let the current take charge again, confident there was now some purpose to his journey. For the first time since running away from home to join the punks, his body was free of alcohol.

All creation—the rushing water, birdsong, a piece of birchbark floating by, the buzzing of a mosquito, the cry of a raven and the hoofmarks of a large animal on the shore—was now infused with an unexpected and beautiful vitality. Even the swamps were no longer sinister quagmires, but were floating gardens covered in white- and purple-flowered water lilies. Filled with exaltation, he felt for the first time connected to his Native roots and to the world as it had existed before the coming of the white man.

Later that morning, off in the distance, he saw smoke rising from a campfire, a tent, and an outboard motorboat pulled up on a large, smooth shelf of rock along the shore. When he approached, an old couple came out of the tent and waved for him to join them.

"My name's Spider," he said after he landed. "The current took me down the rapids from Cat Lake a week or ten days ago and it's too hard to paddle back."

If the elders were surprised at seeing someone suddenly appearing at their camp with no food supplies, no extra clothing and no tent, they were too polite to let it show.

"*Gdi nesh naabem nah?*" asked the wife, asking him if he spoke her language.

"I'm sorry," said Spider. "I don't understand what you're saying. I was adopted out when I was a baby and never learned my language. But I'm from the reserve. My mother tracked me down in Toronto and brought me back a few weeks ago. I've had a tough time on the river but I've also learned a lot."

"Let's have something to eat before we get into all that," she said. "You look like you're starved." It took no more than thirty minutes for the meal of bannock and fried pike to be prepared and eaten. Afterwards, the husband handed Spider a tin mug of hot sweetened tea and asked him the name of his family. When told that Martha Whiteduck was his mother and Raven his sister, the old couple were pleased.

"Your grandparents," the old man told him, "were wonderful people and good friends. And of course we know your mother, Martha, and your sister, Raven. We were sad when the Children's Aid took you away so many years ago. You must have had a bad time down there in the big city with all those white people."

When Spider made no reply, the old woman, who was the more

direct of the two, asked him, "Now tell us why you're really here, and how you survived all those days with no food?"

"The river saved me," said Spider. "It took me away from the community when I had too much to drink and was thinking of killing myself. It talked to me, telling me not to give up when I thought I wouldn't survive."

When the old couple exchanged knowing looks, Spider thought they were making fun of him. "I know it sounds strange, but I'm not joking. Maybe I was delirious but something or somebody saved my life."

"We weren't laughing at you," said the old man. "The white man and many of the people back at the reserve might say you were just imagining things, but we believe you. Your grandparents would have believed you. We think the river brought you to us for a reason."

13

In Search of Oblivion

As time went by and there was no word from Spider, Martha became frantic.

"He probably doesn't know how to swim and he's fallen out of the canoe and drowned," she told Raven. "Or maybe he's hurt and is lying all by himself on some lonely beach. Or maybe he's been attacked by bears or wolves. Whatever! If only I could be at his side when he needs me!"

"I don't think he does," said Raven. "He's big enough to take care of himself. Besides, isn't it a little late to start worrying about him?"

More diplomatically, Joshua made the same point when Martha went to him for help. "He hasn't been gone long. It's summer and there are people from the community camping along the river. Someone will take him in."

Martha was deeply wounded. The only people she could turn to for help were not taking her concerns seriously and it became too much for her to bear. One morning, after spending the first half of the night tossing restlessly on her bed and the second half in a deep and dreamless sleep, she woke as usual at seven o'clock, but with tears in her eyes and the taste of despair in her mouth. It was back—the whiff of dread, the overwhelming longing for oblivion—the depression she had suffered through some thirty years ago when she had returned home from residential school was back.

This time she was not going to let it torture her like it did when she was a sixteen-year-old. But when she tried to get up, feelings of worthlessness and self-hatred spread through her body like a poison, making her fearful of the day ahead. Bursting into gut-wrenching sobs, she forced herself to sit up, pushed her feet over the side of the bed and dragged herself over to the closet to pick out clothes to wear that day.

So far so good. Now if only she could make it to the office, maybe she would be able to dispel the beast in the routine of work. Afraid to say anything to Raven in case she broke down altogether, Martha stifled her weeping, ignored her daughter who was looking at her with concern from her seat at the breakfast table and concentrated all her efforts on making it to the hook by the front door where her car keys were hanging.

Her legs protested. "We don't want to go any farther. Turn around and go back to bed."

Martha refused to give up and forced them to obey, focusing first on one, and on the other, lurching forward like a child learning to walk until she reached the hook. She grasped the keys, lifted them from their perch, paused to gather her strength, pushed open the front door and stepped out onto the stoop.

A wave of dizziness overpowered her and she slumped down against the wall. When the vertigo lifted, she pulled herself to her feet and proceeded slowly and carefully down the steps to her car. Once inside and seated, she grasped the steering wheel tightly, leaned forward, closed her eyes and struggled to regain control of herself.

The cloud gradually lifted and she was able to turn on the ignition, put the car in gear and start driving to the band office. By the time she arrived, she was already feeling better, and she kept her sickness at bay throughout the day by keeping busy. But that evening, driving home, she once again tasted despair.

"I'm really feeling bad, Raven," she said when she entered the house. "Could you make your own dinner? I've got to go to bed."

Without waiting for an answer, Martha entered her bedroom, closed the door and collapsed fully clothed on her bed. Twelve hours of deep, dreamless sleep later, she woke with tears running down her cheeks to fight her way to the band office again. And when she returned home, she went directly to her bedroom, fell onto her bed and went to sleep.

This time Raven came into her room, shook her awake, undressed her and made her eat some soup. Martha obeyed mechanically and was asleep before her daughter left the room.

"You're in trouble," Raven told her mother the next morning when she emerged bleary-eyed from her bedroom. "It's not normal to have to sleep so much. Is it because you're worried about Spider? I'm sure he's okay but if you want, I'll organize a search party. Is that what you want?"

"No, no, it's not about Spider any more. I just need rest. I've been through this before and can handle it by myself."

"You can't do it alone," said Raven. "Why don't you go to the nursing station and get some pills? Or maybe the next time the doctor comes from Thunder Bay, he'll be able to do something? Maybe he'll fly you out to see a specialist?"

Martha, however, refused help and her depression worsened. Instead of dreamless nights of deep sleep, she was now afflicted by restless nights filled with wild dreams involving Father Antoine, the residential school, the bearwalker and the Wendigo. She soon began sitting up late into the night, drinking coffee and putting off the time when she would have to go to bed. The nightmares invaded her waking hours in flashbacks of guilt, rape and loneliness until she became almost comatose with dread and anxiety.

"Why don't I just kill myself and end this agony?" she asked herself. But no matter how much she suffered, something deep inside told her she didn't have the right to take her own life and that she had to live for the sake of her children.

Late one afternoon, thinking alcohol might make her feel better, instead of going straight home after work, Martha drove to Lester's.

Tall and wiry with a scraggly beard on an acne-pitted face, Lester was a few years older than Martha and they had known each other since childhood. Both had passed their earliest years on the land, both had listened to the elders tell the old stories around the campfire in the summers and both had been shipped off to residential school on turning six. Lester had also been one of the big boys who had bullied her little cousin and stolen his food prior to his death. In the years that followed, Martha had made clear to him her disdain, and never spoke to him unless she absolutely had to.

Thus when Lester saw Martha walking in his door, he had difficulty in suppressing a smirk. Despite going to Toronto and supposedly doing well, she's no better than the rest of us, he thought. But what if she wasn't looking for a drink but was going to create a fuss about the way her son had been knocked around on his premises?

"Look, Martha," he said, before she could say anything. "Spider got roughed up here the night he went missing, but it wasn't my fault. Everybody knows I keep my nose clean and don't allow no fighting at my place, but he got belligerent with the others and bit off more than he could chew."

When Martha made no comment, Lester invited her to have a drink.

"We've known each other since we were kids. You went off to the big city to make your fortune and I stayed home and went into the booze business.

"If I do say so myself, even if some people look down on what I do, I've done better than you or anyone else from the old days— new four-wheel-drive truck every other year, new Bombardier snowmobile every winter, widescreen TV, twin V-6 Yahamas on my boat—"

Martha cut him off, saying she'd have some rye.

"Okay, okay, not in the mood for small talk I see. But the customer is always right and if you like hard stuff, hard stuff it'll be. Me, I stick to wine. Can't let myself get too high when I gotta serve my customers."

He pulled a half-empty bottle from a shelf over the kitchen sink, poured a shot into a water glass and handed it to her.

"Want a little ginger with that?"

Martha shook her head, took hold of the glass, closed her eyes and tossed back the contents.

"That's just what I need," she said, shuddering as the whisky burned its way down her throat. "I'll take a bottle if you got it."

Even though Martha had to endure the snide comments of the other customers, she began going to Lester's on Friday nights after she received her pay to buy two bottles of whisky at two hundred dollars each. Once home, she would hand Raven whatever was left of her money to buy groceries and the other necessities of life and vanish into her room. She would then drink herself into oblivion until Monday morning when she would emerge with a splitting headache and feelings of remorse.

Although she dragged herself to the band office each workday, she was now moody, easily distracted and no longer took part in the friendly banter among the staff. When she started to make mistakes in her work, Joshua took her aside.

"Martha, it looks like you're going through a tough time. Do you mind if I speak frankly to you, as a friend and elder, not as your boss?"

"I've been wanting to talk to you myself," Martha said. "I know my work's fallen off. I'm fighting a depression. Probably it's a flare-up of the one I had when I came back from residential school. You remember? The one you helped me with that day when we sat together and talked down at the shore? When we saw the ancestors in the clouds? All those old experiences are coming back. I'm reliving the abuse of that pedophile priest, Father Antoine, again."

"Let's work on your depression together," said Joshua. "But you also have to recognize you've got a drinking problem and if you don't watch out, you'll become an alcoholic."

"I trust you, Joshua. Just tell me what to do and I'll do it. I'm desperate."

"The first thing you have to do is to stop drinking, " was Joshua's response. "I mean really stop. No more visits to Lester's. No more using your depression as an excuse to drink. Promise?"

Martha promised and did not go to Lester's after work the following Friday evening. But the next day, after a difficult, sleepless night, her resolution faltered and she set off to buy a bottle of whisky. On the way to the bootlegger's, however, she passed a small building where a Native preacher from a nearby First Nation held regular church services, prayer meetings and evenings of gospel singing. Preoccupied with her own problems, she had paid little attention to it in the past. But this time, perhaps because she was feeling guilty about breaking her promise to Joshua, she stopped her car and walked over to read a notice tacked onto the front door.

Are You Lonely?

Do You Live a Meaningless Life Full of Suffering?

The Good Book Has the Answers.

Services Every Sunday at Ten.

Martha returned home and the next day she joined a small group of community members who came together on Sundays for weekly worship. After the opening hymns and community announcements, the preacher stepped up onto the raised platform and approached the pulpit, held his Bible tightly in his left hand, pointed his right hand at the congregation and began his sermon.

"Brothers and sisters! Welcome today to this place of worship. I can feel that many of you are troubled. I know that many of you are seeking to lead better lives. I am certain that many among you are trying to understand why you suffer.

"Do you know why you suffer? I can tell you why! It's because you are depraved! You are depraved because you were born into sin! The Devil tempted Adam and Eve and they sinned! They lost their innocence and were driven out of the Garden of Eden by the Lord because they had sinned!

"Men and women ever after were born into sin! It doesn't matter how mighty you are. It doesn't matter whether you are a king, a queen, a prime minister or even a man of God—all of us, my dear friends, were born into depravity and sin!

"Now I bring you good news. Though your sins be as black as coal, though your sins reek of depravity, you can be saved and go to heaven! You just have to repent, believe in the Lord and be born again.

"Brothers and sisters, be good parents to your children. Spend your welfare money on food and clothing for your little ones and not at Lester's. Make your children go to bed early. Make your children give up their evil ways.

"If they don't obey, remember the words of the Good Book, 'Spare the rod and spoil the child!'"

A young man sitting alone at the back of the room then hit a chord on his electric guitar, and everyone rose to sing a mournful old favourite.

> *Nobody knows the trouble I've seen,*
> *Nobody knows but Jesus.*
> *Nobody knows the trouble I've seen,*
> *Glory Hallelujah!*
> *Sometimes I'm up, sometimes I'm down,*
> *Oh, yes, Lord.*
> *Sometimes I'm almost to the ground,*
> *Oh, yes, Lord.*

"Now brothers and sisters, listen carefully to what I now tell you today," the preacher said after the congregation took their seats. "A special burden has been placed on us as Native people. When I was a boy, I used to enjoy listening to the elders tell the old stories about Nanabush, the Thunderbird and the Wendigo. They said man was related to the animals and the Anishinabe people had spirit helpers from the land of the ancestors. They said Gitche Manitou was a divine spirit.

"But that is just ignorant superstition. You have to renounce these beliefs if you want to be saved. For the Good Book says 'Let there be no other gods before me.' And Nanabush, the Thunderbird and Gitche Manitou are false gods.

"The Good Book is the Word of the Lord. It says man was created in the image of God. We must reject the old view that man is somehow related to the animals! Brothers and sisters, we are not animals. God is not the god of animals. If we were animals, there would be no right or wrong. You could love and help someone, or torture and kill him. It would make no difference. There would be no moral order if we were animals.

"Therefore, I implore you, brothers and sisters, save your immortal souls by coming forward today to be saved. Escape the fate of our ancestors who knew not the Good Book and have been condemned to eternal damnation. Reject pow wows with their glorification of heathen practices. Tolerate not drum circles and Native dancing in the community—even if your children beseech you to bring back the old ways.

"Remove from the walls of your houses the works of art featuring Nanabush and the Thunderbird. For they are idols and false gods.

"Now come forward, I implore you! Come forward, I beg you! Come forward today and be saved!"

The preacher pumped his fist in the air for emphasis as he made each point, and the congregation, in a state of growing ecstasy, responded passionately. Some people stood up to shout "Amen!" Others began to shake and to speak in tongues.

Martha was overcome with joy. She remembered only the bad and none of the good times in her life. Her entire existence had been a living hell, and she now knew why that was so—it was because she had been born into sin and had lived a life of depravity, fornicating and drinking and believing in false gods. She wanted to drown her sorrows in the love of God and start anew. A feeling of euphoria and spiritual fullness came over her and she began to tremble. The room filled with a blinding light and she rose to her feet, lifted her arms up toward the ceiling and with tears streaming down her cheeks cried out: "I have seen the light! I have seen the light! I am saved! Thank you, Jesus! Oh thank you, Jesus!"

The preacher came down the aisle and led her to the front. He asked her to fall on her knees and she did. He blessed her and told her that she was saved and that her soul would go to heaven when she died.

Martha said, "Thank you, Jesus," and shouted out, "Amen."

As she rose to her feet and made her way slowly back to her seat, the preacher began singing.

> *Amazing Grace, how sweet the sound,*
> *That saved a wretch like me.*
> *I once was lost but now am found,*
> *Was blind, but now can see.*
> *'Twas Grace that taught*
> *My heart to fear.*
> *Grace, my fears relieved.*
> *How precious did that Grace appear*
> *The hour I first believed.*

The congregation joined in with such gusto that the walls of the modest building appeared to shake.

But when Martha went home after the church service, she had second thoughts. What a fool I've been. What a spectacle I've made of myself. How can I look any of these people in the eye again? Now that I think about it, the preacher's message doesn't ring true. It's no different from what the nuns and Father Antoine used to tell us. Maybe he's right, but I'm not yet ready to write off the beliefs of the ancestors so easily. It makes no sense that a just God would send Native people, who had not heard the Word of the Lord throughout the ages, to eternal damnation. And in my heart, I'll never give up my conviction that Gitche Manitou is the spirit that runs through all things.

Martha was, however, capable of adhering to two seemingly contradictory beliefs at the same time. She thus kept her strong faith in Native spirituality to herself and embraced Christianity on Sunday mornings during church services and on Thursday nights when she joined her new friends singing old-time Negro spirituals with their promise that the oppressed and humble in this life would obtain their reward in the next. Her depression and flashbacks were kept at bay at these times, but came back with greater intensity when she returned home from church and her religious fervour faded. She accordingly resumed binge drinking on Friday and Saturday nights, dimly aware that her behaviour made no sense, but believing she could function no other way.

Without realizing it, Martha began treating her daughter the same way the nuns had dealt with her when she was a girl. She continued to reject Raven's efforts to help her and found fault with everything she did, nagging her about the way she dressed, the way she wore her hair, the amount of time she spent on homework, the music she listened to and the books she read.

"When I lived in Toronto," Martha told her, "I saw two kinds of Native people—lazy ones and hard-working ones. The lazy ones were in the gutter. The hard-working ones studied hard, were proud of their heritage and made something of their lives. They became social workers, lawyers, doctors and teachers. Anything the white man could do, they could do. If you don't straighten out, you'll end up on the streets just like your father."

To escape her mother's tirades, Raven started staying out late at night and sharing her problems with her friends. That upset Martha even more and she would sit waiting for her daughter and berate her when she came home. Raven would ignore her mother and go directly to bed, rendering Martha speechless.

One night, however, as she waited up for her daughter, Martha began to drink. And the more she drank, the angrier she became, thinking back to the punishments she had suffered at the hands of the nuns for offences not nearly as serious as staying out late at night and most likely getting into all manner of trouble. That led her to remember being beaten and thrown into the coal cellar for trying to help Little Joe, and she began to feel morose and sorry for herself.

By the time Raven came home, Martha had worked herself up into a drunken rage.

"I bet you've been smoking pot and making out with the boys," she said, grabbing hold of her, pushing her down on the sofa and lashing her with a belt. "The Good Book says 'Spare the rod and spoil the child,' and this is for your own good.

"From now on you're going to church every Sunday and I'll be keeping an eye on you."

But instead of intimidating her daughter, Martha made her defiant and rebellious. When she tried to hit her again for staying out late, Raven, who was tall and strong, tore the belt from her mother's hands.

"How'd you like it if I hit you with a belt. Try that again and I'll let you have it. You make me sick. Pretending to be religious, crying out in church on Sunday about being saved and coming home to drink yourself senseless and beat me. Spider, for all his faults, was never a hypocrite like you. I hate hypocrites! Now back off and leave me alone!"

Martha gave up trying to discipline her daughter and Raven continued roaming the community with kids seeking companionship and love wherever they could find it. They gathered at night behind the impersonal, windowless walls of the co-op to express their self-hatred and disgust at life and their revolt against their parents by smoking and drinking and littering the ground with empty cigarette packages and booze bottles, by cutting themselves with razor blades, by melting down over-the-counter drugs and injecting them into their veins, by swallowing Oxycodone and Percocet pills stolen from their parents who had smuggled them into the community to feed their own addictions, by inserting their heads into black garbage bags to sniff the fumes of gasoline and hairspray, and by squirting insect repellent straight into their nostrils to get a quick high.

When they emerged from the shadows, they scrawled HYPOCRITES GO HOME on the walls of their overcrowded, polluted and rotting school, giving the finger to the white teachers who arrived each fall promising to be their friends but who often betrayed them by leaving at Christmas and not coming back when the holidays were over. Out at the airport, they did the same thing, writing WELCOME TO HELL on the side of the terminal building to show their disdain for the so-called experts from the outside who flew in regularly to tinker ineffectually with the defective community water, sanitation and electrical systems.

But their rage was not confined to their parents and to the outsiders who had let them down. They turned against each other, like the children in William Golding's *Lord of the Flies,* with the bigger kids pushing around and exploiting the smaller ones. Initially relegated to the ranks of the young and weak, Raven was ordered to steal money and booze from her mother. When she refused, they tried to slap her around, but she refused to be bullied and fought back, defending herself using a piece of two-by-four as a club.

"Crazy bitch," they called her. "You're just as weird as your dingbat brother and mother." But they left her alone and grudgingly accepted her into the ranks of the dominant group.

Some youngsters just opted out and killed themselves. For the suicide epidemic that had begun more than two decades earlier in northern Ontario among Native youth, well before Martha left the community for Toronto, had continued unchecked over the years. But in contrast to neighbouring communities such as Pikangikum, Wapekeka and Webeque, where at times in each place up to half a dozen young people took their lives annually, there was usually no more than one death from suicide each year at Cat Lake First Nation.

Thus when thirteen-year-old Rebecca took her life that fall, the shock wave of grief that rolled over the community was tempered by the expectation that it was unlikely there would be another self-inflicted death for some time. But then two more teenagers, Jonathan and Sara, took their lives, one after another in quick succession. And while they all killed themselves just after their thirteenth birthdays, nobody knew if that was just a coincidence.

Despite her problems, Martha was not so self-absorbed that she was unaware that an epidemic of youth suicide was ravaging the community. Every Sunday she prayed along with the members of her church for the souls of the departed. At the band office, it was the main topic of conversation among the staff and the ever-present crowd of hangers-on in the reception area. She even attended the funerals, and sobbed and cried out with the other mourners as the coffins were carried out for burial.

But in the grip of her depression, and either drunk or hungover much of the time, she shared the grief of the others from a distance, numbly, in a mechanical sort of way, just going through the motions. What was happening was horrific but it did not affect her personally. Certainly she never suspected her own daughter might be involved. Therefore when Raven, shortly after her thirteenth birthday, came into her bedroom one Saturday morning, shook her awake and told her she was part of a suicide pact with the three teenagers who had taken their lives, Martha did not grasp what her daughter was telling her.

"Whaz that? Whaz that? You've joined what? What're you saying?"

"Nothing," said Raven. "Nothing important."

Joshua was eating breakfast with his wife when Raven knocked on their door and entered.

"Look who's here," he said. "Help yourself to some bannock and make yourself at home. Would you like some hot chocolate or tea?"

When Raven sat down on the couch but remained silent, Joshua's wife looked at her desolate face and put on her shawl. "I'm going to leave you to it," she said. "I got a few errands to run" and she went out the door.

"Now, how can I help?" Joshua asked, coming over to sit down beside her.

"Joshua," Raven said, "you were there for me when Nokomis died. Can you help me again? I've no one to turn to and feel really bad. My mother drinks and cares only for Spider and she blames me for driving him into the bush. She never wanted me in the first place and has no use for me now. When I tried to talk to her this morning about something really important, she was so drunk she didn't know what I was trying to say."

"Take your time, Raven," Joshua said. "When you're ready, tell me what's going on."

Raven stared at the floor, struggling to find the strength to share her secret. When she began to sob, Joshua took her in his arms.

"That's okay, Raven. Cry all you want and let me know how I can help when you're ready."

"It's really hard," she said. "It's about the suicides. About the kids who killed themselves."

"Yes," said Joshua sharply. "What about the suicides? What's it got to do with you? I hope you're not thinking of doing the same thing?"

"It's worse, Joshua. It's worse than that. There was this suicide pact and I was part of it. There were four of us and we decided to die when we turned thirteen. Life at home was just so bad we didn't want to go on living."

Raven began crying again and when she calmed down somewhat, Joshua said, "I'm so sorry, Raven. It must have really been terrible. But please tell me more." .

"The others all went ahead and I'm the only one left and I'm no longer sure I want to do it. But if I don't, I'll be breaking my word to Rebecca, Jonathan and Sara. I'm so confused and I don't know what to do. That's why I've come to see you."

Joshua was holding Raven in his arms as she was talking. He squeezed her even tighter, and when he released her, his eyes were full of tears.

"Raven, this is really serious and I'm glad you've come to see me. We got to talk this through. Although you're only thirteen, you've got to help me help you."

When Raven nodded her agreement, Joshua continued. "First, I want you to promise me you won't do anything drastic. If you really feel like hurting yourself, you'll come see me first. I'm not joking. Anytime of the day or night."

"I'll try," said Raven. "But I don't know how long I can hold out."

"Let's figure out what to do," said Joshua. "In a way it's a good thing you've come to me. This reserve has been rocked by suicide after suicide by young people just like you for far too long. But this current wave is heartbreaking. Never before have so many kids taken their lives in such a short time. We've been trying to put a stop to it, but we didn't know who was part of the pact. Tell me, are there any other kids involved?"

"No one else came in with us but there are probably others who are thinking about doing it."

After a minute's reflection, Joshua said, "You probably know that I can't, by myself, solve your problems. No one can. I'm not even sure I can help you to deal with your mother since I had no luck when I tried to get her to stop drinking. What we need to do is to get everyone working together. Because this reserve is sick. And one of the reasons it's that way is because the parents and grand-parents of the children were taken by the government and raised in residential schools. Your mother knows all about this, since she was one of them.

"You were lucky to escape all of that, living as you did with your wonderful Nokomis. You also have a mother who learned her language and culture again when she returned from residential school. But the bottom line is that most of us who attended residen-tial school were never taught to be good parents, and your mother is part of that world. They never say I love you to their kids, and you and your friends feel unwanted. But those are just my views. What we need is to get everyone together to exchange information and look at options."

"But that won't work," Raven said. "Just holding another meeting where everyone talks forever and never comes to any con-clusions won't help."

Joshua went to the window and stared outside for a long time, and returned to the couch.

"There is another way," he said. "What do you think about holding a healing circle and inviting the priest who molested the mothers of the kids who killed themselves to come meet with us? His name's Father Lionel Antoine. He's also the priest who abused your mother. It would be a long shot since the Church is having a hard time admitting its clergy did anything wrong and probably wouldn't want him to come. He might even be dead.

"But if he is alive and he agreed to come, maybe your mother and the others will be able to have it out with him. Maybe he'd say he was sorry. Maybe the women he wronged can forgive him. And if they do, maybe they'll be able to start to heal themselves. They might even be able to show some affection to you kids. I can't think of anything that would do more to bring these suicides to an end. What do you think?"

"I'm all for it," said Raven. "I just hope my mother agrees."

"Let me handle your mother. I think our plan might just work. I've heard the archbishop of Quebec has a big heart and I'll write to ask for his help. But keep it to yourself for the time being in case we can't pull it off."

14

The Church

SHORTLY THEREAFTER, Joshua sent the following letter to Archbishop Laframbroise.

Dear Archbishop Laframbroise,

I would like to introduce myself. I am the chief of Cat Lake First Nation, located 500 miles northwest of Thunder Bay in northern Ontario on the headwaters of the Albany River. We are proud Native people and our ancestors have lived in this area since time immemorial.

We have never met but I have been told that you are the head of the Catholic Church in Quebec. I am writing to you about something that is painful for me even to describe. The government in Ottawa working with the churches decided many years ago that they would take Native children from their parents and send them to residential schools to turn them into white people.

The people of my community had no choice and generations of our children were sent to a residential school run by your church on James Bay. Many of them returned crushed in spirit after being harshly treated by the staff and losing much of their language and culture.

Could you find it in your heart to help our community heal itself? We need to meet directly with a priest, Father Lionel Antoine, to come to terms with our pain. He sexually abused many of our girls in those years. If he is not alive or does not wish to come, could you send someone who is wise and compassionate to sit with us in a healing circle. My goal is not revenge but peace, reconciliation and healing.

Yours Truly,
Joshua Nanagushkin,
Chief, Cat Lake First Nation

The morning Archbishop Laframbroise received Joshua's letter, Bishop Thierry de Salaberry, the impeccably groomed cleric in his mid-thirties who helped him administer his archdiocese, had no idea his day would turn out so badly. As he did every day after mass, he ate breakfast alone in the dining room of his residence. Conscious of the dignity of his office, he insisted on eating on porcelain dishes using sterling silver cutlery on a polished mahogany table adorned with fresh-cut flowers.

His housekeeper served him freshly squeezed orange juice, crisp bacon, lightly poached eggs, whole wheat toast and orange marmalade, poured him a large cup of coffee, added cream and sugar, stirred it gently and handed him the daily newspapers. It was the time of day he enjoyed the most. He loved to drink his coffee slowly and to go through the morning papers, especially *Le Devoir*, favoured by Quebec intellectuals, at his leisure.

The bishop came from a prominent old Quebec family that counted many notaries and bishops in its lineage. It was a source of pride that he could trace his ancestry back to landowning nobility in Normandy, who had sent their sons across the Atlantic to become seigneurs in New France in the seventeenth century. As a youth he had attended the best classical college in the province. Afterwards, although experiencing no particular spiritual call, he decided to pursue a religious life and entered the seminary of Quebec.

Neither he nor his family, nor any of the senior members of the local clerical establishment, who were frequent dinner guests at his family's elegant and well-appointed home, ever doubted that he was destined for greatness. He had been the most brilliant student at the classical college, mastering Greek and Latin with ease, and had excelled in English, French literature and rhetoric. His record of achievement had been the same at the seminary where his grasp of canon law and philosophy, in particular that of Saint Thomas Aquinas, had delighted his teachers.

After he was ordained, it was out of the question that he would be sent into the field as a missionary, or for that matter be assigned like most other newly minted priests to a rural parish. Instead, he became a personal aide to the archbishop of Montreal. And he carried out his duties with such discretion and good judgement that in short order he became a bishop and was assigned to the archdiocese of Quebec City with dozens of priests, most of them older than he was, under his authority.

This rapid promotion he considered his due and he expected to rise quickly to the top ranks of the Church. He had already mapped out a plan for that to happen. He would become a member of the Vatican diplomatic service and then, with his innate talent and winning personality, he would, he was certain, become an archbishop. After that he would become foreign minister to the Holy

Father himself. And then, who knew what might happen?If the bishop was to fulfil his destiny, however, he would have to be called to Rome, and for that to happen, he would need the blessing and recommendation of his superior, Archbishop Laframbroise. He did not think that would be a problem. The archbishop seemed to like him and depended on him for help in managing his archdiocese.

The bishop recognized that he was ambitious but did not consider that to be a bad thing in and for itself. After all, he sought advancement not for himself but for the good of the Church. He had already asked the archbishop to write to the Curia in Rome on his behalf, and Archbishop Laframbroise, admittedly with no great enthusiasm, had promised to give his request the attention it deserved.

In the meantime, Bishop de Salaberry had set out to charm and impress his superior with the depth and sophistication of his knowledge of international affairs, and was always on the lookout for opinions he could appropriate from the newspapers and offer up as his own in their monthly business lunches. This morning, however, he was unpleasantly surprised to see that the lead item in *Le Devoir* was a report that the police were making rapid progress in their investigation into the mistreatment of Indian children by members of the clergy who had staffed Indian residential schools:

> For over one hundred years, the Canadian government sought to deal with the "Indian problem" by trying to integrate Natives into mainstream society through policies of forced assimilation. Generations of Indian children, as young as six, were taken from their families and sent to residential schools operated by the churches where many of them were subject to sexual and other forms of abuse by priests, nuns, ministers, pastors and other supposed caregivers.

The government has now announced that it will pay compensation to all those who attended residential schools and will establish a Truth and Reconciliation Commission to tour the country to compile a historical record and allow Indian survivors to tell their stories. The commission will not be a court of law, and will not have the authority to compel people who have abused children to appear before it.

The authorities are also pressing ahead as fast as they can to locate and prosecute individuals responsible for specific acts of abuse. Many of them are now very old, and it is important to bring them to justice before they die. All former students, of course, retain the right to launch lawsuits against the churches that staffed the schools.

The bishop set his unfinished cup of coffee aside and pushed back his chair. His morning was ruined. Archbishop Laframbroise had asked him some time ago to look into these accusations and to discuss the matter with him at one of their luncheons. The bishop had done his homework, but had not yet raised the issues with his superior. However, the two were scheduled to meet that same day and the archbishop, the bishop was well aware, would have read the same story. He would want to discuss the tiresome subject with him rather than the more interesting topic of his plans for his future.

Just before noon, the bishop rang the doorbell of the archbishop's residence. The archbishop expected his visitors to be on time and would not have been amused had he been late. A silent, respectful nun opened the door and he stepped into the foyer. Everything within he knew well, the pervasive smell of lemon oil tinged with a hint of mustiness, the quiet ticking of an antique grandfather clock, the expensive oil paintings of the Virgin Mary and the martyred Christ on the walls, and the private chapel off to the side of the staircase reserved for the use of the archbishop and visiting prelates from Rome.

After taking his coat and hanging it in a closet, the nun led him up the stairs to the archbishop's dining room. His host, who was wearing a simple black cassock and clerical collar, was of medium height and slight build with warm but watchful dark brown eyes. He would have been content to have remained a parish priest all his life but his superiors had valued his quiet leadership, good judgement and management skills, and he had moved up in rank steadily through the years.

The archbishop motioned the bishop to take a seat at the small table for two that had been set up in preparation for the lunch. Today was macaroni and cheese day and ginger ale was the beverage. The bishop pretended to enjoy his food but was mildly irritated. He could not understand why his host did not provide more varied and elegant meals at these luncheons, one befitting senior clergy, especially someone like himself who one day might become a prince of the Church. But what could you expect from someone who served carbonated drinks at his meals rather than decent wine?

Over coffee, which was when the two discussed business matters, the bishop preempted his superior by going directly to the issue of the residential schools.

"Your Grace, I have, as you instructed, looked into the allegations of abuse by members of the clergy against aboriginal youth in the Indian residential schools we used to administer. It appears that many priests and nuns were overzealous in exercising their functions. Some, it appears, were even tempted into sin."

"Those poor children," the archbishop said. "How they must have suffered, all alone up in those lonely schools."

"To make it worse," continued the bishop, "the Church did little to remedy the problem other than by transferring the offending parties to other residential schools to make a fresh start. Now we are faced with a major problem. You will have seen from this morning's *Le Devoir* that some former students have the right to sue the Church for damages. And they will certainly do so."

"The archbishop sat in silence for a few minutes before speaking again. "What do you think the Church should do? Should it apologize? Should it pay compensation to the injured parties?"

The bishop was happy. When it came to weighing the pros and cons of moral issues affecting the Church, he was in his element. Leaning forward, he spoke to his superior as if he were a junior parish priest fresh from the seminary.

"Your Grace, as the Church Fathers have said, in cases like these, we must look at what option leads to the greater good. The Church is faced with a dilemma. If it apologizes to those who were harmed, it would be taking the moral high road. But in so doing, it would be admitting that it was in fact responsible for the wrongdoing. It could be sued for hundreds of millions of dollars, churches might have to be sold, parishes could become bankrupt, the faithful left with no place to worship, and souls condemned to perdition. But if the Church admits no fault, makes no apology and fights the claims in court, it will be able to limit its liability and continue to serve the faithful."

"In other words," said the archbishop, "you are saying we must decide between doing the right thing for the Indian people or doing the right thing for the Church. I think that's a false choice. In my opinion, in being honest with the residential school survivors, we will only strengthen the Church."

"Of course, of course, you are absolutely right," said the bishop quickly. "My comments were meant to deal with just one aspect of the problem."

"I also think there are bigger issues at stake," continued the archbishop. "How can we help the Indian people heal themselves? How can a country that was built on a foundation of injustice toward the Indian people heal itself?

"Perhaps we can make a start in the right direction if we do the right thing about this plea for help," he said, pulling out the letter from Joshua and handing it to the bishop. "I received this today from a chief in the north of Ontario telling me that generations of children from his community had attended one of our schools, were abused by a predatory priest and are suffering the consequences today. He asked if a Father Lionel Antoine, who was the resident priest at the school in those days, could go to the community and participate in a healing ceremony. Could you try to find him, if he is still alive, and ask him to go? Could you go as well?"

After lunch, the now thoroughly upset bishop returned to his residence. He completely disagreed with the archbishop's position. His superior plainly did not understand what was at stake. The Church in Canada was already in a state of crisis as fewer and fewer parishioners attended weekly services, as revenues dried up, as more and more people, and not just from the Indian community, came forward with allegations about sexual abuse by priests.

Now the Church was facing accusations that literally thousands of Indian children had suffered in residential schools from harsh treatment, sexual molestation and assaults on their cultural identity. It was a distasteful business but he had to consider his options. He suspected the charges were all true. As a bishop, responsible for in-house clerical discipline in the Quebec City area, he dealt with priests who had abused boys and girls on an all too regular basis. To make matters worse, although it made him sick to his stomach, he usually hushed up the cases to protect the Church.

Afraid the archbishop would be displeased, he had not dared tell him he thought it was a bad idea to send clerics to a healing circle. Their participation could be taken by the lawyers for the Indian plaintiffs as an admission of Church liability. He was tempted to sabotage the entire operation. The hierarchy would be as shocked as he was at the initiative to send a priest, who was almost certainly guilty of the charge of abusing children, to engage in some sort of hare-brained reconciliation and healing process.

If he was careful, perhaps he could have a word with one of his well-placed friends in the upper reaches of the Church, and the initiative would be stopped in its tracks. Archbishop Laframbroise would never guess who had let him down, and his career would not suffer. After a few minutes of reflection, however, the bishop shook his head. "How can I think such thoughts? No man of honour would betray his superior." But now he had to travel to the back of nowhere to some place that wasn't even on the map. What about his safety? And the food? He shuddered to think what would be on offer. And the accommodations? Would he have to sleep in a tent filled with bugs?

Father Antoine had rejoiced when the government, with no warning, closed the residential school on James Bay in the mid-1970s. He was, after all, still only in his mid-fifties and too young to retire. Perhaps he would now be able to fulfil his old dream of becoming a parish priest in the province of his birth. He was not certain, however, whether word of his activities with the little girls had leaked out to his headquarters. He need not have worried.

"Father Antoine," the superior of his order told him when he reported for duty, "you have done wonderful work with *les petits sauvages* in northern Ontario, but now we need you here at home. For years, young people have been turning their backs on the Church and not accepting vocations, and we simply do not have enough priests to attend to the needs of the faithful. Could you help out for a few more years?"

"You know I would never say no," said the priest. "But is there not something in my past that prevents me from carrying out such a role?"

"Oh, that little matter," said his superior. "I checked your file and can assure you that your decades of faultless service in the north have wiped your record clean. There is no need to worry."

Father Antoine soon discovered, however, that the Quebec of his youth was no more. His home village and the surrounding farmland had been overrun by the expanding urban sprawl of Montreal and was now plagued with strip malls, supermarkets, motels, drive-through restaurants and giant cinemas. The mighty Canadians, although showing flashes of brilliance under a new generation of players led by Guy Lafleur, Larry Robinson and Jacques Lemaire, were no longer the powerhouse team of old.

But it was not until he took up his duties that he saw how much the beloved Church of his boyhood and youth had changed. The Latin mass that he had loved so much when he was young was gone. The Church was no longer the centre of community life and the priest was not the most important person in local society. Given the shortage of clerics, Father Antoine found that he was obliged to work in three parishes, engaging in a mad rush on Saturday nights and Sundays from one to the other to celebrate mass with a handful of mainly elderly parishioners. The rest of his week was occupied conducting funerals and officiating at marriages on behalf of families, many of whom he would never see again in church, and who treated him as just another functionary, not much more important than the clerks who processed their requests for drivers' licences and Quebec Health Insurance cards.

Nevertheless, Father Antoine worked hard, adapted to the post–Vatican II world, and was soon so highly regarded by his parishioners that attendance in the churches he served underwent a modest increase. But once again, his sexual compulsions caught up with him, and a little girl told her parents he had touched her in her private places. Such was the priest's reputation in the community, however, that no one believed her. His superior thought otherwise, and quietly transferred him to another part of the province where he was not known.

In the coming years, the pattern was repeated. Father Antoine would make a good initial impression, he would offend again, and the Church would shift him elsewhere, sometimes just ahead of the law. Eventually, when he entered his seventies and his sexual urges diminished, he stopped molesting little girls and he became a model priest in every way. And when he reached eighty, he gave up his priestly duties altogether and moved to a retirement home, safely out of reach, he believed, of anyone who could dredge up anything scandalous about his past.

When Bishop de Salaberry called on him and handed him a letter, Father Antoine had no reason to suspect that he brought unwelcome news. Holding the envelope in his hand, he saw from the return address that it was from the chief of Cat Lake First Nation to Archbishop Laframbroise.

He was surprised. Why would the chief of the remote reserve in northern Ontario that had sent so many students to the residential school where he had served for so many years be writing to the archbishop of Quebec? And how was he, a humble retired priest, involved?

Perhaps the chief had sent a letter of thanks to the archbishop to express gratitude for his years of selfless labour on behalf of the children of his community? Maybe he had asked the archbishop to intercede with the Holy Father himself to send him a letter of commendation and a papal medallion extolling his merits?

Yes, that was it. And the Holy Father would certainly honour the request. Now what, he wondered, should he do with the medallion when it arrived? It would be selfish of him to keep it in its case in his room. It would be better to put it on display on the wall of the chapel for everyone to see and admire.

But what if the letter was about something more important? What, for example, if one of his former students had been miraculously cured of some horrible disease after invoking his name in a prayer? Perhaps he was being considered for sainthood after his death?

Bishop de Salaberry told him to open and look at the letter.

"I'm afraid you won't like it."

"I can't believe it," Father Antoine said after scanning the contents. "This is so unexpected! It's all untrue." He looked up to see the bishop looking at him grimly, but he carried on. "How could Chief Nanagushkin say such things! I remember when he was at the residential school. He was such a good boy. He went on to do wonderful things with his life. He was a role model. But he must have changed.

"I swear to you I loved those Indian children. I still do and I saved so many souls!"

"I'm not here to judge you," said the bishop. "But we've been ordered by the archbishop to attend a healing circle at Cat Lake First Nation and we have no time to lose."

15

The Healing Circle

SEVERAL WEEKS LATER, just after suppertime, a volunteer at the radio station broadcast a message inviting the people to attend an important meeting being held at seven that evening at the school.

"The parents of Rebecca, Jonathan and Sara will be taking part in a healing circle," he said. "Two guests from the outside will also be there and the chief thinks they can help us deal with the suicide epidemic in our community."

Shortly thereafter, the people of Cat Lake First Nation began filing into the gymnasium. Spider entered accompanied by his mother and sister and took a seat off by himself in the audience. Martha and Raven continued on to take their places in the circle. Martha had not had a drink all day. She was still struggling with her depression, but wanted to keep her mind clear for the evening.

Joshua, as he had during other critical moments in Martha's life, had gone out of his way to be helpful, taking his outboard motorboat and going down the river in search of Spider. He met the old couple who had befriended him earlier in the summer and they told him Spider had stayed with them for several weeks, learning how to handle a canoe, fish and cook simple meals. And then after borrowing fishing gear, matches, a pot, frying pan and a small supply of lard, flour and baking powder to make bannock, he paddled off in search of his grandparents' old trapping cabin. The old couple had given him careful directions and had no doubt he would find his way.

Although friendly, Spider had greeted Joshua warily when he pulled his boat up on the beach in front of the cabin. He had settled in and was in no hurry to leave, he said. But when told that his sister was suicidal and his mother was not coping well, he quickly agreed to accompany Joshua back to the reserve to attend the healing circle.

His mother had emerged from her bedroom where she was drinking when she heard Spider and Joshua greeting Raven as they came through the door. Martha said nothing and threw her arms around him, crying uncontrollably. Spider hugged her in return but grew concerned when he smelled the alcohol on her breath and she refused to release him. Joshua and Raven came to the rescue, gently prying her arms from around his neck and sitting her down on a chair.

"Welcome back, bro," Raven had then told him. We really need your help now."

Joshua waited until Martha sobered up and then shocked her by saying that Raven needed help to prevent her from killing herself. He had been doing what he could, but in the end, the only person who could save her was her mother.

"Frankly," he said, "with your depression, drinking problems and crying jags, you're in no shape to do her any good. That's why it's important you attend the circle with your family. You might learn things about yourselves you never suspected. At the least, it will be good therapy. And I have some surprises up my sleeve that should help matters along."

Their grief was still visible on their faces when the parents of Rebecca, Jonathan and Sara came in to sit next to Raven and Martha. They were followed by two clerics, a younger one, unsmiling and serious with a purple band around the waist of his cassock, and an old priest, tall and fat with a deeply wrinkled but cleanly shaved face and light blue friendly eyes. The band around his waist was black and a large cross hung down at the end of a long silver chain from his neck. He stood for a minute looking anxiously around the room before sitting down.

Martha could not keep her eyes off the elderly priest. He was someone she knew, she was certain. The priest looked down and began caressing a rosary and quietly praying. His devotions completed, he raised his head and locked his eyes on Martha's and slowly smiled.

To her horror, it was Father Antoine! Martha's stomach churned and she began to tremble. A toxic mix of rage, hate and fear hit her hard, knocking the wind out of her and making it difficult to breathe. This man who had done so much harm to her in her youth was the last person she ever expected to see again. And here he was in her home community looking at her as if they were old friends sharing secret memories of happy times together in the distant past.

The members of Raven's grade eight class, wearing sunglasses to conceal the grief in their eyes, came in and huddled together like so many monks at prayer on seats just outside the circle, their eyes cast downwards and the hoods of their sweatshirts pulled over their foreheads.

The mood in the room was solemn, for the people were still in a state of shock over the deaths of the young people. It was obvious that Rebecca, Jonathan and Sara had been part of a suicide pact. But who else, the fathers and the mothers in the room wondered, had taken the pledge to die? What if one of their own kids was involved? Why were they doing it? Were they really such bad parents? What could they do to bring this epidemic of self-inflicted death to an end?

Joshua opened the dialogue by lifting a talking stick up with one hand signifying that he held the floor. In accordance with custom, he spoke from a sitting position. As he described Raven's visit to him and his letter to the archbishop, everyone listened in silence. But when he said that Father Antoine, and a bishop by the name of de Salaberry, had been sent by the archbishop to participate in the healing circle and were there with them that very evening, the room erupted with shouts of indignation. Men, women and children stood up to get a better look.

"We don't want scum like Antoine in our community."

"De Salaberry can stay but Antoine should be in jail!"

"Let's take him outside and give him a taste of his own medicine!"

Joshua held the talking stick up high.

"Respect the talking stick. You know that the ancestors said only the person holding it can lead the discussion.

"Respect our visitors. You know that our ancestors said that guests, no matter how flawed, must always be made welcome in our homes and community.

"Respect the archbishop. He sent this man to help us heal ourselves.

"Respect the Creator. He had a purpose in sending this priest to us."

When the people had taken their seats again, Joshua handed the talking stick to Bishop de Salaberry as the ranking cleric.

———

The bishop did his best to look happy but had great difficulty in hiding his irritation. The trip from Quebec City had been endless. There were, of course, no direct flights to the remote community, and it had been necessary to change planes at Montreal and Toronto to reach Sioux Lookout, the jumping-off point for the reserve. Just that leg of the journey, he calculated, had taken longer than to fly from Quebec City to Rome.

Through some mix-up, his office had reserved rooms at a hotel in Sioux Lookout that was definitely not up to his standards. There was a faint odour of urine and a strong smell of cigarettes in his supposedly non-smoking room, his bed was lumpy and guests having a party down the hall had kept him awake most of the night. The food in the hotel restaurant was not to his taste: liver and onions, and hamburger steak and poutine were the house special- ities. The poached egg he had for breakfast was overcooked and his orange juice came out of a can and was warm.

At the airport, his heart had sunk when he saw the aircraft that was to take him to Cat Lake First Nation. It was a small, single- engine eight-seater, crammed to overflowing with Indian passen- gers and cases of pop, bags of potato chips, boxes of detergent and groceries. Although he prided himself in being open-minded, he wondered if the pilot, who was Indian, really knew how to fly. And how could people as poor as Natives were supposed to be afford to travel by airplane? Shouldn't they be using canoes?

Matters had gone downhill from there. The plane left an hour late, was bounced around by thermal updrafts and made three stops at other First Nations airstrips before reaching its destination. Bishop and priest emerged from the aircraft to a deserted airport. The car and driver that the chief had promised would be waiting was nowhere to be seen. When they entered the tiny two-room terminal building to use the washroom, there was no toilet seat, no toilet paper, no water in the toilet tank and no water in the faucets of the heavily stained sink. A large sign in English and Anishinabe syllabics warned the public—unnecessarily—not to drink the water.

After relieving themselves behind the bushes, the bishop and his travelling partner picked up their suitcases and hurried down the gravel road in the direction of a cluster of houses they could see off in the distance. Clouds of blackflies, sandflies, midges, deerflies, horse-flies and mosquitoes had come swarming out of the ditches and swamps to suck their blood, to tear off pieces of flesh and to crawl into their noses, ears and eyes. Crows, ravens and bluejays perched on telephone poles laughed at them as they trudged by, caked in sweat and dust and swatting futilely at their tiny tormentors.

Eventually a woman in a passing pickup truck, the cab crammed full of curious children, stopped and said something incomprehensible to them. In due course, they understood she was offering to give them a ride. They threw their bags into the open box at the back, climbed aboard and used a dusty spare tire as a seat as she took them on a jolting, rattling ride to the band office.

Naturally, when they got there, he had given the chief a piece of his mind.

"Don't you understand," he complained, "that the archbishop is doing you a favour by sending not just one, but two clerics to participate in your healing circle? Don't you realize the Church has never agreed to such a thing in the past? Don't you appreciate that I am a bishop? Don't you know that it has taken us two days of hard, uncomfortable travel to reach your reserve?

"And how am I to interpret your failure to send a car to pick us up at the airport? If you are trying to give some sort of message that we aren't welcome, we'll turn around and go home!"

It had enraged him even more when the idiot of a chief had burst out laughing.

"No, no!" he had the gall to say. "Don't get excited. You are most welcome. We need you tonight. As for the car, I guess my secretary just forgot to send it."

When he asked where they were supposed to sleep, the chief told him "at the hotel, of course."

Only the hotel wasn't really a hotel. It was a small building with three bedrooms with a communal washroom and kitchen. To make matters worse, the chief's secretary had forgotten to make reservations and three rooms were occupied by technicians from the outside trying to repair the temperamental water treatment plant. Fortunately, two of them were practising Catholics and he had been able to persuade them, discreetly invoking his rank as a bishop, to give up their rooms.

He had also had trouble keeping Father Antoine in line. When they left Quebec City, the priest had accorded him the respect and deference due to him as a bishop. But as time wore on, Father Antoine gave the impression that he was not listening when he told him about the challenges he faced in carrying out his daily duties, and had the nerve to yawn when he related several witty stories about his privileged ties with the archbishop himself. The final straw was when the priest had resisted wearing his cassock to the healing circle. The people, he claimed, wouldn't care what they wore and the cassocks would be hot and uncomfortable.

He had to speak sternly, making clear that bishops outranked mere priests and Father Antoine would do as he was told. He had sought to soften the blow by explaining that the Indians would be more respectful in the presence of clerics who looked like real churchmen and not like civilians. Father Antoine had reluctantly donned his cassock but had stopped talking to him.

The entire experience had been far worse than he could have imagined. He now just wanted to get this healing circle ordeal over with as soon as possible and leave on the first available flight out the next day.

"People of Cat Lake," began the bishop, "your chief wrote to His Grace, Archbishop Laframbroise, to tell him that your community was going through a difficult time and asked if Father Antoine could come and join your healing circle. His Grace, of course, agreed and asked me to come as well in case I could be of assistance. Both Father Antoine and I were delighted to oblige.

"Now before I turn the floor over to Father Antoine, who is the person I am sure you really want to hear from, I just wanted to say that I know many of you attended one of our residential schools that served the children of this area many years ago. Not everyone, I know, was happy there. Times were different and the Church did the best it could in the circumstances. I hope you will remember this if troublemakers from the outside come to you and ask you to join in lawsuits against the Church for the way your children were treated in our schools."

The bishop passed the talking stick to Father Antoine and said nothing further. He had done his duty by making clear the official position of the Church and the priest would now have to fend for himself.

"My dear friends," began the priest, holding up the talking stick in his left hand as if it was a papal cross and he was the Holy Father himself blessing a crowd of the faithful. "My dear friends," he repeated, twisting around in his seat and looking around the room and smiling beneficently as if the people were as happy to see him as he was to see them. "I have such good memories of the years I spent with so many of you here in this room tonight up at the residential school. You were just children of six when you arrived, knowing only the ways of the bush, and when you left at the age of sixteen, you were civilized, baptized, educated and ready to found families of your own. I am so proud of you."

Cries of outrage drowned out priest.

"Liar! You belong in jail!"

"Pedophile!"

"Monster!"

"You ruined our lives!"

Father Antoine sat quietly as the clamour of the crowd continued. "How can you say such things?" he said, trying to make his voice heard. "How dare you say such things!" he said, this time shouting. The room fell silent and Father Antoine smiling weakly, once again attempting to establish a personal contact with the people.

"I made so many friends from this reserve at that school. But you have to forgive me if I don't remember all your names. I am now an old man and my memory is not what it used to be. But I know you," he said, turning to Martha. "You are my *petite Marthe* and would never betray me. Tell them they are wrong. Tell them they have forgotten how good I was to you and to the other girls!"

Martha looked away. Perhaps what had happened had been her fault? Perhaps in some way, she had tempted Father Antoine? Perhaps she had deserved what she got?

"Is there no one here who will help me?" he asked, his face ashen, when Martha did not speak. "Is there no one who remembers how gentle I was with everyone who came to see me in my office?"

"Don't you understand?" Joshua said, taking back the talking stick. "Nobody can help you unless you admit you did wrong, unless you apologize to the people you abused so many years ago."

"But I gave them my love," said Father Antoine, "even if today no one wants to admit it. I would be the first to apologize if I was at fault. Would it help if I were to say I regret so many children were lonely at that school, that the food they ate was bad, and that the nuns in their desire to educate your children were sometimes harsh?"

"I think I know what you are trying to say," said Joshua. "But your type of love involved abusing the little girls. Don't you see that?"

"No! No! Absolutely not! I love Indians. My own grandmother was a Huron from Wendake near Quebec City, so the blood of an Indian flows in my veins. I can trace my family back to fur traders who travelled in this region over three hundred years ago. Many of them married Indians. Many of the last names of the children who came to the residential school were Antoine. I always thought of them as distant relatives."

"My friends," said Joshua, addressing the people. "We have heard from our visitors. Now it is up to the families of the dead to have their say."

The mother of Rebecca, the first of the three children to die, embraced the talking stick and said nothing as tears rolled down her cheeks. She twisted her hands and shifted her weight from one side of her seat to the other, as time went by and she did not break her silence. Finally in a small lisping voice, she started to speak, holding her hand in front of her mouth.

"I feel so bad. She was so young. Our only child. Who would've thought it? I've not spoken of my pain before. It was too hard."

The mother sobbed openly, abject and animal-like in her misery, and leaned her head on her husband's shoulder. He, too, began to cry and held her tightly.

"I was the one who found her," she said, straightening up and no longer attempting to hide the gap in her mouth. I'd been drinking and me and my husband were fighting. Don't even remember what it was about. He'd slugged me in the mouth knocking out most of my front teeth and opening my lip, and he hit me again giving me a black eye. I went out and got a piece of firewood and gave him a taste of his own medicine. I guess we were both pretty drunk.

"Rebecca came in yelling for us to stop. She was crying like crazy and saying she couldn't live no more like that. She'd decided to kill herself, she said. It was a cry for help, but I didn't believe her. She'd said the same thing before but had never done nothing. She'd always been a handful and I thought she was just acting up. I laughed at her and told her she had it easy compared to the old days when we lived on the land when it was a life-and-death struggle to survive. I told her the government gave us everything. The government would give her everything. So what was her problem? I turned her away.

"She was hanging by a wire from a clothes hook in the closet. I blame myself and feel bad. I should have listened to her and told her I loved her."

A long silence followed, disturbed only by quiet weeping from someone in the audience, and the woman began again.

"When I look back, I realize I was always too impatient. She could never satisfy me. I wasn't there to fix dinner for her. I never encouraged her to do good in school. I was always shouting at her, just like the nuns used to do to me at residential school."

Her husband held his head in his hands and loud, convulsive sobs racked his body. "It gets worse," the woman said, reaching over and trying to wipe away the tears of her husband with her hand. "When she was just a little girl, she told me her grandfather was touching her in her private parts and doing things to her. I freaked out because that's what Father Antoine used to do to me, only worse. But to my shame, I blamed her for tempting her grandfather. I slapped her just as I had been slapped by the nuns when I asked them to tell the priest to leave me alone. She must have felt bad. Just like I felt when that happened to me. I know it went on for years and I never did nothing to stop it. I'm so ashamed."

It was then Jonathan's father's turn and he started speaking in a low voice. Not a sound could be heard in the room and everyone strained to hear his words.

"I feel awful," he said. "He was our baby. Our other kids were a lot older and they spoiled him. The last time I saw him he was smiling. He hugged me and said he loved me. I should have told him I loved him. Maybe he wouldn't have done it. He was so happy and full of mischief when he was a little boy. When his brothers and sisters left to live on the outside, he got real quiet and sad. In the letter we found after he died, he said he had no hope and life wasn't worth living."

Holding tight to the talking stick, Jonathan's father looked down at the floor, unable to find the words to continue. Ten minutes of silence followed and he began again, this time shouting angrily.

"How do we give our young people hope when they have lost their language and culture and they don't know who they are? When they see us adults lying around all day with no work and doing nothing? When there are no books in the school library to read? When they're not learning to read and write in school, what are they being prepared for? Their role models are the bootleggers and young Native hookers, the drug dealers and gang members in Regina and Winnipeg they watch on television programs. They see people on television driving fast cars, living in big houses and eating in fancy restaurants, but they know they'll never have any of that stuff.

"We gotta help them. We need to find a place where they can hang out and do fun, healthy things, like listen to hip hop music, play Ping-Pong and shoot some pool. We need recreation facilities.

"As parents, we need to pay more attention to family life. I bet if we were to eat together at least once a day it would draw us together. Why not take the kids hunting and fishing on the weekends? Why not spend the summers with them on the land? That way we'd all learn about how life was in the old days, before all these suicides. Most of all, we gotta stop blaming all the bad things the white man did to us for all the bad things we do to our kids. The last residential school closed in this province almost thirty years ago. We got to move on and get a life!"

When Sara's mother took hold of the talking stick, the words burst from her mouth like air from an overinflated balloon pricked by a knife.

"I know why she did it. She went out to Thunder Bay and spent the winter with my sister. She went to school and did good. She went to pow wows and to events at the Friendship Centre. She loved the big drum and Native culture and became a jingle dancer. At my sister's church, they respected Native spirituality. They said there was one creator for everyone. When she came back, the other kids said she was putting on airs about her good grades and made her feel ashamed of them. The neighbours told her not to practise jingle dancing in front of the house and I didn't stick up for her. They said it was superstition and a dance of the devil. When she played pow wow music in the house, the other kids said their parents told them not to listen to it. It was pagan. She felt bad 'cause they took away her pride in being Native and she decided to die. She told me she was going to kill herself and I went to the nursing station for help. I know the staff there 'cause I got diabetes real bad and they're always helpful. But they said they had no resources to work with suicidal people. They telephoned the doctor at the hospital in Thunder Bay. He asked them if they thought she was really serious and they said they didn't know. Kids were always threatening to kill themselves they said but not too many followed through. He prescribed some pills and said he'd interview her the next time he came to the reserve.

I saw her take a rope that day but I didn't do nothing. I've never been any good at making decisions especially since I came down with diabetes. I was looking out the kitchen window and saw her climbing a tree. She tied one end of the rope to a branch and the other around her neck. She looked at me and I looked at her. I should have run out and told her to come down. But I froze. I couldn't even cry out. She hung on to the tree for a minute looking at me and I tried to call the nursing station to ask them what to do and she jumped before they came on the line. I'll never forgive myself. You know I never even told her I loved her. She was only thirteen."

Out of breath, her eyes expressionless, she could say no more.

16

Embracing Life

"I WANT TO TELL YOU HOW THIS ALL STARTED," said Raven. "A bunch of us were hanging out one night behind the co-op like we always do. Some of us were sniffing and everyone was feeling bad. We never had anything to do and we were bored. Most of our parents sat around doing nothing all day but watching stupid shows on television like Jerry Springer and Judge Judy and didn't care whether we were home or not. They didn't care whether we got drunk or not. They didn't care whether we went to school or not. They didn't care whether we learned our language or not. They bought booze on welfare days and drank until they ran out of money. It didn't matter to them if there was no money left over to buy food for us, and they didn't care if we went to school hungry.

"Someone said, 'What a life. It's not worth living. Maybe the white people who say Indians are just a bunch of savages are right. Maybe we'll grow up to be just like our parents. Why don't we just kill ourselves now and get it over with. It'd be a good way to get even for all the bad things our parents have done to us. They'd come to our funerals and regret they treated us that way.'

"And when Rebecca, Jonathan and Sara killed themselves, their parents got all upset. They paid more attention to their kids dead than alive. There were big funerals with real nice plastic flowers, pictures of the dead for everyone to admire, long speeches and choirs of elders singing the old gospel songs in Anishinaabemowin. At school there were memorial services right here in the gym and kids wrote poems about them and their pictures were hung on the walls as if they were heroes."

"And what makes you the big expert," Jonathan's father said, interrupting Raven. "You had it good, living with Nokomis all those years."

"Yeah, and why didn't you tell us if you knew all about it?" asked Rebecca's father, who had not spoken to that point.

"Leave her alone," said Martha. "How do you know how she felt? If you got to blame someone, blame me."

"No, they're right," said Raven. "I should have said something. It's just that I couldn't."

"Lay off the kid," Rebecca's mother said. "It takes a lotta guts to face everybody like that and what she's got to say is important."

The other parents nodded their agreement and Raven continued. "Rebecca, Jonathan, Sara and I made a deal to kill ourselves when we turned thirteen. We all knew thirteen was the right age to die, when we were no longer kids but before we became grown-ups and parents. We knew that in the old days, thirteen was the most important time in the lives of young people. They went into the bush and built shelters to meditate in and stayed there for days without eating or drinking until they received their spirit name and vision about their future from Gitche Manitou. They then went home and got married and started families of their own. They knew what they wanted to do with their lives and it was a time of celebration for everyone.

"But that was when Native kids had a future. Now we don't become adults when we become teenagers, but drift along with no hope. We had nothing to lose and so why not die?

"Maybe I did have it better when I was a kid than the others," she said, turning to Jonathan's father. "But I joined in because I was having so many problems with my mother. She only came back from Toronto because she had to. She went through the motions of taking care of me, but I knew she wasn't sincere because she never showed me any love and started to beat me.

"There's something else, something I haven't dared tell anyone before, not even Joshua. After each suicide, the dead started to visit those of us who were still alive. Now I'm the only one left and Rebecca, Jonathan and Sara are coming to see me every night. They stand around my bed looking at me sad-like, never saying anything but I know what they want. They want to be sure I understand they'll never find peace in the spirit world unless I join them. I gave them my word, and if I don't go through with my undertaking, I feel I'll be letting them down. And they were let down so many times when they were alive."

Sara's mother shrieked and began to wail. The other parents joined in, rocking back and forth in their chairs, their eyes clasped shut, and keening in black despair. The suffering of their children was continuing in the afterlife and there was nothing they could do to help them.

Raven, desperate to explain herself and bring their anguish to an end, rose to her feet and shouted at them: "Stop! Stop! Let me finish. I never really wanted to die," she said, fighting back tears, "I just wanted my mother to say she loved me. I think the others just needed some reason to live and the love of their families."

The parents, jolted back to reality, straightened up in their seats and began hugging each other. Someone brought them a box of tissues and they wiped their eyes and started crying again in cathartic release. Members of the community were now doing the same thing. Tears streamed down under the sunglasses of Raven's classmates.

Father Antoine held his head in his hands. The bishop looked down at the floor, unable to meet anyone's eye.

Martha took Raven in her arms and hugged her and whispered that she loved her and that she had always loved her. Then, grasping the talking stick in one hand, she took the floor.

"I sure hope some good comes from all this suffering tonight. If it does, it won't be because Father Antoine and the bishop showed any remorse. But I say, so what if they and people like them don't say they're sorry? Our pain is so great, we shouldn't waste any more time on them. It looks like begging."

"But that's letting them off easy," someone called from the back of the room.

"I don't agree," said Martha. "It's easy to say you're sorry when you don't mean it. And we're the ones carrying the burden anyway, not them. The only way to get it off our backs is to forgive those who harmed us, whether they accept their blame or not. That doesn't mean we should forgive and forget, but we need to forgive to be able to start healing ourselves and get on with our lives." Martha then dragged an astonished Father Antoine to his feet and hugged him, saying, "I forgive you." She turned to the bishop and hugged him as well.

The parents of the children who had killed themselves, one after the other, left their chairs and followed her lead. And when the mothers put their arms around the priest, each of them said in a voice so low that only Father Antoine and the bishop could hear, "Don't you remember? You raped me when I was a little girl but I forgive you."

The members of the healing circle took their seats and the room was still.

"I have one last thing to tell you," said Raven, picking up the talking stick again. "Last night, I visited the spirit world in my dreams and met Nanabush, and I told him I had come seeking guidance on whether I should fulfil my vow to join my friends on their journey of death or whether I should live.

"Nanabush looked at me for the longest time before answering.

"'That is a decision only you can make,' he said. 'But just remember, the Creator put you on earth for a purpose and you will be going against his will if you kill yourself. I know you believe your life has no meaning. But have you never thought that just living gives meaning to life? Is not the experience of life the real meaning of life?'

"Nanabush then took me by the hand and told me to look deep down into the waters of Cat Lake. When I did, and the ripples on the surface cleared, I saw myself obeying the spirits of Rebecca, Jonathan and Sara and hanging myself by a rope from the black spruce tree that stands in our front yard. I saw my mother screaming and running out of the house and falling on the ground when she saw me swinging there. I saw Joshua coming to cut me down and hugging my mother. I saw the school close and all the kids running out crying, just like we did when the other kids killed themselves. I saw the people coming with gifts of food to my mother to try to comfort her. I saw the preacher talking to my mother and trying to help her.

"I saw the police come and take me to the nursing station where they put me in a body bag just like they always do. I saw them shipping me out like a piece of freight on a charter to Thunder Bay for an autopsy. I saw myself lying naked on a stainless steel countertop in a laboratory as a doctor wearing a white lab coat looked at the marks around my neck and cut me open to take samples from my organs to test for drugs and who knows what—just like they do on

CSI Miami. I saw people from a funeral home take me back to the Thunder Bay airport in a black hearse. I saw my mother being comforted by Joshua and by the preacher at Cat Lake airport as my body was unloaded from the plane and taken to the school gymnasium for the funeral service.

"I was then in a coffin with its lid open, dressed in my best clothes, my head and my body resting on soft red velvet cushions. Weeping members of the community passed by to kiss me and to say goodbye, just like they did at the funerals of the others. There was a guard of honour of kids from the school and my mother was standing at the head of the coffin wringing her hands and Spider had his arm around her shoulders. Someone read a poem I had written back when I was happy with my life, and the families of the other kids who had taken their lives were so upset they left the room. The preacher delivered a sermon telling everyone to be joyful, for I had gone to heaven, a choir of elders led the crowd in heartbreaking songs and someone started to play *Amazing Grace* on an electric guitar, just like they always do at all the funerals.

"I looked up at the faces of my friends from school as they crowded around, and I knew that it wouldn't be long before some of them followed me.

"Then the coffin lid slammed shut and everything was black. I felt the coffin being picked up and carried away and I was ever so scared.

"I called out saying that I had changed my mind, that it had all been a mistake and I didn't want to die. But no one heard me.

"A few minutes later, I heard the sound of the coffin being pushed onto the back of the pickup truck we use as a hearse. I felt the vibrations of the engine as the driver turned the key in the ignition and every bump as he shifted gears and moved off over the trail to the cemetery. There, I knew, an open grave awaited. Soon

I heard the preacher say 'Earth to earth, ashes to ashes,' as clods of dirt rained down on the wood over my head.

"No, no! I cried. I didn't mean it! I don't care if the Church treated my mother and the others bad at that residential school. I don't care if my mother drinks and beats me. I don't care if the people can't get their lives together. I don't care if they spend their welfare money on booze and drugs.

"I want to take my chances with life! Thirteen is too young to die! I want to smell the air after a rain. I want to see the waves battering the rocks on the shore. I want to hear the call of the loon. I want to fall in love and get married. I want to touch the soft warm skin of my own baby. I want to sing and dance. I want to experience bad as well as good things. I want to travel, to live in Toronto, to see the world and come home and help my people. I want to grow old. I don't want to become a spirit!

"But no one paid any attention for I was dead and buried.

"The image faded, leaving me with a feeling of absolute dread and hopelessness.

"Nanabush then spoke.

"'It is now for you to decide whether the joy of living, even in pain, outweighs the finality of death.'

"I chose life and woke up feeling happier than I had since my mother came back."

The members of the community sat in silence. They now understood that the land they lived on was sacred, and by forgiving their enemies and connecting with their ancient culture, they could find the strength to heal their wounds. And that night, before the people went to bed, they told their children that they loved them.

EPILOGUE

WHEN MARTHA WENT TO BED that night, she closed her eyes and Father Antoine came to her, just as he had so often over the years. This time, however, he was not the corpulent priest with bad breath who haunted her nights with flashbacks of abuse. Instead she saw him as he had become—a pitiful, ageing pedophile, unwilling to acknowledge, let alone apologize for, the harm he had caused her and the mothers of the children who had killed themselves.

Earlier in the evening, Martha had told him that she forgave him. Now, several hours later, the rapture induced by the dynamics of the healing circle was fading. But that did not matter, for she did not regret making her gesture of mercy, and more importantly, she no longer feared him. The pardon she had extended to Father Antoine had banished the monster of hate within her, freeing her to deal with her depression and alcoholism and make a new start with her children.

She was ever so proud of her children. The strongest member of the family, Martha recognized, was Raven, but she would still require much nurturing to reach her potential. Martha just hoped that she would find the mothering skills within herself to meet the challenge.

As for Spider, she had been ecstatic when Joshua had brought him back. Even better, he told her he had not had a drink since the night he left the reserve and felt at peace with himself for the first time in his life. He knew himself, however, and would soon resume drinking if he returned to the city or remained on the reserve. He planned to return as soon as possible and live a traditional lifestyle away from alcohol in the trapping cabin of his grandparents and he hoped that his mother and sister could come to see him often. He wanted their company, and would need their help in mastering life in the bush and learning the traditional teachings.

Father Antoine went to bed a deeply troubled man, for despite his words of denial, his encounter with the mothers of Rebecca, Jonathan and Sara had thoroughly upset him. Who could have guessed that his actions of so long ago would shatter their families and lead their children to kill themselves? As a priest, he knew there were few if any greater sins than murder, and taking your own life was self-murder. How many people had he destroyed over the years?

The enormity of his sins made Father Antoine tremble. It was not as if he had not known that he was doing bad things. He had, however, convinced himself long ago that he was different from other men, and had been compelled by some blind force within himself to act as he did. Other priests were doing similar things without being punished by the Church, and this to him had been a sign that the hierarchy, if not approving his actions, at least understood his predicament.

Now for the first time, he was ashamed of himself and realized that he had used his faith as a tool, an instrument, a means of rationalizing his unacceptable conduct. For during his years at the residential school, after the passion of his encounter with each little victim had dissipated, he would descend to the chapel late at night overcome with shame and remorse, get down on his knees, clasp his hands together, turn his face to the statue of Christ and pray fervently for forgiveness and vow that he would never again touch another little girl. In the course of the night, a feeling of great peace would come over him, and he would know he had been granted absolution.

The nuns, when they entered at dawn for the first mass of the day, he was well aware, would see him there still on his knees, praying earnestly. How fortunate they were, they must have thought, to have a priest of such exceptional piety and goodness as their spiritual advisor. But often that same afternoon, after a long nap, he would wake up refreshed, the urge would return, and he would summon another little girl to his office.

Years later, when he returned to Quebec and resumed his exploitation of little girls, he had sought solace in prayer and had confessed his sin after each encounter. And each time, he had been absolved of his sin—or so he had thought. But now he saw that he had gained a peace of mind that was at best self-delusion, and at worst a divine joke. For he had never felt pity for the little girls and he had deceived himself when he assumed they had loved him, mistaking their compliance with his demands for genuine affection. He now had to find a way to make amends to his victims before he died. But in his heart, he knew he had pity enough only for himself.

Bishop de Salaberry went to bed in a thoughtful mood. Something had happened that evening, he knew, that would change his life forever. When he heard the stories of the suffering mothers who had lost their children to suicide, he had been overwhelmed by the deepest sorrow and sadness, and a feeling of compassion such as he had never before experienced. His ambition to rise in the hierarchy of the Church was no longer of any importance. He had felt the presence of the divine, and this, he knew in his innermost being, was because of the spirit of forgiveness shown by the families of the children to the representatives of the white society who had done so much harm to Indian people over the centuries.

Perhaps, he thought, before he fell asleep, the archbishop knew this would happen to him when he had asked him to accompany Father Antoine to Cat Lake First Nation.

And that night, the spirits did not come to ask Raven to join them on the other side.

IN THE NORTH of the province of Ontario, there is a land so vast that it could swallow up France and still have room left over for Belgium. It is a region of stark, harsh beauty, green and lush in summer, and white and cold in winter, with deep blue skies by day and with countless stars turning dark to light by night. It is the source of several of the greatest rivers in Canada, the Severn, the Winisk, the Attawapiskat, the Albany and the Moose, that rise in the uplands of the Laurentian Shield and flow northwards to the sea through the immense, swampy Hudson Bay Lowlands.

It is also the only part of the province occupied to this day largely by Native people—in the boreal forest by the Anishinabe (Ojibway) and their close cultural cousins the Anishininimouwin (Oji-Cree), and along the Hudson Bay and the James Bay Lowlands by their good friends, the Omushkegowak (Swampy Cree). The Nishnawbe Aski Nation, where this novel is set, is a grouping of forty-nine First Nations whose traditional lands make up more than sixty percent of the area of Ontario running from the height of land to the James and Hudson Bay coast and from the Manitoba to the Quebec borders.

A drama of death and sorrow has been playing out for generations in this region. From the late nineteenth to the latter part of the twentieth century, the people of Ontario's remote boreal forest, like their Native counterparts across Canada, watched helplessly as the federal government removed their children, often by force, and sent them to Indian residential schools to be turned into brown-skinned white Canadians. All too often the children were abused by predatory caregivers and returned home broken in spirit and devoid of parenting skills. In the infamous "'60s Scoop," the Ontario Children's Aid Society and its counterparts across Canada entered the reserves and seized children by the thousands and adopted them out to white families across Canada and the United States. In the 1980s, the traditional life of the people was further undermined by exposure to the culture and anti-Native sentiment of the outside world when winter roads were pushed into their communities.

With their parents, grandparents and great-grandparents before them traumatized by their residential school experiences, the youth had no one to turn to in their families for love and support as they confronted these monumental shocks, and they began to kill themselves in staggering numbers. From 1986 to 2010, almost five hundred people, including sixty children under the age of fourteen and one hundred and eighty youth aged fifteen to twenty, took their lives in the territory of the Nishinabe Aski Nation out of a total population of fewer than 30,000 men, women and children. And this despite the frantic efforts of chiefs and councils to stem the epidemic of death that continues to this day, out of sight and mind of the outside world.

In some communities, survivors speak of the ghosts of suicide victims who come calling in nighttime dreams seeking to persuade young people who had joined in suicide pacts to fulfil their part of the bargain and kill themselves. Too often, the appeals are answered and more deaths take place.

For many people, Native and non-Native, dreams, especially about people who have passed away, are not imaginary phenomena but powerful depictions of reality. In the land of the Anishinabe, of the Anishininimouwin and of the Omushkegowak, young people who participate in suicide pacts have spoken to friends and relatives about visits from the spirits of the dead, just before they too killed themselves.

This is a work of fiction and any resemblance the characters may have to people living or dead is entirely coincidental. The Cat Lake First Nation is actually a proud Native community of some five hundred people located on the shore of Cat Lake one hundred and fifty miles upstream from the Albany River and one hundred miles by winter road to the west of Pickle Lake. The airport, band office, school, cemetery, rapids and shoreline depicted in the book are, however, composite creations drawn from more than a dozen fly-in Anishinabe reserves in northern Ontario.

The residential school in this novel is also composite based on many residential schools across Canada, including the St. Anne's Indian Residential School at the mouth of the Albany River on the James Bay, which was in operation from 1904 until its closing in 1973. On May 29, 2002, arsonists, believed to be former students at the school, destroyed the long-abandoned structure.

ACKNOWLEDGMENTS

MEEGWETCH TO MY WIFE, Marie-Jeanne, and our children, Anne-Pascale, Laurent and Alain. Meegwetch to my mother, Maureen Benson Bartleman, and Hilda Snake for the translations of key phrases into the Anishinaabemowin dialect of Chippewas of Rama First Nation, my home community. I also thank my mother for telling me tales of Wendigos, bearwalkers and witches that she heard the elders relate on winter evenings around the old box stove in her grandfather Benson's kitchen when she was a little girl on the Rama Reserve in the 1920s.

Meegwetch to Shirley Hay of the Wahta First Nation for her comments on the aboriginal cultural context and to Grand Chief Stan Beardy of the Nishinabe Aski Nation who introduced me to his people. Meegwetch to the residential school survivors who courageously provided me with the details of the sexual and physical abuse they suffered while attending Indian residential schools in the 1950s and 1960s. Meegwetch to Goyce Kakegamic of the Sandy Lake First Nation, a residential school survivor, former deputy grand chief of the Nishnabe Aski Nation and leader in the

249

fight to combat suicide among Native youth. Meegwetch to Nokomis (Grandmother) and elder Lillian McGregor, Crane Clan, Anishinabe of the Whitefish River First Nation, for her help in preparing the prayer to Gitche Manitou. Meegwetch to Raven Redbird for her insights into the problems faced by Native women new to Toronto and to the staff of the Anishinabe Street Patrol and the Salvation Army Breakfast Mission for allowing me to accompany them over the years to witness first-hand the help they provide to the homeless, Native and non-Native alike. Thank you to Nanda Casucci-Byrne who travelled with me to the fly-in communities in northern Ontario and who made many helpful suggestions throughout the drafting process.

Thank you to John Macfie who spent many years in the 1940s and 1950s in the territory of the Nishinabe Aski Nation and who was willing to share his insights with me. The book he co-authored with Basil Johnston (*Hudson Bay Lowlands*, Dundurn Press, Toronto, 1991) and the research paper of Edward Rogers (*The Round Lake Ojibwa*, Royal Ontario Museum, Toronto, 1962) also provided useful information about community celebrations in the 1950s, including details about the construction of water drums that I drew on in the novel. Professor Donald Smith also kindly read the manuscript and provided helpful comments for which I am grateful.

Thank you to the individuals, especially Eric Van Pelt, who were prepared to share with me their insights on life on the streets of Toronto in the late 1980s and early 1990s. A thank you to Alistair MacLeod, Deb Mathews and Shelley Peterson for reading the manuscript and encouraging me to publish it. And most important of all, special thanks and gratitude to Louise Dennys and Diane Martin for their friendship and guidance.

JAMES BARTLEMAN is a member of the Chippewas of Rama First Nation and rose from humble circumstances to become Canada's first aboriginal ambassador. After a distinguished career of more than thirty-five years in the Canadian diplomatic service, in 2002 he became the first Native Lieutenant-Governor of Ontario. He is the author of four bestselling works of non-fiction including the prize-winning memoirs *Out of Muskoka* and *Raisin Wine*.

A NOTE ABOUT THE TYPE

As Long as the Rivers Flow is set in Monotype Dante, a modern font family designed by Giovanni Mardersteig in the late 1940s. Based on the classic book faces of Bembo and Centaur, Dante features an italic which harmonizes extremely well with its roman partner. The digital version of Dante was issued in 1993, in three weights and including a set of titling capitals.